"A defiant and tend
thousand lifetimes :
breath-taking, and h
as at once the most high-fidelity and stylized of mediums."

—Ken Liu, author of *The Paper Menagerie and Other Stories* and *The Grace of Kings*

"In *All Flowers Bloom*, Kawika Guillermo has achieved an ambitious feat: to chronicle a memory—and its vast empire of battles and love, constant guises and surprises—that spans over four thousand years through a narrator who, like the beloved, is blessed, or cursed, with hundreds of lives, each rebirth announcing a different milieu, a different role. One of this daring book's themes is desire as reincarnation redux! With its crisp prose and continual shifts in time, place, and of narrator's gender, I could not help but compare it to Virginia Woolf's *Orlando* and David Mitchell's *Cloud Atlas*. But this novel does more than that, for at its core, is a lover's discourse on desire, its multiple masks and power to make lovers and strangers, and traitors and rescuers out of us."

—R. Zamora Linmark, author of *Rolling the R's* and *Leche*

"*All Flowers Bloom* is a beguiling book, with an inventive narrative unlike anything I have encountered before. This is an emotional journey through lifetimes and loves and losses. Kawika Guillermo delivers wonderment and surprise, a complex universe, and an unforgettable cast of characters."

—Doretta Lau, author of *How Does a Single Blade of Grass Thank the Sun?*

ALL FLOWERS BLOOM

KAWIKA GUILLERMO

Westphalia Press
An Imprint of the Policy Studies Organization
Washington, DC
2020

Westphalia Press
An imprint of Policy Studies Organization
1527 New Hampshire Ave., NW
Washington, D.C. 20036
info@ipsonet.org

ISBN: 978-1-941755-12-9

Daniel Gutierrez-Sandoval, Executive Director

PSO and Westphalia Press
Updated material and comments on this edition
can be found at the Westphalia Press website:
www.westphaliapress.org

For Y-Dang & Kai

In remembrance of Daniel Durwood Patterson

The Heading Images are under Creative Commons and are fair use for commercial purposes. Authors and websites listed below:

Image 1, page 1: http://www.supercoloring.com/ja/nurihui/hua-mo-yang-nomandara-14, by Lena London.

Image 2, page 30: http://www.supercoloring.com/ja/nurihui/hua-mo-yang-nomandara-17, by Lena London.

Image 3, page 64: http://www.supercoloring.com/ja/nurihui/hua-mo-yang-nomandara-16, by Lena London.

Image 4, page 95: http://www.supercoloring.com/ja/nurihui/hua-mo-yang-nomandara-14, by Lena London.

Image 5, page 129: http://www.supercoloring.com/ja/nurihui/hua-mo-yang-nomandara-13, by Lena London.

Image 6, page 181: http://www.supercoloring.com/ja/nurihui/hua-mo-yang-nomandara-12, by Lena London.

Image 7, page 240: http://www.supercoloring.com/ja/nurihui/hua-mo-yang-nomandara-10, by Lena London.

Image 8, page 291: http://www.supercoloring.com/ja/nurihui/chou-xiang-de-namo-yang-nomandara-1, by Lena London.

Image 9, page 324: http://www.supercoloring.com/ja/nurihui/hua-mo-yang-nomandara-21, by Life of Riley.

Image 10, page 334: http://www.supercoloring.com/ja/nurihui/hua-mo-yang-nochou-xiang-de-namandara, by Painter.

Image 11, page 344: http://www.supercoloring.com/ja/nurihui/hua-mo-yang-nomandara-26, by Peaksel.

CONTENTS

I've always had a poor memory. From the first moment I opened my eyes, I've let others remember for me, steer me in a pre-programmed cruise, while the past dwelled within my peripheral vision. My past lives entombed by time. What I cannot remember I imagine.

Taste's pleasure sparks, but I can't recall what. How does one salvage all those fleeting moments, years past expiration? How to begin foraging through discarded memories, those mounds in an infinite landfill? Whatever I wanted I imagined before me, everything besides you. Perhaps in these pages we will persist, a place to point and say—*there*.

I made all the wrong choices. In each life I perished in spasms out of time. But with every death, you became clearer. You were the wild one, uncatchable, untamable, deservedly outside my realm. I hope to keep you as you were, before I connived you to love me back. It's true what Cryss says: men prize the thing ungained. Things won are done. Joy's soul lies in the doing.

Four thousand years, hundreds of lives, and one night to write you back. I must be quick, unfixed, unafraid, let memory come like vapor, heart in throat. I will jot down whatever comes, no matter how unreal, how silly or malicious. Let it all come, whether it be the violent or the transcendent hurrah. Let it come, love's dolorous fog, forming in dewed drops.

Book 1

#871

花開不同賞,	Flowers bloom divergent pots
花落不同悲。	Flowers fall their own dread
欲問相思處,	I've been meaning to ask: will I miss you
花開花落時。	When they bloom, when they fall?

薛濤	Xue Tao

Life

What do you think?
Babylonians? Jews?

A

Bred, born into servitude,
Around 600 BCE,
Siege of Jerusalem.

Light/Dark. And Each of Them Dark as Night

Memory pools into a reflective surface of my first life. Perhaps I see you in it, but if it was you, it was a you I had not learned to recognize, a you of bubbles and ripples.

I remember waking in my master's bedroom, hearing them playing in the veranda. My hands shook at their laughter. Every laugh sounded heartless, an amnesia-induced glee. Any time I opened my eyes they had been there, their footsteps rustling to and from my door. Children. Children who needed breakfast and baths and someone to tell them lies and break up fights and clean their mess and entertain them with my harp or a game of rackets. And then I had to eat and care for myself too.

I remember the boys, Noy and Levi, playing with wooden swords, watching the alleyways, hoping to catch a peek at another slaying. And then, in the beat of a fly's wings they turned from hysterical laughter to emotional meltdown.

"Go away!" I shouted at them from my mistress's bed, but they kept prattling near the archway. Perhaps they were hungry. "Shhh!" My lungs ached from screaming as I imagined theirs were from crying. Perhaps the soldiers outside

3

would hear them and chuck spears through the window. A wind blew open the curtains and the sun peeked at me over Solomon's gold-tipped temple.

No, not the children, it was wrong to think that.

I slept in bits on silk sheets. The war that had trapped us starving and helpless in my master's estate wasn't even mine. I should have left as soon as soldiers rammed the gates open, should have flung myself onto the nearest and eldest Babylonian brute. But instead, those kids.

Stirred awake by the children's clamor, I recalled that two of them had already died; they could not be hungry anymore. Now, with only six mouths to feed, we had a sporting chance.

God, those children were dead. Dead.

Someone knocked on the bedroom door. The cedar-wood croaked. It was Eden, the eldest, easing the door open. She wore a blue patchy dress she had stolen from the mistress's closet. It draped over her body, hiding her protruding bones.

"Auntie, wake up," she called. "Someone's coming up the garden."

I pulled the master's pillow over my head. She knew the rules: keep the doors locked, tell anyone who comes that there's no room here. And definitely no food.

"Auntie?"

"Wake me again and I'll bury you in the desert."

"It's that soldier, Auntie."

"Oh."

I staggered up, my head as light as my stomach. Into the mistress's closet, I rifled through her dresses and picked the turquoise muslin cloth she wore to weddings. Too bad the jewelry box was missing—that petty prune must have hustled it into exile. I let my hair fall over my arms, but could find no bronze. The mistress hated her own reflection, it only reminded her of the scar on her upper lip, a minor flaw, but there nonetheless. We, her handmaids, were her only mirrors.

"Eden!" I called. "How do I look?"

"Beautiful, Auntie."

I felt my hair, mossy from lack of nutrients. "If he laughs at me, I'll know why."

A soft knock. Too late.

The children joined me in the foyer to meet you, the squat soldier. You had first arrived on our doorstep three days before, hoping like the other scavengers for something to eat or barter. But unlike the others, you left promising to bring back whatever food you could obtain. You looked the same as before, scraggy beard, your spear too fresh to have been combat-tested. This time you brought more food than we had seen in weeks, a veritable feast: olives, goat milk, two loaves of unleavened bread. I sent Eden to store them in the hidden cabinets of my old servant's quarters, while the other children divided a bread loaf in the master's hall.

I trusted you now and introduced you to the children. Shani, who was of the house, and her friend Hagar, who happened to be visiting when the siege began, both six. Then the boys, Levi and Noy, seven and four, who still believed their parents would come back for them.

"Chew slowly!" I said, slapping Levi's hand as he reached for another piece of bread. "Savor each bite."

"I thought there were seven children," you said through

your thick black beard.

"The other two girls are out scavenging," I lied. "They doubted your return."

"They shouldn't have." You placed a sack on an empty chair. A small brass shield poked out. "It's dangerous out there, especially for young women."

I heard Eden rush down the winding staircase. The children, too focused on savoring their first meal in days, could not catch your eyes on Eden, on the loose wisps of her walnut hair, the hem of her ankle-length skirt. I'd had to train myself to stop thinking of her as a child, as somewhere between child and woman. Then your eyes turned to me, on my mistress's jewels, strewn through my patchy hair.

"Is that a sword?" Levi asked, pointing to the bronze hilt at your side. "And a slingshot!" He grabbed at it, yanking the weapon from your belt. "You use this to bash in Babylonian heads?"

"No," you said, taking back the leather sling. "It's for herding and scaring away wolves, mostly."

As we ate I wanted to ask you everything. If I had known this was the last time I would see you, I might have abandoned the children.

You said all of Judah was witnessing the same destruction. It was clear that the chosen people never should have rebelled, that god went to their heads. You spoke of the war, and I wanted to tell you how it had been for me. How, when the children got so unruly, I pricked my fingers with a knife to relax, and once used the blood to scare them into silence. How, when Noy lost his tooth, we had to burn the master's silver to seal the wound. How often I disappeared into the bathroom. Perhaps if I were vulnerable in the right way, you would stay with us. And maybe, after the war, if I was still alive...

"I'll come visit again," you said, standing. "If I can. You're lucky in a way. They don't seem to know what to do with children. You're just the odds and ends, especially you," you pointed to me, and I remembered that I was the outsider in this place.

We spent the next three days without much incident, living off your bread, praying for your return. The two children who went missing, the young girls, had left for the worst reason—to go to the temple to pray for god to save them. I had taught them such nonsense before, but to see them act on it, to be so foolish. There was no reason to search. They were gone. I had to change the story: The First Temple, Solomon's sanctuary, is no holy place. Pray here. If you leave, the devil will take you.

The worst was putting them to sleep. The children who were never unruly suddenly turned inward, remembering what was lost. They cried frantically. The worst—Levi and Shanti—gained a frenetic nervousness that kept them from sleep. Levi, always afraid of the dark, demanded candles be kept lit, keeping the other children awake. Soon enough one child would remember their parents and they'd all start sobbing into their bed of fluffed pillows.

I told them new stories, similar to the ones I had heard the Jewish handmaids tell, of a place in the sky. Tales of vengeance and bloodshed.

"There are two worlds," I whispered to them, circling the veranda. "One of light, the other, an unformed darkness."

"And the Babylonians?"

"From the dark world of course."

"Is there food in the light world?"

"There are gardens. With bushes holding every fruit and vegetable in such abundance. And goats for milk, and cattle for us to tend the land."

I told them stories of light rabbits and dark wolves, of light sheep and dark snakes, always with these two worlds, one we knew only in our memories, the other imprisoning us within our own city walls.

"What about the soldier?" Levi asked.

I imagined you, with wavy brown hair. My soldier, sweating, swinging iron.

"The soldier is from the light world, of course!" Eden shouted.

"Shh!" I hissed. "I don't think they heard you in Bethlehem."

"And what does he wear?"

I saw only skin, smelled only sweat. In my dreams a garland of daisies billeted your head.

"He wears absolutely nothing," I said.

Once the rations were gone, and the children asleep, I woke Eden and we embarked together, unshod, into the city's quiet night, wearing only our gowns. With the Babylonian soldiers clanking through the streets in iron boots, silence was our protector. Eden climbed the rooftop palisades while I took the alleys. We lurked in the dark, canvassing through the school and the marketplace, both scavenged clean. I passed chattering soldiers and lost track of Eden.

Tiptoeing into an old dwelling, I heard the long, haggard snores of the elderly.

Where people were, there was usually food. On my hands and knees, I crept across the beaten clay floor of the small abode, my sounds covered by snores. I crept up a stairway and crawled prone onto a rooftop laden with thatched baskets, each one empty. I discovered a row of straw baskets covered by planks of wood and cautiously removed each plank and lifted each basket, feeling their weight. Hidden beneath scrolls and tableware was a loaf of barley bread, a clay pot of dates, and boiled locusts. I swiped what I could carry into my sling.

From the rooftop, I spotted a troop of soldiers huddled around a man, dead in the street, his blood already dried in the dirt. On a nearby rooftop, an old woman screamed at the invaders. Hunger had driven her to provoke the enemy, unafraid of the consequences. "There will be justice!" she screamed. "You'll see!"

I didn't stay to watch. As the troop shuffled to the rooftops I headed into the alleys, trusting Eden was smart enough to do the same. In the empty market, a woman gestured at me from one of the barren fruit stalls. I ignored her at first. But she held a glistening object—an emerald.

"What do you want?" I whispered. A stupid question, and she looked at me with a deserving sneer. I tore off half the loaf of bread and snatched the jewel.

"I'm glad it went to you," she whispered. "Someone so young."

I found Eden waiting nearby the garden entrance. Only I carried the key.

"What is that?" she remarked, eyes on the emerald in my sling.

"What does it look like?" Her askew glance told me she could tell the children, give me a real riot. "Maybe we can trade it later," I assured her. "For bread."

The next day I hit the last straw, Noy pulling on my dress, not letting me eat, and then almost ripping my ear off. I stood to leave, sick of them all, and hit my head on a lamp. I was losing my mind.

I tried to sleep in the master's bedroom. The sound of crashing, smashing, slipping rocks. I couldn't tell if the children broke the dining table or what.

"Auntie! Come outside!"

On the rooftop garden we watched Solomon's Temple crumble into a smoldering fire pit. The smell of a year's stockpile of incense wafted through the city, a thick, heavy smoke. A boulder flew through the air and punched into the temple's side, leaving behind a small whirlwind of vapor.

"Are they killing god?" Shanti asked in a lilting voice.

"God can't be killed," Eden said, taking Shanti in her arms.

"Shh!" I reprimanded. "They can still hear us."

Another boulder flew, this one from beyond the walls. A marble pillar crumbled, quaking the earth. Stomachs rumbled. We chewed the dried-out tomato plants.

"Auntie," Levi said, "can you tell us when the temple was built?

"It is called *Solomon's* Temple, dummy!" Shanti broke in.

"But who was Solomon?"

"He was our greatest king," Eden said.

"My mother said he had a hundred wives," Levi said, chuckling. "All dark as night!"

"Women hold the seeds for the new world," I said, repeating words the mistress once told me. "But we can only be planted once the weeds have been uprooted." I wasn't getting it right.

"Why do they want to destroy us?" Eden asked, perhaps to no one. Tears formed in her eyes, and I curled her into me before the children could react.

I had no idea what to say. "Because we're good, and they're bad."

Shanti seemed annoyed by my remark. "My father said the Babylonians came because we refused to pay tribute."

Her confidence roused the children; they looked to me to respond.

"Belief is not a sin," I told them, trying to appear certain. "But it can be made into a crime."

"So what, Auntie," Eden said, sniffling. "We should just stop believing in anything?"

Thankfully, another sound distracted us. A boulder flew up in an arch following the sun and disappeared into the smoke. Then, a loud crashing of what could have been the temple's second pillar. The blocks tumbled through the city, breaking in screams that echoed into a future where they would be picked up and studied and re-aligned by men who would believe they were more than just stone.

I drew myself inward, unable to bear another moment pitying the city or its people. My memories of Solomon's Temple were not theirs. I was ten when the mistress first took me there, not long after I arrived in Jerusalem. She brought me to watch a goat sacrifice, which seemed no big

11

thing. But to see it in such a grand hall, with gold overlaid walls and bronze pillars, was something. Goopy innards cleaved out of the animal and I saw its soul sucked from its eyes.

Another boulder smashed into the golden temple's inner courtyard. We're all going to die, I thought.

"It's the people from the land of shadows!" Shanti shouted, pointing off the ledge. She hung from the balcony, her fluffy hair an easy target for a spear.

"Get back here!" I scolded in muted tones. "Eden! Take her!"

Eden muffled Shanti mid-scream and forced her from the ledge, but too late—the other children were already leering at the street below, where a group of six soldiers pounded on our neighbor's door. They used their shields as rams to force their way in. I recognized one of the shield's images: Marduk, their spiteful god.

"What are they doing?" one of the children asked.

Screams followed the soldiers' entry. Screams as useless as prayers, and just as easy to silence.

One of the soldiers lingered outside. His shield was different, with the image of the god Nargal, a man with a lion's body.

"Hey, evil ones!" Levi shouted.

I ducked instinctively. "Get down!" I whispered, grabbing Levi by his belt and pulling him against my side. I closed my eyes and thought of you. The soldier, our soldier, bringing us food, getting us out of this hell.

"Pray for the soldier to come," I said. "Pray he takes us to the light." If only I could change everything about myself, everything about the world I was stuck in. If I survived, I decided, I would do anything to escape my place.

I held Levi so close he struggled to free himself. I couldn't help but wrap him into me.

The soldiers left our neighbor's dwelling, leaving us a banquet of unspoiled morsels. I took Eden with me. We shuffled over rooftops laden with ash. We snuck through a dried-out garden, a dirty bath, a cluster of buckets left to capture rain, rows of clothes left to dry. We prowled, just quiet enough and just high enough not to be noticed. For the first time in days my stomach quaked in hunger, alive again, just thinking of the crumbs we might pick up.

The steps behind me drew silent. I saw Eden face-down in the alley, her head and leg bent to the left, mid-jump. Something metal, perhaps a nail, had pierced her foot. I called her name but her only response was to cry like a bleeding calf. Idiot! I thought. What good was it to wail— who could she be wailing to?

At the sound of shaking iron, I fled.

What could I say about Eden's loss? That she was killed by a nail? She had walked the rooftops a thousand times, her legs a thousand times nimbler than mine. Killed by what? The ash strewn about every rooftop? Or did hunger make her less perceptive to her surroundings? Or—did she see the soldiers, and finally, also see an end? It was like her, wasn't it, to dive into the arms of an iron-wielding barbarian. Her cheeks, flushed from impact with blood, could be called rosy.

On the rooftop garden near our home I found a full olive leaf. I would tell the children that the leaf came from the world of light. That's where Eden went. A place where tables were always being set and wheat was forever ready for harvest.

As for myself, I was beginning to believe that the entire world had ended. Stone was no longer stone.

The day didn't come by itself. We had to push the sun up, lift it with our arms to keep time from standing still. Since Eden disappeared, the children had been looking for cracks in the dark world, where they could squeeze through to the world of light. Every morning they woke up, toes to meet the sun, and saw the temple still gone, the spires and houses still a pile of rubble. Only one of the temple's towers still stood, ready to collapse at the next breeze. Even the bricks were pummeled into pebbles.

Hunger bit me. I imagined Eden's fate. Perhaps the soldiers shared her. Perhaps, like me, she would be sold to a rich family. Perhaps they would force her to bear for them as well. These wealthy women who refuse the pain of childbirth, but still grow jealous of the pregnant maid. Like my mistress, abandoning their least-favorite child, the one too dark to join them in exile, as dark as the maid who gave her life.

I grasped for that emerald hidden in my mistress's pillow. The jewel I saved for you, and all the other beaded anklets and necklaces I scavenged, awaiting your return. With no mirrors in the house, and no Eden, there was no one left to tell me how they looked, adorned on a creature like myself. I would know from your face, when your lips formed into young roots. If there were even a remote, thin filament of possibility of your return, I would survive.

The children no longer woke me. I pushed my body into their room where they lay stuck onto wet pillows like mussels on sea rock. Starvation was not how I thought. Their bellies looked full, distended, pregnant even, but their arms were like cracked branches ready for kindling. Levi had lost his fear of the dark. Shanti no longer talked back. Years of famine taught us to live on bread and wine, and often without bread. It also taught us how long the human body could last.

"Do you want to hear about the light world?" I asked the children, joining them on the pillows. "In the light world. They live a thousand years. They have entire cities full of offspring. Their fertility never ends. One day, those dark men will be blotted out. All flesh on this earth will perish. Remember."

I looked into Noy's eyes. The weighty sleep seeds gunked his eye slits, deepened and black. Dead eyes, until they blinked. I cried over what would soon be his deathbed. I wept for him, but not for my own child who never knew I gave her everything. Where was the line with the universe? I kept forgiving, expecting a deliverance that never came. But where was the line?

The sound of shuffling metal outside. Had they finally come for us? I saw three shiny helmets, waxed by well-fed underlings. Soldiers were now living inside the brick house near the neighborhood gate. I saw them tossing out relics from inside. Menorahs. Scrolls. Altars. More men appeared with their giant shields, their iron breastplates. The sunlight shone off them bright in white flames.

At dawn, I made for the commandeered house. If I were caught, I would tell them everything. None could say I went willingly.

My body shook on the wooden rails between our houses. My vision saw the sky in a bruise, and as the sun set, it turned into a welt. My body felt heavy, wavering, like Eden's

15

before she fell. Somehow, I made it onto the house's tiled rooftop. I heard voices and hid behind the lattice overlooking a small garden canopy. I tottered through the battered back door. A strange sound bellowed from the bedroom, sobs that became a loud wail. I used the noise to cover the clack of my feet as it met thin blue tile.

"I'll do anything," the sound went. With each word, I shuffled forward. With each scream, I crept another inch. When the wailing stopped, I grabbed onto a wooden pillar and held my breath.

Snatches of words came between wails: "... please, no ...please."

The courtyard was full of dirt where plants once grew, but even the weeds had been picked clean. I maneuvered into an empty dining hall. The wall across from me pounded, so I crawled on all fours, afraid the wall would break and that would be that. When the sound stopped, I stopped. When it came, I moved.

More sounds: "it hurts...please stop."

A basket! I couldn't help myself—I dove for it, opened it, saw the glorious feast—the bread, the salted meat! My cheeks wettened in gratitude. "Thank you Lord," I whispered.

The screams continued as I made my way out. I thanked God for the screams.

Food lasts only as long as will, and my will plodded forward for weeks, until I died covered in stones they would one day call precious. As death crept upon me I watched Solomon's Temple, a fortress once impregnable, reduced to a pile of stones. The children, their indignant howls, looped in my memory.

The temple's light was the last thing I saw, a holy beam that was indifferent to us, the maids and their children. But deeper than that, deeper than god was the feeling that you had risked everything to help us. As my heart beat its last, it furnaced a love that would one day tower over us all. My hope that you would return bringing bread and lamb, arms trembling with excess, smiling as my children ate their fill, had kept me breathing, until you were the only light left in the universe.

I could have waited eons for you living off the power of love alone. But, god knows, one has to eat something.

Life

B

Romans, the Han, the Parthians? Pre-Augustine? 100 BCE?

A battle. Barely a memory, could be invented.

"You" direct address, confusing Flimsy False Hope!

This life doesn't project well. Not images but sensations, smells, tunes, all lodged in memory's passing. I remember fighting, but I cannot name the war.

Faces are hazy. Impressions of the opponent: tough, lofty soldiers, emerging from the forest into the open country. Then pulling down their pants to taunt us—their saggy red-spotted cheeks riddled with disease, shaking at us from the mud. Our general told us to stare at them; his bald head was covered by a red insignia of a bird. An eagle? A phoenix? A dove? He assured us we would skewer those barbarous cads. We believed him, for when it came to meting out death, our army had no equal.

The barbarians began to rally near the fortification walls. They dragged three of our captured brethren nude in the mud. Blood seeped from their bracers like slug slime, and their sages proclaimed that the blood-signs augured victory. A unit performed drills, hurling spears at wooden dummies decked in our bloody armor.

"The more you watch," the general said to me, "the more weaknesses you will see."

When daylight dissipated over the dew-dripped trees we heard their war cries. I felt the fear that had once paralyzed my village with tales of foreigners coming to claim us. The stories of their determination were true. The barbarians had brought their women and children with them. They would pave over our city with their offspring, or die trying.

When the sun rose, we woke to see our enemy: an entire nation on the move, waving at us in our fort. It never occurred to us that they could just walk by.

One taunted us, waving his dick in a circle. "We will say hello to your wives at home!"

Had I a wife? I dream of your face, burned into my mind. You *were* there, in this life, though I had scoured you from memory. When I died, I shouted past the battlefield, to the eons gone by, somewhere in the unfolding of time, where you might hear it.

Let me try again. When I first saw you, you were tousling your hair to release its moisture. Whether black, brown, or blonde, your hair fell in tresses along your collar, down your back, and bound with a thread, perhaps gold. Whether straight and angled or circular and ripe, your face had not a blemish. In your eyes, whether blue, green, or brown, paradise stood, love in one iris, beauty in the other. You sat upon a stairway, your body grave and stately, your heart tender, and all you looked upon were made the same by your gaze.

I saw you at a village festival and your beauty was matchless. I, a young man who had never loved, gladdened at your sight, and grew grateful for life. I paced the fields near the revelry, watching you. From which village did you hail? Had you a husband, a lover? Every person that spoke to you subdued me. I felt fire, scorn, love, all at once. When our eyes met, you gave me an awkward glance, as if to say "and why these eyes, and why me?"

I was reborn in the glint of your eyes. I had no defenses against it—what love! It assailed me, dragged my heart against the seabed, sent me rolled and shaken, rudderless, adrift with no sight of shore. What type of malady was love, that it could turn fire to water and then to fire again? I felt myself drown; I felt flames stroke my blood. I felt the life, the energy, and the rage, swirling over every mote of your soul, even as you covered it with laughter. I would love you until my heart incinerated.

Away from your sight, desire blazed. I strained in my bed contorting in silent agony. My uncles believed I was diseased, but neither potions nor leach-craft could squelch the inferno that enveloped me. Its embers were crusted onto my heart, melding us together. As soon as the heat drew back, images of your face, your lips, came like oil to erupt another flare.

This was how I was when the barbarians attacked: in a trance between desire and despair, ready for love's wrath to bring me to the port of death. But this agony also made me fearless. So, when I heard the clamor of bells and women shrieking and marauders pillaging, I was not afraid.

I flew into battle with a wooden shield and a dull axe and hacked a man just outside my door, staining the wood with his blood. Another charged me, lashing the shield from my grip. But I caught him, my free hand girding his manhood, and I struck him in a frenzy, hacking at him until calm washed over my body and desire began to recede.

The foreigners fled when a phalanx of soldiers on horseback appeared. The trails that stretched to the edge of the village were filled with bodies of livestock and children.

Survivors stood nearby. Every villager was in a true fright. And I had woken from slumber, courting death to the pinnacle of desire.

Calvary rode by in a troop of ten. There I first saw the general—hacks splayed upon his helmet. He glowered at me through the gap in his helm, saw my bloody axe, my shield hacked to pieces, and not a plate of armor on my chest. He saw my flame, my strength, my hardened flesh. He saluted me, clasping his gauntlet to his breastplate.

It was valiant for a man to wage one's honor and that of his family's five generations back to the one they loved, and to go to battle in their name. I did not know your name, but I vowed that you would forever be master of my heart, until the day I fell. I went the way of many love-struck subjects of the vale: to field! Battle after battle, I played the part of a noble gentle knight, toiling toward an honorable death. I asked for neither deeds nor riches. I waged my heart into war.

After the last column of barbarians passed our fort, the general signaled us to move out. It took many days for their columns of men, women, and children to pass us by, and only then, with their backs turned, when they were sloppy with drink, did we move to strike.

I led a troop of men, hawk in hand, between the hills of a sparsely grown valley. I felt myself reaching that sacred river, where your spirit would meet mine.

With sword, shield, and fist, we ambushed their backline. We caught a group of them bathing in a pond and we poisoned the waters with their blood.

At daybreak, a soldier pleaded to the general for permission to return to our fort. We had expended our water, with no way to resupply. The general pointed to the far-off lake, behind the enemy. "Let your thirst drive you."

We charged the first column. Their leaders had chained their ankles together so they could not run away. We cut through them like sifting through straw. Some of the men came loose from their chains to retreat, only to find their wives, at the rear of the columns, holding axes, ready to kill any cowards in their midst.

The women slaughtered their husbands, their brothers, and then themselves. Their entire nation died in front of us. It was either kill us, or become nothing.

Blood clung to my ankles. We slaughtered them and called it sacrifices for the gods. The muddy field was strewn with blood, even that of their children, who they had killed to keep from mixing with us. We killed one person and absorbed the silence, waiting to hear a gurgle, a groan, and moved on to the next. Once the battlefield was quiet with death, I could no longer remember your face, but I heard your spirit sing.

I meant to die. Alive, I could not return to you, for I was more afraid of love than war. Without war, there was nothing to feed the fire. Cruel battle was my only salve. In the atrocity of war's end, I was still among the living.

Night fell and I marched along the length of the lake, treading blood and mud beneath the stars. Deep in the enemy encampment, I drew into a hut that smelled of sour wine. I disrobed my armor, my clothing, my helmet, and lay down on a burly cot, covering myself with the enemy's straw blankets.

I heard the general's men nearing my abode, rifling through every hut, cutting down any survivors. They were trained to kill in an instant, to draw out death like the sweep of a broom, with a single easy stroke. The moon's pale gleam shone through the hut. I wondered who you would be in the next life. If fire grew around you, or if you grew it in your palms.

Life

88 BCE - Rome.
The last life before blooming.

C

The first encounter with desired object. Fetish develops.

This is a whole Lot of Olives

I recall this life all too well. My first vivid memory was the day I saw your face against a dazzlingly bright afternoon sky. There you were in Rome's Forum, standing upon a revolving stand of servants.

I was on an errand from my master when you caught my eye. Despite your misfortune you looked poised upon that stage, regal even. The way you drew back your shoulders and gazed imperiously upon the marketplace. And something else. Your skin, gleaming with sweat, strummed my insides. The white wooden mask covering your face snapped me loose. Your arms were chained to the pin of a rotating stage that seemed to stop just for me. When they tore off your mask to sell you, your eyes shot out with Minerva's lustre, a frightening glare that would remain burned into my memory for the next three millennia.

The Quaestors had engraved your identity on a plaque:

Origin: Palestina.

Character: Obedient, loving, family-oriented. Will serve you in the best way with the best heart.

Skills: Able to do general housekeeping and take care of

children. Cooks Persian cuisine. Very good with purple olives.

Language: Judaic. Limited Latin.

I stood watching you from the middle of the Forum for what seemed like hours, as one by one, the other slaves were sold off. The buying started with the most educated ones, who went to the Antonii and Furnilla families to tutor their children. Then the smiths and child-bearers. Ever since the previous round of slaves that emerged from the war, Patrician families no longer needed cooks. If you were not sold soon, you would be a mistress to the spas.

I sped from the crowd, embarrassed that you, this dark beauty before me, might spot me in my coarse and dirtied tunic. I found my brother Juvenal carrying a batch of bath towels. "Have we no need for another maid?" I asked him. Juvenal was a bath servant with access to the equestrians, who, overfed and indolent, relied on servants to share gossip. "Listen," I told him. "Can you get some gossip to my house? Is there a wife? A daughter? A mistress?"

"My duchess—" he started.

"—Just the same. Tell her this. The new thing for maids. Palestina women make the best cooks, because…they have the biggest hearts."

"Gha! who'll believe—"

"No problem, ok? Persian food. Cures—alcoholism, let's say.

"Is that—"

"And, purple olives rid disease. Or, no—they give energy! Ok. Now *Hurry*!"

Juvenal went disappearing behind the playhouse. Everything I told him was the opposite of the usual gossip.

Horse-sense wisdom dictated that Palestina women were aggressive, known to harbor questionable thoughts. And Persian cooking was far too salted for the Roman palate. But gossip was most effective when it shocked, when it seemed ahead of its time.

Days later you were in my master's house, a silent woman who knew not a word of Latin, and who the lady of the house had taken to calling "the Persian." You appeared bashful, gentle, simple of attire, an unordinary pleasure. But your brown eyes transported me into scorched lands of gods and beasts. Every morning, after teaching the children, I followed you around the estate, holding ladders as you dusted marble, sampling from the hummus and pitas you cooked. Inexperienced with such exquisite beauty, I menaced you. I criticized your oily meals and asked you to adjust your unkempt figure. I reasoned that I was helping you, giving you fair warning before the masters found a reason to punish you. But as a servant myself, I knew not how to combine the power of my position with the love in my heart.

What I could never criticize was your skill with the purple olive. Some part of your essence seemed to speak to the plant, convincing it to lend its sweetness into your breads, cheeses and wins. Not a drop was wasted. You even used the oil to keep the shiny glaze on our master's tables. During lavish dinners, the family showed off your kebabs and olive soups, while I grew closer to you in the servant's quarters eating nuts and bread. You poured the least diluted wines for me, and did not protest when I inched closer. In your sleepy eyes I returned to the lakes and mountains of my village, and in your kiss I knew the bliss of my mothers and sisters, whose debt had cost me my freedom.

For two years our masters visited the Italian provinces, leaving you and I in an empty mansion without fear for punishment. By then I had grown kinder to you, stressing my position only to impress you. You never learned Latin, yet I found a deeper language in your body: the curve of your back as you poured wine said, 'my darling.' Every posture expressed your nature, and I learned to read your body as we dressed in our masters' clothes, made love in their beds, and took to raising their children as our own.

When the masters returned I remembered my position, but you never forgot the taste of comfort. You left abrasions in the cutting board as you split each olive apart, the purple liquid spilling out of its skin like regurgitated wine. I tried to instruct you in obedience. Our master had provided for us, kept his promises, paid off our debts in exchange for a few years of our lives. In his house, we could experience luxury like nothing our villages could offer. Our master was so good he even promised that upon his death, we would all be free.

One night our master crept into your room. I remained, hiding behind a curtain, as his tall shadow spread upon the candle-lit walls. "You will go with me to the provinces this time," he told you, sucking on a dessert of olives. "I simply cannot tear myself away."

When the master took you from me, I believed it was in his right. Even still, as the days passed, remorse grew like layers of dust upon the marble walls.

My compliance made no difference. Not long after you left, our master's body was carried into the Forum, his corpse so full of stab wounds that not a drop of blood remained. Before they could confine us to our quarters, I fetched Juvenal and his gossip. Our master hadn't even crossed the Antium before he died of poisoning. In his right hand, still, the purple skin of crushed olives.

"Palestina slave!" the gossipers whispered, assuring themselves that they had known all along. Some hailed you as a hero, a slave who killed for freedom. But there was no freedom to come, just unmitigated punishment. The law stated plainly:

> *If a slave murders his master, then not only him, but all the slaves of the household shall be tossed off the Tarpeian rock.*

You were to be freed from your chains only for the moment between being hurled off the cliff and hitting the rocks below. And the rest of us, sixteen servants, were to follow. Your desire for freedom consigned us to graves shared with murderers, traitors, and arsonists.

At dawn, a crowd of sympathizers followed our procession through Rome, some rankled by the injustice that all of us were to be executed. But most had come to see you, the Palestina maid whose will was Medea's vengeful wrath. For us they felt pity, but for you, their eyes remarked upon your skin, your lips, all that had made you.

The summit overlooked the Forum, where I first laid eyes on you, when all I saw was your beauty. At the cliff's edge you stopped struggling, perhaps captivated by the view. The executioner read your warrant and you stared at the sky with a quiet defiance.

Your silence accomplished nothing. The executioner hurled your body toward the market where you had first come into my world. But the gods did intervene—somehow your body lingered in that moment between your granted freedom and the rocks below. I recalled your eyes the first time I saw you, brown gems on the white mask you wore.

As your body sank slowly into the air, your pink-tinged eyes locked onto mine. Not to assess or despise. It was a soft, aching look. In your lips I tasted your olives. In your irises I felt your fire and smelled the bread you had smuggled for me and my children. Taste, fire, scent, over and over, every sensation absorbing your essence, flooding me with some eternal magic. Sailing toward death, your body tore through air, unguarded and powerless. That look was our parting gift, absent of parting words. As your body hit the rocks, I felt your soul stab through the fabric of our world, tugging mine along.

Then the executioner flung me from the cliff. I aimed for the rocks marked in your blood. The debris of time stripped away until I collided with your corpse.

In the thousands of years since I was tossed from that rock, I've come to imagine what happened next went thus: an otherworldly aura bound itself to me, flailed me through the cosmos, aimed my soul toward no particular place, but was drawn to something: a ship in the middle of an empty blue sea, in that dissected center where my bright star-like shield sent me skidding across the water until I landed inside the berth I would revisit for thousands of years to come, the place where I now write these very words.

It was a soft landing. My first breath inhaled the scent of jasmine and pine. My body rocked upon waves, my head cushioned upon swan-feathered pillows, beneath the heavy blue and white sailor-striped comforters so heavy, much heavier than the scratchy wool in my servant's quarters back in Rome. I recalled feeling without memory; hitting the stone, my limbs snapping, my head cracking open, touching your lifeless body.

I was thrown, and my first thought was that nothing had saved me, that I was still paralyzed, my fingers curling around rock. But in this strange world, my body had reset, unbroken and embraced by silk. I curled into it like an embryo. The warmth, the comfort, the chill of cool sheets beneath me. If there ever was a bed to lie in for days, while blood crept slowly to my brain, then yes, I was in it, and lie is just what I did.

The room contained me in eggshell-white walls. Through lace curtains, I saw a pristine blue ocean. The room itself was strange—walls made of iron, not wood. How did we stay afloat? Across from the bed stood a sink with a ceramic Parthian waterspout in the shape of a man's head. I yanked on a beaded cord and water came out, easily, like a pump.

On the foot of the bed lay a scroll that read in an opaque cursive, THE GRAND MEDITERRANEAN PLEASURE CRUISE. The next page carried a readable script bordered by realistic drawings of young men and women, some nude, some with eyes like sharp arrowheads, some whose bodies were painted over in black symbols. Below the drawings, the scroll read:

Grata Domum

Bienvenido a Casa

Wilcuma Hām

歡迎回家

Bienvenue Chez Toi

بہ خانہ خوش آمدی

Welkom Tois

Below these words was a painting of bulky hills covered in mist, and in the corner, a man ascending an icy ledge.

ROCK CLIMBING

Another image held the dark figures of Egyptian pottery, a goddess supine upon a sea.

FULL SERVICE SPA

I skimmed through the remaining amenities, each matched with the image of a god. The only one I recognized was the goddess Cybele, enthroned with lion, cornucopia, and mural crown.

FITNESS CENTER

ORATIONS

MARKETS

CASBAH

WRESTLING MATCHES

ICE SKATING

ORGIES

24-HOUR SURF SIMULATOR

CASINO

POOL GAMES

TOURNAMENTS

WINE

This is how it all ends, I thought. I felt needles prickling my spine, kneading at me. In the mirror I had the same face, the same chiton and shawl I wore before I tasted air.

Then I remembered you, the Persian maid. Even in that heavy sent of Jasmine, I could still smell your olives. My mind sparked in pain. Your jaw hitting the rock with an awful crack. We had no idea we would end up here, but if we had, surely, you wouldn't have rebelled as you did.

But where were you? I pictured you, but could not recall your name. It began with an "S."

I shot from the room into a lightly perfumed hallway as wide as the Rhine that led deep into the ship in both directions, so far I could not see an end. A pair of men strode by, their ornate clothing as strange as the figures in the drawings. In Rome, I believed I was in the center of the world, but had never seen such people. One of the men wore clothing as regal as an Eastern Emperor's, with a long silk tunic, patterned all over in diamond shapes, ornamented with bands at the wrist and neckline. The other wore a mauve tunic snugly secured by a loose, low-slung leather belt at his hips, girded with a buckle decorated in jeweled medallions. When they took notice of me, they reviewed my clothes, my chest, my legs.

"A bloomer?" they whispered.

They passed me with smiles and I followed them down the hall, emulating their stride as I passed numbered doors.

"Welcome," a voice said. I turned, but saw no one, just the barren white hall. The voice came again, feminine and ethereal.

"*Oceanus*: we ride the stream that encircles the world."

The voice seemed to come from all directions, a voice from my thoughts, perhaps, but real nonetheless.

"You can trust me," the voice said. "This is a world without pain, without judgment or division."

I moved through that hallway that never ended. If I was dead, where was the Styx? Where was Charon, the ferryman?

"Let go of fear," the voice said in a whisper. "That is the string that ties you to worldly passions."

I came to a wide oak door. It had no number, but a steatite plaque of a serpentine beast. Through it, I entered a gymnasium of inlaid marble paneling with steam baths on one side and a track full of young runners on the other. I walked atop a grassy path, believing I was in a dream. I was in a realm of gods, each concerned only with lifting weights and inhaling steam.

"Rid yourself of impatience," the voice came again. "Here, time is infinite."

I was back in the empty hall. Black ghost figures filtered through the hallway. I followed the scent of baked bread and pushed into a crowd, searching for you, a Palestina whose name began with S. I felt your presence, slicing tomatoes over a stove, giving me the first bites.

I found myself in a large oval hall as spacious as the coliseum, with tapestries of centaurs and large carpets supporting circles of people, their lips gummed with redcurrant. They took fruit offered by servants dressed in loose garments.

"To serve is to know humility," the voice said. "*Asepsis*: cleanse ourselves of all patina."

I passed large muscular bodies conversing in food-filled grumbles, giving no attention to their speech, so I could hear nothing but cacophonic chatter. I wove myself between sitting bodies. None ate greedily, none seemed amused by the rare delicacies: sliced mangoes, scored lamb outfitted with prunes, muskmelon seeds. Among the gourmandizing of pork and the slurping of soft white cream, were people dressed as priests, monks, Pharaohs, soldiers, and a cadre of crowned beings I could not recognize. Souls from past lives, but all here—doing what?

"Each of them has lived in suffering," the voice said.

"Each has known the impermanence of the stream. They have each earned their place among us."

I zipped through an archway of long purple drapes to another banquet hall, this one covered in a canopy of smoke and steam. At eye-level were rows of circular tables, each one centered by pots of boiling water and small grills to cook thin cuts of beef and lamb. Near the cackle of fried meat and vegetables, an acting troop performed The Bacchae on a raised arena stage, with Agave holding what looked like the real human head of her son.

"In the Ilium we are all the same. No prejudices exist. We accept the harmony of the structure."

The hall's window displayed that deep blue ocean, its surface as still as untouched bathwater. I took leaping steps up a grand marble staircase, out of the smoke and steam and then I was in it, a real sun that warmed my body, in that cool breeze without smell or the tinge of cold. And that yellow sun—polished, fragile, and indefinable, as if it were made by the same hands as landscape tapestries. I stared right into it and felt no pain.

The ocean sea rocked the boat in easy waves. No men handled the oars, and for that matter—no oars. Nothing on the ship seemed seaworthy. There was only a sail as large as a temple and just as stable, its taut material the soft texture of a white rose petal. This was no galley. Something unreal kept the ship from foundering.

The boat tilted right, and I leaned against an iron rail, near rows of reclined chairs that supported tight-bodied souls. The boat tilted left, toward that incredible light of the sun, and I saw not the bodies around me but the harrowing pain of memory—Solomon's Temple burning, my sword crushing a barbarian's skull, my imprisonment inside my master's triclinium. I was once that servant who offered snacks of cheese and pheasants to the guests. The boat tilted right again in an easy sway.

"S!" I thought. But none of those souls could have been you. I knew it as soon as I looked about, scanning every high-breasted virgin beauty. None of them reclined the way you did, never relaxed but never on edge. None slept the way you slept, with balled up fists squeezing a candle or the leg of a stool, as if to anchor yourself to the dirt. There was always something uneasy about you, something sharp about your shape. But these souls were at ease.

"All you loved has not yet bloomed." This time the voice came from a tall woman clad in Valkyrie armor. Her golden hair was braided through a leather pouch bulging with wood and stone that rocked back and forth with the ship's dull sway.

"She is down there," the goddess said, eyes on the ocean below. "Along with all the pain and suffering you once knew." Her bangs cupped her forehead like a lion's claw, her crystal eyes keenly on me. "No use thinking of those who continue to writhe within the stream. They are, well, inconsequential."

My heart clenched. I couldn't remember your name, but I saw your face, felt your kiss, tasted your tears. The ocean screamed as water slapped the boat, and I heard you fly from the Tarpeian Rock. Sweat trailed the blue veins leading to my fingers and I fell upon the iron rail. I felt only you: born into a new life, rising in unspeakable beauty. Then: the men who would conquer you, who mustered all the ingenuity they knew to lure your heart into their net.

"To remain here," the goddess said with those full, ambrosial lips, "you must learn to suspend your baseness. Your insatiable shadow. Your lustful heart."

In the sun's sparkle I heard a strange cackling, a chorus of souls struggling together in chains, the wind lashing them in waves upon the ship's hull. I felt your magnetic embrace, though the drop to the ocean below was daunting. I had come into this world falling. Perhaps, in the same way, I could return to you.

Life

D

You will doubt my memories here. I doubt them myself. Trying to remember this far back, events blend with tall tales. Can a memory, unclear and unreasonable, simply be discarded?

This was an age when nothing was written, for the future had nothing for us. Even the great empire had retracted into squabbled chaos, retreated behind fortified walls, long abandoning me and my great chase. Yet I still pursued her—you, of the same soul but different nature. I hunted you through ancient, war-torn cities, rarely stopping, rarely sleeping. I was an old man when I sensed you again, after years in the empire's badlands, scouring the world for your tracks.

All the hospitality had gone out of Perd. The ancient magician's city had faded to a resting place for weary warriors and monks. I smelled barbecued otter near an old portrait of the restricted God Ka, with smears of dried grease atop the canvas; I passed the remains of a torched inn, its burnt wood smeared with the blood of the empire's enemies. Once locked inside with the fire, their charred remains traced the archaic symbols its priests had died to protect.

Even the magicians' schools near the mountains were converted into forts, towering over the snowed city, poised ready to turn against their own people. The children pointed to me, spotting my dirtied cloak and empty eyes; they knew I was among the last generation of magicians, those once branded as heretics. The children took no time for me, they knew who I was hunting: you, the last dragon. And I, the last fool fighting for an empire that had already begun to crumble.

My silver staff glowed as my spell of direction picked up your scent. The children followed my furred boot-heels to the city gate, but they could not go any further. Not yet asleep, I followed your diminishing cry.

The petrifying wind of the north stanched my thirst and froze my grip to my staff. The direction spell led me outside the imperium, toward land hemmed-in by icy cliffs scrawled by dragon's claws. You knew I lurked behind. Your trail took me on a mystic eddying ride down steep cliffs and ice. I was determined to follow you anywhere, even after my spells drained. To death, to the greatest reach unmapped.

I proceeded through the imperium's last icy archway, chewing on clumps of oats and walnuts. With my death, the magicians would fade into memories of pleasing songs, ritual dances, and parades. Our descendants would be held up, weak and sputtering, for the crowd's gaze. The empire outsmarted us. They dwindled our numbers, not by attacking us directly, but by enlisting us to fight. They gave us a prophetic war. It brought purpose to our schools, and gave us meaning beyond that of heretics. We felt useful, locked in a battle with a beastly enemy. The war between us, a war the empire had begun, would be our end.

Bereft of the spell of warmth, I continued into the cloud-speckled light, onto the flatness of a frozen lake with green pecks of hardened seaweed. Standing under that heavy sky upon the remains of a vast, dim moor, I saw your shadowy figure—Evald, the last wild dragon. After all my will to end your life, I could not help seeing how beautiful you were, how you were growing more beautiful. Your rugged skin was so unlike your domestic brethren who played fire tricks behind iron bars. Your wings shone in the gray sunlight like a crescent moon. Your nose expelled a deep bright orange flame. Cornered in the harsh tundra, you sought to frighten me away, the last primitive impulses of your life now caught in a perfervid dance of smoke. I cast a multiplicity illusion so that I appeared as a hundred. You took aim at my copies, crushing them with fierce fireballs that split crevices into the frozen lake. Then you aimed at nothing, your crazed dance a fire-spitting pirouette. And amidst that chaos I heard your savage laughter. I followed it with the fuzzed traces of my own incantations, ice spells and weather alterations that brought hail and lightning to strike your wings. Battered across the hard surface of the lake, your body buckled and heaved, your escape put to rest by the cold, your tattered body too numbed for chasing.

I left your corpse and walked alone across the snow, stepping languorously across a spacious sky, my staff clicking sharply against stone. The cold slowed my breath, shocked me into panic. With too little strength to return to the imperium, I marched northward, through the silver-imprinted runes of an even more ancient civilization: the Tydes, legendary high priests who we magicians once expelled from our dominion. The *Song of Wharre* told of the Tyde necromancers from the north with the powers of possession and resurrection, powers we could neither understand nor hope to master. But they were much fewer in number. In one generation of war, we wiped them out, nary a single surviving Tyde child to beg for repentance. Now I, the last magician, would join them in their frozen heaths, with my boots on death's step, far from the imperium's reach.

The ruins were frozen over, inhabited only by smog and mist, with no voice to remind us of its history. Sloughed into a frozen Tyde dwelling, I let my breath sink beneath the snow. The light of my staff waned, emitting a firefly's soft glow. As it darkened, the gleam of that luminescent diamond sky brought me familiar, mindful offerings.

Life

E

First time the Destroyer contacts. Must be before 1100.

733 - The Battle of Tours

Need Trans. "No shelter for the People"

Perhaps half a dozen lives passed, each only half lived. And in each the yearning I carried for you grew, scorching any type of kindling it neared. For over a thousand years it burned brighter and brighter, until in one life, it caught the attention of an entity who came to see all the things my love for you could devour.

When it first revealed its true nature to me, I was a child sitting atop a wagon. A cobbled path opened before our caravan, led by mules and horses that pushed past the city trenches, then the row of beech trees outside the city, and into the afternoon sun's striking heat. My imagination took off, forming adventure upon the flat earth before me. I envisioned a spear sticking from a patch of blue and pink flowers, the only color in sight. The ground was the dirt where Christians could be hiding. The sky was filled with high, unreachable branches of cork trees, where Christians could be hiding. And just ahead of us, the princess screamed, begging for rescue.

I picked up the pretend spear, lobbed it at Izîl, saddled all rosy clean on his mule, and it pretend pierced through his chest cavity. "Gawwwd!" he pretend screamed. He

42

broke the wood as he tried to draw it out, pretend splinters cutting through his skin.

"Tariq!" My older brother, Muhammed, called to me. His arms were folded upon his dark tunic tied with a crimson sash turned bright red by the sunlight. "Get out of the sun," he said, kicking his feet up on the wagon's side. "Your rash."

Just being reminded of my scraggy skin made me itch. I scratched my arm until it hurt.

"Stop scratching," Muhammed said, his wheat-brown eyes on me. As his head receded into the wagon, a pretend dune lark perched on his ear and pecked into his temple.

The caravan moved through another cork grove. The shade cooled us.

"How much longer now?" I asked.

"We've barely left Cordoba," Izîl responded from his mule. Behind me, six Amazigh recruits followed silently, their red keffiyeh headdresses trailing behind us. Behind them I could still spot the capital city's bright brown spire.

Izîl added, "Feel free to walk off any time, kid." Two of the mule-back soldiers shared a laugh.

"Ice that son of a goat!" I pretend yelled. And there she was—my trusty, pretend goddess, Amunet, unclad and all-woman warrior, her body covered in red ochre. The goddess bounded from the top of a cork tree and scythed Izîl's head off, caught the head in mid-air by its beard, swung it like a lasso, and chucked the frozen-in-shock face into a lark nest. "Die vermin!" Amunet screeched in a reverberating voice as she kicked dust onto the broken eggs. She fell laughing, kicking her legs up to churn out every guffaw.

"Wait!" she came to a halt, sniffing the air. Her yellow cat-eyes struck from place to place. "I smell death." Assailed

43

by the scent, she shoved her nose into the birds, the eggs, and Izîl's corpse, as the unfazed mule dragged it over the dirt. "The smell of death. By my divine grace." She heaved from the smell. "Yeah, that's still where it's at. It's hard to describe—ok, you know a date, when it's about to mold?" She flew in the air brisk as a kite, the yellow silk from her cape draping down. Four white feathers from her gold necklace encircled her like leaves caught in a web.

Our wagon passed an old mosque. From a plot of trees, we were back in the unforgiving sun. Pretend bubbles floated up from the loamy mounds of earth. They popped above us, cooling us with sprinkles of rain.

Amunet tapped her fingers on her neck. "Top notch, Tariq! Your imagination remains potent. I got the pulse and everything. Shall we play with some fish?"

Fish swam by in swarms of blue, pink, and glittering gold. Over the years, Amunet had trained me to imagine them, each with unique differences—golden scales, crocodile jaws, wolf tails. Following alongside the wagon, Amunet spun her scythe in a death dance, blood spilling from every sliced fish and then dispersing in puffs of red smoke.

A pretend band of Christian terrorists emerged from the mosque, a growing fire behind them, its smoke flowing in a spiral toward the sun to give me shade. From inside the mosque, a woman's voice screeched in pain. "Arrraahhaagh!"

"Amunet!" I commanded her, "Save the princess!" I scratched my skin as the Christians heaved spears at Amunet, her spinning scythe splitting their bodies in half, ripping through their iron armor and helmets like papyrus.

"This is fun and all," Amunet remarked. "But why do you always imagine this *princess* piffle! Humans and your bathetic savagery. And killing these people? This is disgusting. Your mind, the dirt of a shoe." She levitated into the cork trees, the Christians taunting her from below. She hurled rocks at desert birds, hitting them every time. Square between their pretend eyes.

"It would do you good to read something," Muhammed said, taking me out of the daydream, back to the silent earth. Our wagon turned into a small canyon covered in vines. The canyon's walls loomed over us, and our soldiers kept their hands at their sabers. "No sense being the first literate person in our family," Muhammed said, sitting cross-legged to comfort himself through the bumps on the road. "And spending all your time musing and staring at the desert."

"I could be of some greater use," I said, a bird landing on my shoulder. Dozens more came. They lifted me up so that I circled the wagon on a throne of fluttering hawks, doves and falcons. A flamingo, my magistrate, followed my circle from the dirt below in wonky steps.

"Allah has always protected our lands," Muhammed said, though I could barely hear him from the sky. "In Cordoba, you sit and learn with Jews and Christians. Does it matter to Allah? No. In Cordoba, you have something entirely new, but it's normal for you, so you don't appreciate it, head always in the clouds."

From my levitation height, "But we've always been—"

"—never mind that." He tapped on the ruby and sapphire jewels embedded into his saber's hilt. "Just learn and study, like the Arabs. It's not fair only they should become wise, while we fight."

The birds lowered me, puffed out in black smoke. "I wish I had never learned to read," I said.

Muhammed shuffled through the galley of weapons at

the base of the wagon: small scimitars, bows and arrows, maces and helmets. He pulled out a dried codex and after dusting it off, handed it to me. "The clerk said it was easy to read," Muhammed said. "Even for Berbers."

I had only ever read from the Quran, yet I could read the words better than I expected.

"Out loud," Muhammed said. "I want to see those lessons put to use."

"I should be training," I said. "The battle is only days away, isn't it?"

"While the sun is up, you read."

I read:

> Time has gnawed at me, bit me and has cut me.
> Time has harmed, wounded and injured me,
> and has destroyed my men who have died together.
> This has made me restless.
> They were not a harbor for the cruel
> Just like the sun, which is no shelter for the people.

I read on, glancing from the codex to look at Amunet. Her naked legs hung over a canyon rock wall. Christians surrounded her, pointed spears at her, and behind them, encased in a prison of stone bars, the princess screamed to be set free.

Amunet ignored them. Even as the Christians pierced her, she ignored my game, her yellow cat-eyes whispering to me in a voice only I could sense. "All the time I've wasted training you," her voice said, spears jabbing at her skin, her body refusing to bleed. She sniffed the air, eyes closed, smelling a fruit in that sweetened moment, on the cusp of rotting.

"Tariq!" My brother scolded me with one last quelling look. "Read!"

I read again:

"Just like the sun, which is no shelter for the people."

The caravan made camp in the canyon, with daylight enough to start a fire. Muhammed instructed me to light it while he fed and watered the horses. "We Berbers may be warriors now," he said, leaning on a rack of dried meat. "But for centuries we have been wanderers. Any Berber should know how to start a fire."

I struck the flint in a pinch. Its smoke turned black as it incinerated a handful of leaves. I fed it bristle. It gasped for air, swallowing sticks, and then took a bite of the wood. Finally, it sparked in joy. Muhammed rubbed my head and lay down on that brown rug spun by our mother.

From the edge of the fire, Amunet sat in a fetal position, naked legs covering her mouth in a veil. Fish swam by, got roasted in the smoke. "It's a hell of a thing," she said. "The smell of death just before it strikes." She stood, her supple stomach flashing the gold of the fire as its ash flew through her naked body. She covered her mouth and inhaled. "Oh, Tariq, it's everywhere."

The princess appeared beside the fire, dancing, wearing a kuchi of coins around her waist. In the silent shade of the canyon, the coins tinkled in soft echoes. Her eyes reached out to me from behind her blue mask, heaven in her eyes. A spark from the fire landed on her shirt and spread onto the gold brocades at her shoulders.

"The princess is burning!" I pretend yelled. "Amunet, save her!"

"Forget her!" Amunet shoved the princess into the fire. The flames engulfed her before she could scream.

"What are you doing?"

Driving the princess's face into the pyre, "Forget her already!"

—*Tariq?*

A wave bore into the fire. A torrent of rain. A river. A cyclone.

"Amunet, please! Save her!"

"—Tariq!" Muhammed yelled, breaking my dream with a toss of a prayer mat that rolled out at my feet. "Time for Salat!" He sneered.

In the light of the four fires of our caravan, I saw the other soldiers bent on their knees, hands pointed east. I swiped dirt from my hands and began my own prayer. My mouth recited a verse, but meanwhile thinking: Let me prove myself, let me be admired. Let me save the princess. Let me be good in the eyes of the Lord.

Amunet stood before me, in the direction of Mecca, hands covering her mouth and nose. "You might as well be worshipping rocks," she said beneath her palms. "All this smell of death around you, and this is how you react? Delusions of a princess, and now, of a god?" She squat to my level, the last slice of sunlight in her yellow eyes. "Tariq, I shouldn't say, but there's no harm in telling you now. I am a supernatural being. Not a pretend one. A real one. You might call me a god. But don't, you might worship me. That would be embarrassing. And ethically unsound."

"You're in my imagination," I said. A fish sailed by her. A nest of birds appeared in her hair.

"I am, but I'm also in my own." She shook the birds,

out, annoyed, and sat below a canvas of stars. "For my kind, imagination is a form of travel, much faster than a caravan. The beings in my world—we live on the bark of a tree. We see everything outside it, while you are just part of the wood, smashed into each other, too dense to see much. But imagination, that's how we can tap into you. I appear in your daydreams. Doesn't sound like much, but there's no greater power in the universe."

I looked away from her, toward the ground, but Amunet remained in my vision, shrinking when I looked down, larger than the moon when I looked up. Was she attached to my eyeball? I shut my eyes and she remained, her gold tinsel twirling about. Snakes on a black background. I should have been quoting a verse, but I was paralyzed with fear.

"You've always been in my daydreams. How can you be otherwise?"

She sniffed the air. "You know, nothing beats the scent of death. Like yeast on the crux of its rise. You know how much I love it."

"It is weird."

"Well, right now, you reek of it."

I bent my head onto the mat and sniffed the air, but smelled nothing.

God is the greatest, God is the greatest
I bear witness that there is none worthy of worship but God

"And the princess," I pretend said, head toward the darkening sky. "Is she real too?"

Amunet scoffed, her hand waving away the question. "You're such a dolt!" She pushed me on my back. "For six lives I've followed you, watched you grow up, given every chance possible, like a cat fed only on fish." She paced in mid-air. "And what happens? Every single time. It's 'oh, my beautiful maiden!' or 'oh, one day my prince will come!' until you die and piss yourself silly."

> I bear witness that Muhammad is the prophet of God
>
> Come to prayer
>
> Come to success

"You can't seem to get out of it," Amunet continued. "Every life, even though you can't remember your own rotting tits from the life before. It's always love, love! Fie on love! Just cliché and starry eyes. Don't you realize how—"

She prattled on. I refused her my imagination.

> God is the greatest, God is the greatest
>
> There is no deity but God.

I rubbed dirt from my pants and began rolling up the prayer mat.

"But is she real?" I whispered.

Amunet's voice returned. "Yes, you sod. Like you, another barren-brained barbarian. She's just a—just a *human.*"

"But is she real?"

—*Tariq!*

"Oh god, the smell, holy hell. Can't you smell that? Even your fish scatter away. See? Your imagination seems to know what's what."

"Is she *real*?"

"—Get down!"

I felt dirt, Muhammed's body on top of me. Fire lit our wagon with an intense orange light. "Inside!" Muhammed screamed, lifting my waist. A horse neighed and the ground shook; I collapsed in the entrance of purple rugs.

I scampered into the corner of the rectangular tent as the sound of battle burst from all directions. No clashing of armor and swords, just screams and galloping and screams. I saw Muhammed's silhouette on the tent's entrance, dark and disproportionally large. I heard the metallic rasp of a scimitar being unsheathed.

"Tell me what you're feeling," said Amunet, sitting atop the sharp curve of her scythe, balanced upright on the rug.

"I'm going to heaven," I said, looking over the tent for a weapon. Fruit, bread, clothing, rugs.

"Mmhmm."

"I'll meet her there."

"Wow."

An arrow zipped through the entrance rug and stuck into the earth. Not pretend. Its wood was sanded down fine, and carried small red leaves on its end.

"She's real, isn't she?"

Amunet leapt from her scythe, and swung it at a pretend desert lark, decapitating it. "Gods condemn you!" she shouted at them.

"She's *real*, right?"

"She's not as you imagined."

"Show her to me."

"Amazing, even moments before death, you still—"

"—how will I find her in heaven, if I don't know what she looks like?"

"What a retort. Fine! Here she is."

51

For the first time, Amunet used a power not of my imagination. Time and space distorted into a blur as a portal bordered by amethyst jewels appeared in the center of the tent, a window to another realm. Water poured through, the rush of rain. A thunderstorm. When my eyes adjusted I saw an old man covered in chains. His skin was pale and white hair ringed his spotted scalp.

He was you, S. In this life, you were a gray-bearded prisoner sitting cross-legged on a stone floor, staring out a window blocked by metal bars.

"What is this?" I asked.

"Your princess. Don't feel too bad for him. He's had worse. In other lives."

"Show me the princess."

"That's *her*. Not as you expected? Well, she is in a prison. You were at least right about that."

Your white hair blended into your short beard. On your chest was a tattoo of the cross.

"He is Christian," I said. "You're lying."

Another arrow sliced through the tent, pinning down a food mat.

Amunet's yellow cat-eyes settled upon me. "It's time you stopped, don't you think? She's not worth another life."

"You're lying. It's a lie!"

Another arrow pierced the tent. Through the rip, I saw Muhammed on the attack, his silhouette growing smaller.

I pulled one of the arrows from a straw basket, unsure of what to do with it, and peeked through the heavy rug entrance. Muhammed's head rolled toward me, his expression calm, accepting. I saw none of our soldiers still standing, only Christians, clad in iron armor and swords larger than my own body.

Something happened—a jolt of pain, then I fell into rocks and dirt.

"Try not to look at your body," Amunet said, though I couldn't see her. "Pinch your fingers. Don't pass out yet."

Screams came from farther down the caravan. Two Christians on horseback galloped by, torches in hand. One lit the tent.

"Those are my things!" I said. The fire grew, inching toward me, but I couldn't move my legs. "What happened?" I pined.

"Don't use your real voice," Amunet said. "Save your energy. Tell me in your imagination. What are you thinking now?"

"They're burning my books," I pretend said. "That's *mine*."

"That's rich! What else?"

"The Princess."

"There it is."

"She's alive."

"That's a bit of a stretch. Well, yes, he is alive, technically. But so is a potato."

"Why is she in prison?"

"*That* was an old, decaying man. Not a *she*."

"Why is *he* there?"

Amunet hovered above me, peering at the body I could not lift my neck to see. "I shouldn't say. But I suppose you won't remember anything in the next life, will you? So. That old man, he grew up on a farm, his father was part of a peasant revolt. He was captured."

"He's been in prison all his life?"

"Six years as a servant-boy. Four serving in the mines. Two more as a servant, then sixteen in the mines, the rest in chains. He tried to escape of course, attacked fellow inmates, and a handful of guards. Once, before he was released, he spat in the face of a nun. Chained again. Now, here he is, desolate and alone, another life well wasted."

Amunet opened the portal again. I saw you, your eyes staring at the turbulent wind in front of your cell. Your stomach in rippled red rashes.

"That's her," I said. "She's real. In the flesh."

"Fascinating."

"That's her. That's her." My breathing escalated; I could no longer control my lungs.

"Tell you what. I'll leave her with you, Tariq. In the next life, try not to imagine any birds. You know how much they freak me out."

The weary fire began to suffocate, in want of wood. The Christians' laughter and victory chants echoed in the canyon. I died watching your body shake from cold. It was a pity, I imagined, to never know how much you were loved.

Life

*Name origins flannfluga,
Kjar — interv. as nee.*

*885-6 (Siege of Paris)
Scandinavia /Vikings*

No Boundaries

Misfit.

F

The scent of pig stew wafted in, waking me. The key hanging from my waistband opened the blue-patterned clothing box beside my loom. I took out the blouse layered in deep blue cotton, bound with a ribbon of glittering gold crust, and hurried to slip it on. The stew's scent made me weary with hunger, another cluttered mess of peas, carrots, turnips, and bone. I shooed Edda, one of my white cats, off another locked box and withdrew a cube of incense. Lighting it brought back Kjar's scent. I slammed shut the bedroom door with my foot and absorbed you in a pleasant fog.

In this life, the townswomen called me flannfluga, the woman who flees from men. But I spent every morning with you, my Kjar, wrapped in your scent, wearing the clothes you sent me from abroad. I conjured your breath when it was really my own exhale; I recalled your fingers tracing my veins. After fifteen years of your absence, I had mastered this art.

At the age of twelve, I married a stranger. At thirteen, he went viking and never returned. Our marriage began as an alliance, but grew into an excuse to cloud my body in transformative linens and wools, in silver jewelry, in patterns

55

made from my own loom. I was often left on my own to tend the cattle and to make medicine for the winter illnesses. But I was not lonely. Like Freya, I became accustomed to sharing my life with cats.

I was sixteen when I visited the long house for my first þing, where the leaders of all the tribes went to vote, argue, and posture. Women could not speak there, but we felt little need to. From the audience, we sent our servants to serve bran-packed bread to the men, so that nature might interrupt their arguments before their axes did.

That was when I first smelled your deep musty scent—the scent of some faraway earth. I could not have prepared for the dreams your scent would confer on me. My heart in a blaze, I watched you, a bawdy, broad-shouldered man, as you spoke of going viking again, this time deeper into the great fertile lands, seeking a place that Christians called Gaul. There you would build settlements, and perhaps never return. The women seemed furious with this proposal. How could you men do this, when no women went with you? Who would you marry?

Even when the þing denied your proposal, it was already done: I was a ghost striving for your scent. That night, my sharp-purple kerchief yanked you to me in the dark recesses of the long house, then behind the trees bordering the plains, then into the mining caverns. We pulled at each other's clothes. You twirled your tongue around my nipples. I gave you bruises; the walls gave me scrapes.

For a year you visited my husband's farm, bringing me clothing from your viking expeditions. You came bringing dresses in bejeweled orange and vermilion, garments in colors of sun-yellow and sea green that I could spin, weave, and dismantle at whim. You brought me shawls and turbans from the Steppes, leopard-skin from traders beyond the great sea. When you noticed I took to your smell, you brought stacks of incense from some faraway land you could not pronounce.

"Perhaps I will give up viking," you told me once, after our lovemaking. "You cannot run this farm by yourself. Your husband is probably dead—it is no shame to marry again."

As soon as my heart leapt, so too my passion died.

"What wasted girth," I told you. "You ask me to marry someone whose battle axe, blunted and worn, is only good for logging?"

At the next þing you won your proposal. I was true to my word and married you, only to see you sail.

I folded a thick bear-fur scarf around my body as I paced through the fields with Tostig just beside, carrying buttermilk for my servants. In the fields, Sven cut corn with an iron sickle, while Ingrid swept and bound stocks of wheat. All my servants were captives from your first viking in Gaul, their hair darker than any others in our village. They gathered around me, sitting on folded corn and sipping buttermilk, reporting the status of the yields. Before taking my leave, I reminded them of their quota.

I last saw you fifteen years ago, upon your brief return, when you brought me walnuts, grapes, and wine. I went to meet you at the dock, wearing a pair of oval brooches of gilt bronze. You sent me so many textiles over the years, each woven through so many gowns. For over ten years I yearned for your return, ripping the clothes you sent when I was in anger, breathing deep your incense when I hoped to reminisce.

When your ship arrived, I saw my reflection mirrored in the gray waters of the bay. I went home and refused to see you. When you came to my door, the servants kept it locked. "Your rule," I told you through the doorway, "only begins outside these walls." You asked me to promise that in Asgard, in the halls of Valhall, we would find each other. "No," I told you, wiping my tear-streaked face upon the purple brocade you had sent with the last haul. "I will not go into Odin's banquet. I will wait for you in Freya's heaven, our Folkvang." We did not have time to argue, and neither of us were the types to change our minds.

Just before death claimed me, birds had augured my passing, and I was prepared, body and mind, to lose the thread of life. The servants helped me plan my most exquisite dress, the one I would be buried in. Only days before, I had received word of your death at the hands of six thousand barbaric Christians—an exaggeration, no doubt, or worse, a lie, just like all the lies told when a man starts a family elsewhere. But if you were really gone, then I too had to pass on, if we were to meet each other in the next life. In Odin's abode, or Freya's.

I spent my last day on my spindle, assorting textiles from your conquests. Dresses filled every room of my house, each one clawed by my cats and ridden with their hair.

I lit the last mount of incense and began to thread the wickerwork. I cut loose strands, wove in emeralds, jewels, diamonds. It could take hours, maybe days, but in the end, I would make a rope so beautiful, so exquisite, that not even Freya could deny my skill. Its jeweled pieces, I prayed, would attract your spirit with the promise of a treasure far-away.

Life

1,100 AD? Only est
from order, incl. prev. life & Illum.

G

A tropical archipelago,
high mountains. Many possibilities.

Lodes Untouched by Common
Empires

O, 871's Poor Recollection Is On Display...

In my next life, I was more of a tool than a human being—
something to be bandied about, used or unused, to be kept
down, to be worried over. I was the chief's estranged son
who preferred crafting and weaving to hunting and killing.
But only women weaved and cultivated. Men fished, hunted, and raided.

I was a child when thoughts of you ensorcelled me,
pleading me back to my previous life. In the growing cold
of winter, as the snow sculpted the distant mountain of our
island, I could not help myself in picking up the woman's
craft. As the fruit died from cold, I too was remade.

In my fifteenth winter I refused to hunt; I was a corpse for
the hunt of our rivals. To be of my people was to be hungry with vengeance. I hated going on the hunts, slapping at
mosquitos, and having to perform the role of a domineer-
ing warrior. So I took an attitude carefully designed as dis-
missive when I wanted to listen, unhelpful when I wanted
to assist, and violent as it was possible for a man to be, all

wrapped up in a casted persona, unmeasured in its aggressive posturing. There was no greater pain than this.

When the northern breeze of my eighteenth winter came, I was still unable to find a wife. Until then I had never considered women for my passions.

A shaman came to our house. Tattoos of crescents smattered her skin. Banging on drums made of pig hide, she summoned the spirits, invoking my unseen past. She sang in a voice from my dream.

"You were in love before you were born," the shaman told me. "Your past life was of sweetness and ice, a life of eternal winter. In that life you promised yourself to another. Your husband. You promised to find each other in the next life. This life."

Then the shaman and my brothers tied me down, leaving my stomach exposed as she cut along my ribs with a sharp blade and let pour the blood where my spirit's memories survived long after death. "Love is in the blood," she rasped as my body went numb in winter's cold. On the brink of death, I forgot your scent.

"You must be cleansed again next winter," the shaman told me in a creaking voice. "And every winter hereafter."

My twentieth winter was of sunshine and surf. One could barely tell the time of year, but I still went through the bloodletting ritual. I was married to Oarcea that spring, but the thought of sex still made me nauseous. The sight of a woman's body was all visual rot. And how could I be disloyal to you, the husband of my past life?

When finally I could see snow from our house, my wife came to me in disguise, her face masked in the war paint of a huntsman, her body clothed in the fur and feathers of our chief. I wore nothing save a cloth that I had weaved in my youth. At first I did not know who she was, yet something filled my senses. I felt your hands traipsing their way down my stomach. I felt your manhood, deep in my throat.

"I've seen you somewhere," I whispered. "Somewhere far away."

It was on an early morning of my twenty-ninth winter when the enemy raided my family. I told Oarcea to stay huddled in the house with our five children. I had seen them before, the warrior tribe, in their ungovernable lust for blood. To take my wife was part of their ritual to manhood; to take their heads was part of mine.

They entered my house, salivating at the sight of Oarcea's exposed breasts. I hid crouched in the corner. Like snakes they snipped at her, forced her closer to my concealed axe. When I began lopping off their heads, my children joined my battle cry.

By my thirty-ninth winter I had learned to be discreet. In summer I dressed in the clothes of our great chief, but in winter my wife dressed in them as we grew intimate beneath fur blankets. What else was there to do in winter, when every cold breeze felt like your voice whispering into my earlobe? We were isolated then, our children grown and with their own families. The bloodletting ritual was no cure; its numbness only brought back your scent; the feeling of blood pouring down my skin left me in an avalanche of desire.

On a sallow afternoon during my forty-fifth winter, I watched clouds like fish-scales over the ocean. On the beach, I arranged men made of straw as my eldest grand-child practiced his straight blade. His younger sister bent to yank a dagger from the weapon rack.

"No no no," I told her, taking the blade from her.

"Granddad, why?" she asked.

"It is forbidden." I returned to stringing the bow that would be used in my grandson's hunt, where he was expected to bring back his first hog.

"Can I help build it, granddad?" My granddaughter asked, pointing to the sheaf of arrows within my sash.

"It is forbidden," I said.

My fiftieth winter. I spent my remaining days crafting head-dresses, using Oarcea's weaving tools, though she was long passed. The winter troubled my memory. When the air felt calm, I stole away from my children and marched up the snow-capped mountain.

Halfway up the hill, I met the village shaman at a small creek bed, the trees tinged with frost. She wore a gloomy gray cloak, and faded red flags flapped across her chest. "Do not forget," she told me, handing me a sharp hailstone blade. "Bleed yourself to death, and in the next life, you will remember nothing. His scent will pass by you with the spring breeze. Your spirit will be free." I had survived three shamans since the first bloodletting, and I knew my destiny better than she. I kissed her coarse hand, thinking that I could have been like her, chief's son or no.

A great cloud covered all that I could see from the mountain. The snow had numbed my feet. Hard-bitten by cold, I began to remember all my lifetimes, people after people, furious with lust, mad with murder, pillaging each other's towns, celebrating death. I tossed the shaman's dagger into a bed of snow and fell on the iced dirt, waiting for your thick arms to hold me to sleep.

At the entrance to heaven's gymnos center, I formed myself into a firm, toned body, with a wide chest and bulging bronze biceps. Nearby, a sexy slice of Spartan man-muscle skipped on a jump rope, his skin rippling in perfectly timed repetition like a moon circling an object of deeper gravity. The gravity in question: a veritable cornucopia of genitalia, the lure of which thrust me into greater fervor as I entered the beast ring and brutalized a bull into submissive caws.

After washing off the blood, I reformed my body into a handsome, well-muscled twenty-two-year-old, with a snug outfit around my sinewy torso. It was a stark contrast to the coughing, flabby body I left behind in my last life, a body fed and watered with the plants.

I was told that my first arrival through the Ilium was a miracle. But the second time I landed inside stateroom #87101945 of the Grand Mediterranean Pleasure Cruise, the souls that filled the ship wondered if I was a god, if the structure had chosen me for some ominous purpose. Many began to pray again, to whichever deity they could remember.

The one who monitored me during my first visit, before I impulsively leapt into the stream, knocked on my stateroom door just as I was beginning to recognize my room's egg-white walls, its oak desk, and the flat blue ocean outside. I opened the door and saw not the golden-haired Valkyrie, but a daintier figure, less goddess and more empress. She wore a narrow-cuffed, knee-length tunic tied with a sash, and beneath that a narrow, ankle-length skirt. Her hair, now black, was still woven through that swaying fist-sized leather pouch, which now peeked from her right elbow.

"I shouldn't be wasting time on you," she snapped, sitting cross-legged on the stateroom divan. "In the millennium since your last arrival, my role has optimized. But you, you were something of an unfinished puzzle. As far as I know, no soul has ever leapt into the stream and returned."

Her voice inhabited an unusual but mesmerizing cadence, finishing unnecessarily opaque words with an even more unnecessary drawl of every syllable. I ran my finger across the ceramic horsehead spout of my room's sink, avoiding her probing gaze. "Luckily for me," she said. "You're rather easy on the eyes. Hnh. Ok, I'll take you as my ward. But this time, don't be so easily *stooped*."

Her name, she told me, was Cryss. And though it would take a century, Cryss would teach me the art of living graciously within heaven's Great Mediterranean Pleasure Cruise.

My first arrival was a mistake, she said. I must have inched my way in, bartered too heavily with death. "You were besotted on worldly delights," she told me. "And took love for the hot desire of passion. The pleasures of heaven, you will find, go far beyond what mere love can provide."

For the next nine decades, Cryss taught me to suspend myself within the Ilium's harmonic bliss, letting time breeze by in a cloudless open sky. And for nine decades I could have been in the stream looking for you. Instead, I chose a polished afterlife, with thousands of souls who had once lived an effortlessly prolonged existence. I too was a success in that sense, for in my last life, I was given a bad hand, as the blossomed say. But I had the gusto to play it right, to forestall death until the proper moment. Though it was never clear what exactly I had done to earn the Ilium, the proof was in being here.

And for nine decades I waited for you to join me. After one hundred years, if a soul were unable to forget, memory would take them, infecting them like a disease until they lived forever immured within their pasts. And just like clockwork, after nearly a century, my past lives began to return with greater clarity. They came like lost dreams, sparked to life by a scent or a song. I tossed a discus across the gymnos lawn and recalled a past life as a cavalryman, tossing a spear at a naked, charging barbarian. With each twist of my body, I felt the motion of the horse beneath me—a black, magnificent creature.

The sports park extended deep into the cruise ship. I passed a small beach of high point break waves, where bloomers surfed and paddled. Just across stood a glossy rock wall with dashes of ice and snow. Blurred sunlight hazed out from the ceiling of smudged glass. A guide passed with a group of new enlightened souls—hunky men who seemed too shy for their bodies. Like Cryss during my first entry, the guide was dressed as a goddess, the Virgin Mary, slender with wide eyes and a luminous blue shawl. She spoke in an ethereal voice: "The deckhands aboard the cruise ship range in the thousands. Janitors, doctors, mechanics, research technicians."

"But did they get into heaven as well?" one of the hunky men asked.

"Sometimes," the guide said. "Those who pass from the stream know patience. Work generates patience."

Another life sparked in my mind. I too was once a servant—*we* were slaves together, domestics for a Roman family. Who was *we*? There was me, but also a woman, an import from the Holy Lands. I remembered your scent of olives. I remembered the letter S.

With no limit to my energy, I may have exercised for months. Eventually I tumbled out of the gym and ventured to the ship's night end, The Beauty Bay, a hall dressed like a Moroccan casbah bathed in a fragrant smoke that colored its glass lamps purple and gold. A lit menorah met me at the entrance, and I weaved between bronze chandeliers, passing a group of revelers wearing strips of orange silk in their hair, carrying tilted pipes, their eyes drifting like puffs of smoke. The charming aroma of a hookah lured me into Cryss' private sedan.

I ducked though a silk drape, into a tent lit by a single torch that levitated in the room's center. Cryss appeared across the room from behind a veil of vapor, her progeny Jezebel beside her, chewing on a piece of smoked fish, her hair covered in an over-the-top golden crown made of in-laid kingfisher feathers and decorated with gold dragons and beaded pheasants. Jezebel took a look at me and burst into laughter, hiding her smile with a chunk of salmon. In the soft glow of a bronze lamp, I saw myself: Greek, male, sweaty.

"Don't be skittish," Cryss said, her throat starched with smoke. "Keep your skin on, baby boy." Her body was wrapped in a purple rippled dress with a bold studded leather belt accenting her waist.

"Something's wrong," I told her, circling the torch fire. "I think I'm going crazy."

Jezebel leered at me, scolding me with her eyes. She did not speak—her tongue had been hacked out in her past life, an old debt, and the soul preferred silence.

"This is a fire temple," Cryss said, cradling my face in her hand. "It offends the gods to turn your back on the flame." She turned my eyes to the fire. "*flōs*: blossom from the mighty."

"I've come for counsel," I said.

"I'm reluctant to moralize you." Her mind trickled oil onto the flame. "So I'll be unfaltering in my injunction." Her head tilted, letting the words linger out of her mouth as the torch fire brightened. "Or have you forgotten how to receive pleasure?"

In the mirror above a tray of incense, I saw the new body I had unconsciously built for myself: a long-haired brunette with a veil covering my nape. It had taken decades for me to control my imagination, to generate myself into new forms. For this form, I took a craftsman's love of detail, designing its skin as the pinpoint where all sexual preferences overlapped. The first time I showed this skin to Cryss, she said I was one of those bloomers with a writer's imagination. With practice, I could will anything to life.

Cryss took my arm and yanked me to her, pivoting me on the point of my red heel. Her ribs rubbed against my breast; her lips whispered into the shell of my ear: "You shouldn't turn your back on the fire. Some believe it holds some scrying magic, able to foretell fortune—but you must follow its lead."

The flame cackled and a flood of memory shook me. I breathed and felt your exhale. I let a tear squeeze through my eye, certain that somewhere, you were in pain.

Cryss gave a maniacal laugh, her hands around my

neck, choking me, but not entirely stifling my airways. "Too eager to peck," she whispered. She bound me there, forcing me to face the torch, as Jezebel's hand stroked my thigh.

"My past lives are becoming clearer," I whispered to Cryss. "Have you ever heard of two spirits encountering each other, again and again, throughout their life cycles?"

My words sent Jezebel's desire away, and she went to lazily unthread a throw pillow. Cryss traced a slender forefinger across my nape. "Let me guess," she said, cupping my chin to keep my eyes to the flame. "This spirit you remember, again and again. She, or he, is still caught in the stream. Yet you've been here for nearly a century. You have the honey, but not the gall to drink it."

A spark cackled from the fire.

"I need to find her."

"Damn you're dull!" As she spoke the torch burst to life, exposing the glossy mosaic floor. "Why, overtaxed by the gift of light, you have become blind! One hundred years is nothing. Time, that old common arbiter, crowns all."

"But I've only ever been waiting for him."

"What is he seasoned with so well, that you cannot find the approximate mixture here? Beauty? A tight shape? A wise mind? Gentleness? Youth? Free thought? Passion? We have all assortments of these."

"Will he ever make it out?"

"Not all flowers bloom," she said. It was a common adage on the ship.

I circled the fire so I could see Cryss lounging on the back of her red velvet booth. "What if I went back?" I said. "Is it possible to save her from the cycles—to bring her here?"

"Cartographically speaking, we are in a riddle." She stretched out on the couch, bored by another common newbie question. "If you see someone walk into a burning house," she said, a coy smile on her lips. "Would you follow their path?"

I ventured to the balcony overlooking the vast ocean. The lights of the casbah coated the water below in a ringlet of gold-shot smoke. The ocean held a constant stream of souls, life after life in infinite repetition. So far, everything that had befallen me seemed distant, random, meaningless. But you were there, in every life, striking a chord that resonated across heaven and earth.

My fingers felt wrinkled. Somewhere, you were bathing. My face turned red and I felt you weeping. My eyes caught a bird of prey, a dark blot against a blue sky, and I felt that relentless urge to catch it.

Life

Where would Edessa be?
A code? A real place?
Near the Christians?

H

1140 AD.
871 is accurate with proper nouns
From the Seljuq empire in Edessa

The Destroyer Comes !
A Phantom Of Free Will   - Jahtiha !

Many lifetimes passed without you. Love receded from me, ebbing like a tide, until fortune gave me another chance. I was near you, but I could not see beyond the boundaries of war. Two days before my death, I rode a mule to the barren hills, and crossed a rivulet that marked the no-man's land between the Seljuq empire and Edessa. I would return to Edessa, the once bountiful city of my birth, then strewn with cadavers and poisoned by Christian devils.

Rumors of the uprising against the crusaders led me from the northern plains to the outskirts of the city. My mule was laden with sacks of food for the insurgent camp: baklavas, pomegranates, nan, and hamir. At the dip of the desert valley, I felt the eyes of my Sunni brothers upon me from behind shrubs and rocks, espying my intentions. I led the mule slowly with my left hand, tilting my body to show them my right arm, where my hand was maimed in Edessa's first battles.

"A friend," I called to them, raising my flat stump.

The insurgents came out from the bushes like weary ghosts. There were three of them, their bodies enervated, their eyes focused on the sacks slung from my mule, tasting

71

the bread with their eyes. I recognized one of the men as one of the many boys I had helped train years before, one of the few who escaped the first battles when the crusaders overpowered us. Last I saw him he was a child. The insurgency camp had dissolved his youth.

"I know you," I told him. "I have news from the empire."

"You are the second messenger today," the man said, scratching his dusty beard. "So I wonder then, who is the real messenger, and who is the spy?"

A silence fell. I observed their situation—they had already eaten their mules, and no gravesites littered the hills.

"I know Volkan," I said, walking my mule closer to the young man. "He still leads you, yes? We were friends, before the siege."

The young man scoffed. "Volkan has never had friends."

"He had me."

The wrinkles on his face disappeared as his brittle jaw cracked. "Did he?"

In this life you were Volkan, my childhood friend. And though you grew up to lead an insurgency in the name of our great prophet, you were never very pious, except when it came to matters of the body. An orphan, you had to seek out a life without antecedents, making yourself up as you went along. As an adult, this gave you a boastful pride, as if you had made the whole world in your image. While I struggled to survive in the refugee villages, your insurgency fought for our ancient city. Before the Christians, Edessa's university rivaled those in Persia, and our mosques were known even in Mecca. Edessa, city of Abraham and Job. For you, Edessa was the world.

I followed your men to a circle of thick cedar trees where you sat cross-legged in your warrior's black tunic, a red sash holding your saber. Unlit candles sat at your sides, and before you stood a bronze shield smoothed into a mirror. You were always like that, looking at your own image in ponds, rubbing the fat below your chest as if this would make it firm. Without the aid of Edessa's teahouses and yogurt, you looked far more aged than when I last saw you.

"The empire plans to finally send reinforcements," you said, spinning a long knife upon a rock. You seemed in the habit of doing so, for the rock was so flat that the knife spun easily, until you stopped it, pointing toward me. "At least that's what the first messenger already told me. So, I have to ask—why have you really come here, Kareem?"

When you said my name, I could no longer hold my longing. You said it fully, your tongue twiddling at the long "e" sound. Even in your squat old-man stink, I wanted you—your skin, dried and patched like a sack, soft flesh lurking underneath.

"I bring word from the empire," I said. "But also from Gaye, your wife. You remember her?"

The three men who had escorted me put their hands to their swords. You were silent and took to spinning the knife again.

"Or your children?" I taunted.

"Answer my question, Kareem," you said, grabbing the knife, and thumbing the hilt against the rock, as if you could flatten it further.

I unbuttoned the satchel at my side and brought out three dolls made of twine and dyed yellow. "Look, one from each of your children. Ipek, Ece, and—"

You drew the knife up, slamming the sharp end into rock. The echo reverberated through the grains of sand at my feet. The three men behind me pushed me onto my knees. One held a knife at my throat.

"Leave us!" you shouted at them. You sun-stared them until they sheathed their swords and headed off to eat the bread from my mule.

"You're going to stop being a silly little cur?" you chided.

"If I must," I replied, tossing the twine dolls. You let them bounce from your wide chest. My hands drew upon it.

"Never again," you said, pushing my hands away. "We are embroiled in a war against fanatics. Every impure rumor about us loses a regiment."

"Then why do you fight?" I pounded your broad chest, then gripped your flesh. Your chest always seemed further to the left side of your body than it should have been, your heart unprotected by your ribs.

"You know better than to ask." Your sober eyes finally drew me back.

I sat up on my knees, tears forming in my eyes. "I came here because of a dream I had."

"Shocking."

"I didn't want to come. Gaye, after hearing of my dream, pleaded for me to find you. She knew you would refuse to see her, but that you might make an exception for me."

"No good has come from your dreams, Kareem," you said, standing. One of your chest hairs clung to my fingers. "A voice speaks to you through them. Sometimes it is a goat, sometimes a viper. You know what the holy Quran says about these Djinn."

"But his words are always true. My Djinni does not lie."

"Does he not? How wise of you to take advice from a soul-harvesting demon," you retorted, face unruffled. "The Djinn try to replace God. We can never know their intentions."

"They guard our mosques," I said. "They built Solomon's Temple."

"*Our* mosque was burned to the ground by Christians!" you shouted, stiffening your shoulders. "Your Djinni foretold of its burning, yet did *nothing*."

"Nevertheless, he has another message." I sank my head, hoping to quell your rage. "He told me that you would get reinforcements from the empire, that you would have everything you need to take back Edessa, and that you would fail. You will all be killed."

Your nose turned up at the scent of the bread hardening over a small fire.

"You'll still fight, won't you?"

"For Edessa? Always."

"Your stubbornness is astounding."

"We must be stubborn. A thousand years before now, there was no me. No you, either. Not even your Djinni. Before the prophet, even."

"So?"

"So." You clapped your hands, announcing the start of dinner.

We ate nan straight from the sacks, watching the desert winds pile sand. There were six groups of men sitting in small circles, with the bread and fruit I brought in the center of each. You sat high, overseeing the camp, your breath heavy enough to hear amid the mashing of lentil soup. Your only companion was the bearded young man who I had helped train, the man whose name I could not remember, and did not care to relearn.

Though my dreams were always true, my Djinni never mentioned him. Your new man, who was just a boy when I knew him. My Djinni foretold everything else: how I saved you when Edessa was attacked by the Christians, my wrist absorbing an arrow aimed at your throat; how I prevented you from eating tainted goat meat, which you chewed but did not swallow, for you had no sense of smell. Everything that you would not reveal about yourself, the Djinni prophesied. He spoke to me through daydreams, in the fabric of imagination. I dreamed so often of your marriage that I enjoyed myself at the ceremony, despite your inebriation. The marriage was just as the Djinni had foreseen: the multi-colored herbs of poppy seeds; the angelica and black tea leaves that garnished appetizers; the burning coals that almost lit Gaye's thin blue dress. Even Gaye, with her brown veil and her own consistent, silent worship of the prophet, would never plead against what you and I shared. The Djinni had predicted that too—the three of us sharing each other's lives in a forbidden matrimony. He told me first of the children, Ipek, Ece, and Demir, covered in a constant dust. Then of Gaye, welcoming me into your home, building a fire to keep us warm.

How could I know that, when the Djinn's prophecies came to pass, I would have no right hand, and could not build a fire by myself? Or that the children were covered in the dust of a refugee camp terrorized by sandstorms? The Djinni's dreams withheld details. My heart would be with you, my Djinni told me. But how could I guess that our love would be so strong as to drive you toward the insurgency, leaving Gaye alone and pining for you? How could I know that the children would be from my seed, though we would still call them yours?

During the two years when you and I lived together, before your marriage, the Djinni gave me dreams of places I had never seen. Mountains of white dust that burned to the touch but enfolded me with a strange cold. Dreams of sand upon deep, infinite water, where we had fished together. When you were a woman, when you were a beast, when you were a Christian, you were always my lost love. The Djinni gave me the dream of you and I, yoked together through time, through every life in Allah's vast creation. We met only to touch and part again, to move and pull away.

All those dreams, and yet, the Djinni never told me of this boy, not once. Damn this little son of a cow with his lean body so taut as he broke a piece of bread in half to give you the larger piece! The Djinni never gave heed to my longings. I could only wait for his prophecy to pass.

The next morning, reinforcements from the House of Seljuq arrived at the camp, their horses decorated with gold bands. Each cavalryman carried piles of spears and arrows strung together like firewood. Their blue robes seemed untouched by the desert sands; their bronze helmets shaped skyward to mimic a mosque's spires. The insurgents, now well fed, had transformed from the enervated apparitions of the previous day. Now they sharpened their arrowheads with focus and practiced shooting through crusader helmets. Even you, who knew my dreams were never wrong, commanded that we eat our fill, for victory was assured. Your voice inspired belief even in me, as I imagined in a blink that we were back in Edessa's familiar alleyways. No desert, no mules, no other men. Only us.

When I saw the white horse, a gift to the insurgency, panic struck me. Just as the Djinni had foretold: a white horse with a blue scarf, with red leather reins. A servant walked the animal ceremoniously, and the camp's insurgents stared in admiration as the horse passed. The insurgents cheered. The young man, *your* new man, clapped in a daze, riveted by the horse's wavy blonde hair. "A horse fit for a king!" He raised his fist toward your statuesque body.

The Djinni's dream was branded in my memory. I could still smell the wound from your stomach, your intestines ripped apart by a spear, your screams as you fell from your white horse, your black blood steaming like meat pulled from a smokehouse. The dream did not end there. I heard your heavy breathing stop. I watched as the crusaders piled your body atop other cadavers to make a mountain. I smelled your fat as it melted in the harsh desert sun, mixing with the others in a mash.

But I found myself holding a bowl of milk, in praise. Your young man made a toast to our forthcoming victory— the bloodbath, the terror that awaited us.

That night, right from under the noses of your grisly soldiers, who were tired from food and drink, I snatched your white horse, wrapping its leather strap around my maimed right arm, and rode toward Edessa.

"Fate does not buckle under." His voice came as I rode through the desert night. "Not yours, not his." The Djinni. Perhaps he spoke through the horse, but no—his visage appeared on a desert mount, a figure as tall and as slender as a cypress, a white tunic veiling his face. His voice rippled the sand, an echo through time. "I suppose," he said. "This is not the best time to chase your imaginary fish."

"You artless hustler," I said. "You never told me about the boy." The white horse below me grew sedate by the sight of the phantom. Animals always recognized a higher power.

The Djinni inhaled, drawing wind toward him. "So, fish. Out of the question?"

"Tell me what you really want from me," I said, gritting my teeth. "Why do you whisper about the future, but expect me not to react? What type of Djinn are you—evil or good?"

The visage remained in place, his light drowning out the white crescent moon. "I would not say I am a Djinn, and yet, out of all the made-up gods that your kind have impressed upon me, Djinn may well be the most accurate."

"What are you, I asked you! Evil or good?"

"How would they answer you, your compatriots?" His visage grew into a pillar, rising skywards and making northward, to Edessa, its walls a barely visible rectangle. "How might they respond to such a question, coming from you, a man they believe should not share the same Earth? Your deformity already makes you more a hindrance than a boon. But what of your desires? They are your own people—yet they would hack you to pieces, if they only knew."

"You are deceiving me."

"Deceive?" He curled over. "This image you see is but a pallid envoy for my true nature. I am *Dulcarnoun*, the unseen, the unknowable, but you give me shape and form. I am an emotion, a thought. *Alam al-mithal*, the imaginal plane. I only tell you what your body already senses. You possess all you need."

"You tell me he will *die*!" I could not control my voice. "You tell me they will all die! Our city, our people, everything! And nothing can be done! What am I supposed to do with these dreams? Why me?"

"You can smell it too," the visage said. "You're just a bit slow on the uptake." As his head lurched skyward, his bright veil bathed the desert sand in sparkling white light. "It's overpowering, the scent of a life's end."

He vanished in the waves of a mirage. As the light fizzled from my eyes, I saw again the distant torches on Edessa's city walls. The white horse paced toward it, though I gave no cue.

In the early morning, I rode back to the desert valley, where a great cloud of dust remained splattered upon the blue horizon. As I neared it, I saw Seljuq soldiers in their blue robes marching through the desert fauna, alongside rows of mameluke warriors and cavalry archers. For a moment I remembered the pride of the Seljuq and the majesty of our people.

I reached the pikemen just as they charged, their trilling battle cry striking the land, their war horns singing praises to men about to fall. I maneuvered west of their position, just in time to miss the stampede of the men surrounding heavy siege weapons like coats of blue armor. In the thick of it I found you, Volkan, leading the cavalry's charge, holding a pickaxe to climb the city wall. Your new man rode beside you, holding a red flag signaling to advance.

I wrapped the reins of the white horse around my right arm and gave chase, couching upon my saddle to keep from feeling the violent pounding of the earth.

"Volkan!" I screamed your name, nearing the front-lines. You snaked away from me. My left arm reached for the advance flag, but your man bustled away, his horse kicking up clods of dirt. I wrapped the reins even tighter about my right arm, letting the limb go numb, and gripped my horse's golden blonde hair. "Volkan!" I screamed over the din of battle. "The Christians know you're coming! They know!"

Your eyes met mine, disturbed at first, your hand moving to your scimitar hilt.

"What are you doing on my horse, Kareem!" you shouted.

"The crusaders know you are coming!" I cried in a rasp. "Their ballistas are positioned straight at you! Their archers lie in wait! Stop the charge!"

You sneered without even glancing in my direction. "And how do they know this!?"

Sweat poured from out of my blue cap in a ring that stuck the cotton to my head. I heard the whistling arc of arrows.

"Just stop, Volk, *please!*"

Your body rumbled upon your horse, but your head was stiff, pointing to Edessa. Arrogant and proud, you were deaf to my pleas.

"Volk, *please!*" I screamed, nearing you. Your bearded man kicked me from my left side. I fell, but was yanked up by the reigns strapped around my arm. The white horse hauled me along on its side, not whinnying or straying, but charging with you, unburdened by my deformed body. I groped upon its hair with my left hand, flailing like a doll, my boots skidding along the dry desert sand until finally the horse veered away and stopped.

The strap loosened on its own. I saw someone mount the white horse. Liquid flowed between my eyes. Blood sapped through my armor like a squeezed pomegranate.

"Volk," I said, seeing your squarish figure on top of the horse. "You cannot win. Stay. You must stay with me."

"Kareem," you replied, "A thousand years from now, we will not be here. But for now, we can still act."

"But we can be—"

"—don't tire yourself. The wind will blow on without you."

Coughing sand, I crawled toward the horse's white legs. I reached for you, your beautiful chest, knowing a spear would soon run through it. You looked as if you would say more, but you didn't. A new trail of dust lifted, carried upwards by the army's winds.

Night had fallen by the time I reached your empty insurgency camp. I collapsed onto your matted bed, surrounded by a sea of stars, my wails too late to join you in the next life. I gazed at the divine lights, given to us by god, but it was not god I saw. It was that cackling fire, sprouting on pure sand without kindling or smoke. Perhaps it only existed in my mind, but it was in my mind that I received the Djinni's last dream.

In the desert, a nude carcass was strung up. Vultures and hawks circled it. The decayed body was missing its head, and the ripped skin of its neck was so jagged it could have been beheaded by a dull paring knife. Flame had caused the figure's feet to furl into itself and thicken. In its crotch was a deep cut where its manhood should have been, its burnt tissue like a skinned goat hung out over a steaming brew.

I awoke shivering. Who was that man? Why did he deserve such punishment?

The corpse had no right hand. Instead, a maimed stump.

I waited for them, the survivors, whose desire for vengeance smelled like a spoiled apricot. I wept, but not for my own death. For a thousand years the dust would rise, with no Kareem, and no Volkan, to see it blow by.

Life

N Africa — Consistent monotheism led to monoamoury.

I

1256 AD. Vatambe no records.
"Bornuland"

"Only Loves Strangers"
Atypical Commands from a Deity

In life after life, my body was consigned to work for some encroaching empire. Travel seemed particular to great powers, so it was no coincidence that I encountered you again along my routes.

I met you during my eighth year as a Kanem military officer, when my caravan drove southwest of Lake Chad. To evade the vast deserts of the North, we went treading in the long yellow grass that grew from nearby oases. Further south and the oases turned to streams, then to rivers, and finally we were in the tall forests of Bornuland.

I went about my business receiving tribute for the empire, while those in my caravan went to work: the merchants traded pots, seeds and mamelukes; the imams searched for locals to convert; the mercenaries built hostels for Muslims on their hajj to Mecca. I was the only one representing the Kanem Empire.

While I packed for the route to the next tribute station, an aged farmer arrived, though he carried no tribute. Rather than take his land, I asked him about a woman who had come with him. She was you: a radiant being with long flowing hair, large eyes, and a black onyx necklace.

"That is Ugbabe," my servant said, translating the farmer's words. "She was given to the goddess Oya to pay her father's debts to the goddess. When she was young, she became a slut, and had a child. She refused to marry the father. An infidel and a whore, she only brings sin to men."

I could not tell if my servant was unnecessarily cruel in his translation. Raised in the desert lands myself, I wondered how these forest pagans imagined the divine. Perhaps Allah worked through your kind in other ways.

"I speak your tongue," you told me, bowing with a rushed inelegance. Three scars spread like lightning strikes across both sides of your face. "Everything your slave said about me is true," you said haughtily. "But you don't care, right?"

"You may address me as Santjyot," I told you, hoping to regain the Empire's formality. "I am charged as ambassador to your lands."

"I don't have the heart to consider you," you said. "The Goddess Oya, who has protected me since birth, only allows me to love strangers. So, I can be yours only for tonight. I owe this farmer anyways. He saved my life once."

People said that a woman married to a goddess could not be controlled. Such sayings usually accompanied stories of pagan fathers marrying their daughters to false gods. The belief was one of the many hoary nostrums of sacrifice, animal spirits, and wizardry that cohered into a sinful, backwards view of the world. But I never imagined one of those sacrificed daughters could grow up to love her fake goddess, and give her heart not as an obedient wife, but as something else entirely. Of course, I knew not of our past lives together, and my mind said to leave you, this impure woman. But I also felt something divine in your color. I became enthralled by the idea that your darkness needed my light.

We met in the wheat fields that night. Our love was so ecstatic that I barely noticed the cracks of lightning from an oncoming storm. I throttled in pleasure as the rain beat upon our meshing bodies. A pleasure I had never known, at least, not for several lifetimes.

My wives could never give me the ecstasy I experienced with you that night. So every summer for the next thirteen years, I made the voyage to the lands Southwest of Lake Chad receiving tribute, hoping to encounter you again. Then one muggy summer day, there you were, walking along the desert path near the long yellow grass, leading a trade caravan that crossed my own. I recognized you immediately, a large-eyed woman leading a train of servants who carried baskets of grain and millet on their heads. You had a proud stomach and thick arms, and the loose yellow buba wrap hanging off your shoulders barely clung to your curvy figure. The scars on your face appeared like the whiskers of a lion ready to pounce.

I could not help myself. I stopped to trade.

I had my servants build a makeshift covering of logs, stones, and tree leaves to block the sun. As I watched you set-up trading goods, I recalled my trespass thirteen years prior. I stuck my hand into my pouch to grip the small amulets that protected me from sin, cowry shells with special verses of the Quran. I repeated the verses silently as I watched you sort your wares. The Noble Quran 24:30. *Men must lower their gaze, protect themselves from the impure.*

As soon as you entered my covering, you seemed to know what I felt. My beard, my Taqiyah cap, my white robes, none of it could cover my lust. You crept toward me on the long rug, ignoring the bowl of dried fish and millet.

"We mustn't," I gasped. "You are an infidel."

"But we both want to." You spoke my tongue with your jumping accent. Your hair swept down, tickling my legs.

"We must first wed in front of Allah," I said, eyes closed.

"But I am already wed to the goddess Oya. By her command, I can only love strangers."

We kissed. You blew a great light, a great life, into my lips.

"Please. Marry me. We are not strangers. We loved each other, many years ago."

"We did?" You sat up, looking me over, your large legs cushioning your body. You squinted at me, unable to recall the memory.

"You *know* me!" I said, passion now bursting into anger. "I am Santjyot! We made love thirteen years ago and I have never forgotten it! I don't care about your goddess Oya! We must marry. You will live in luxury. All the clothing you desire. Servants, goats, wine, oils."

"I can only love strangers," you said, turning away.

I gripped your shoulder. "The Kanem Empire will expand. When we do, your false goddess cannot protect you. Everyone will worship Allah. Come, marry me now and escape your fate."

"You may not believe in Oya," you said. "But I hear her. Even now. She tells me…oh! So. You must be the one, yes? She told me about you. That you have been chasing me for a long time, even when my soul was in another's body. You have sought to kidnap me, take me from the things I love."

"False!" I shouted. "I would never do such a thing. Your spirit is a demon. I can offer you true happiness."

You pushed back the vines that made a doorway to my abode. "I don't know you."

"If you leave now, you'll die. Only through me—I mean, only through Allah, can you survive what's coming."

"Goodbye, Santjyot."

"They'll kill you!" I shouted, but you were gone.

Your caravan left as the sun set over the yellow grass. That night I tossed in a bed of leaves and sticks as my heart called up steamy dreams of night oases and I felt loud cracks of lightning shuffle me over and over like debris caught in a violent wind.

Six years passed without seeing you. I pined for you in times of loneliness, whenever I heard violent thunder. Within those six years, as I had warned, my empire called a Jihad on the Southwestern lands. Our warriors slaughtered many, and I guided them into the forests so they could loot maize and make slaves, until we were deep in the Igabalands. Too old for battle, I awaited messages from our soldiers and scouts, who returned to my tent from your lands, exhausted, having finished yet another gruesome battle.

"The Igaba are converted," my scout grumbled, scratching the streaks of dust in his beard. "Only a few remain to be our slaves."

I tried my best to hide my agony. "Did you see a large woman among the living?" I asked.

The scout shook his head, his attention on the soldiers sneaking sorghum into their cups outside my tent. I excused him and clutched my cowry shells. You were an infidel, led by the whims of a goddess. And yet I loved you, I would have married you. All you had to do was convert. I cursed you, your goddess, your people. Then I cursed Allah, cursed the prophet, cursed my rotten heart.

As the sun rose over the canopy of dried-out tree leaves, soldiers rushed to form the long caravan of men that would bring us back to our desert home. Their faces were bright with joy, and even below their beards I could see their skin flushed with the victory of our conquest. Our religion had spread to the ends of the earth, to the great sea. What could we do but rejoice?

I walked at the end of the line, letting dust fill my lungs. Wide-stepping over a skein of brush, I sauntered into the long grass, rehearsing my many trespasses. To desire, to love someone with every cell of my body, meant more to me than the love of god himself. Now, how could I remain in this world? When I returned to my Imam, I would beg for Allah's mercy, and admit my sin. I would spend my remaining life pleading my soul to paradise, thinking always of how my heart had strayed to a land of goddesses.

Life

Religions / Christian,
Starvation. Germany —

1535 — King John & the siege of Münster

False Gods With Power Over Life.
The Thousand Paces - Is That Romantic ...
kkkkkkk

This life was one of starvation and belief. The two often gripped each other, circling my past lives as blood strings through the body. I was either blessed to eat from the fat of the living or condemned to starve while waiting countless hours for the release of death.

I remember scavenging in the city square, hungrily watching a stream of ants that crawled snake-like over the juice of stomped on redcurrant berries, the leftovers from King John's procession through our besieged city. With the religious pageantry now gone, those of us still clinging to life searched the streets for anything edible dropped by the courtiers. I paced around and found that small stick of berries, squished open, tamped by a dozen feet, and covered in a squirming black mass of ants. I grabbed the berries and shook the ants off in crumbs. Six of the redcurrants still seemed edible.

Do all ants think the same? Do some ants go to heaven, some to hell?

I hid the fruit in my palm as I sped through the red brick city square, once inhabited by stray dogs, before we realized that dogs were edible. Since our religious rebellion a year before, the devil had tested our faith, and sent the old Bishop to lay siege to our city. Now we searched for other things that could be edible. Ponies. Cats. Corpses.

With the berries' red juice staining my palm, I arrived in my small cottage near the city gates. There you sat: Corina, wife of the shepherd Walther, stirring grass soup at my empty wooden table, your child in your arms, an unnamed child, for so few survived. Until the miracle we were all waiting for happened, anything could be made into a meal.

"I was able to save six," I told you, opening my palm. You put two of the berries in your child's mouth and two in your own. When you cried, you let your tears drop between your child's lips.

"Please swallow," you muttered.

You were a regular customer at the bakery where I apprenticed before the siege, and for years I loved you from a distance: your wavy hair just touching the counter when you bent to smell the almond pastries; your slender fingers as they squeezed the bread, testing the dough. You requested extravagant cakes made with rosewater and cinnamon, with chocolates and raisins sprinkled throughout.

"Michella and some others are still determined to go," you told me, tongue licking your teeth, ridden with stains from the grass soup. Teeth: not edible.

"They've lost their faith already," I responded. "We will never see them again on earth or in heaven."

"If we beg the Bishop to let us live, perhaps he will have mercy."

I watched your unnamed child. Dark spots had formed around his eyes, his skin jaundiced.

"And what if the Bishop refuses you?"

You pointed your thin, freckled arm toward the city gates just outside my window, near the chapel, to the thousand paces of grass. The once bright pasture had become a no man's land for the impure heathens who had given up on the city but had also been refused by the Bishop's army of drunken Catholic idolaters.

"We will leave tonight," you said. "Will you join us?"

I licked the soup ladle clean until I felt wood on my teeth. You will all die, I thought. I considered convincing you to stay. Telling you I loved you. But that would change nothing. Thoughts of heaven blocked my vision like the edges of a window. Loving you was all I felt; yet loving you would not give us His blessing.

Your group of heathens wandered the thousand paces for days, escaping the archers from both armies. Our city's leader, King John, declared your kind condemned to hellfire. Those of us who ventured to the thousand paces were moved by something other than belief.

Clouds of river fog flowed over my ankles as I sped past the city gates, crossing over the boundary beyond which one may not speak. Six others came with me, each of them the sister, brother, son, or cousin of an exile. We managed to bring bits of food: small patches of berries, unleavened bread, vegetables from the roof gardens. In the thousand paces, nothing was edible. Not the dirt. Not the grass.

It was cold and growing colder. A few birds roosted near a single pine tree, each one as edible as edible could be. I passed the pastures smelling of horse dung, my lantern bobbing in the fog.

We found your group of exiles beneath a lone pine tree.

Archers had killed all the men. A dozen or so women remained, huddled in a tight circle with children in the center, absorbing the group's warmth, bunched together like a cornucopia.

Those of us from the city said nothing for fear of catching your disbelief, like a flu of the soul. I searched for you until my eyes met a woman with button dimples cradling a child in her arms. Her woolly eyes glazed over my figure and I placed my piece of unleavened bread just near her whitened legs, which were crossed and folded onto her body to secure heat. Each of the women had the same tired eyes, the same protruding cheekbones, the same twitching neck veins. None were ugly, none beautiful, none lucky, none unfortunate.

That afternoon I kneeled in the city square alongside hundreds of other worshippers, each of us bowing to the cross. Beneath it, King John stood solid as a spruce, speaking with an ecstatic energy. "At the end only we remain," he preached. I watched the faces in the crowd, everyone clustered around the prophet, taking in his words like lapping up honey. The King continued his litany: "We are God's chosen! We will be rewarded like a flower that only blooms when closest to death."

Where was the line with God? How much did we have to suffer? When was enough enough? I no longer believed. Even close to death, it was a relief to think those words. If given another chance, I would not choose piety, but sin, if sin were all it took.

A stream of ants marched between my legs, heading toward my head flat upon the earth. I stuck out my tongue and invited them into my mouth with the juice of my saliva.

They formed a line, and I felt their unwavering march. First on my lips, creeping slowly up my tongue, then dropping in my throat and into my stomach. I swallowed to keep from coughing. Perhaps they didn't deserve this fate. But who could tell the difference? They all digested just as easy.

Heaven has alcohol. That's what makes it heaven.

By the third time I landed in the stateroom where I now write these recollections, my love for you defied all sense. After two millennia of living in the stream, I could not effort to return, but neither could I enjoy the afterlife. Re-creation was out of the question. To love is to be in extreme solitude, to wait patiently for death—but here, where even flowers would not decay, death offered no release. Of all the places where I encountered you, I could never defeat tradition, religion, family, life's maudlin decorum, each promising the thing none could provide.

I hid in my stateroom sepulcher for years, supine, staring, dumb, inactive. How many years, I could not count. I remember it in flits of blank pages sifted through by a callous wind. For a year I picked at the tan-colored carpet of my stateroom. For another year I watched the fruit on the opal corner table. Every month I watched a new element: how the ripe green grapes lunged over the apples like a noxious cloud, how the oranges shone in different shades as the sun rose and set. In the many years I spent letting the days glaze over me on that stateroom floor, the fruit never decayed.

And I recalled my past lives. I remembered my brothers taking vengeance upon me, forcing my own manhood down my throat. In another life, I was a vermin of a woman who cast you away. In another, I was vicious and certain you belonged only to me.

For a year I watched the sun and moon pass. In the early morning, the sky's dark purples gradually turned to light yellows until the window cast a warm circle on the wall. I saw the figures from my life near Edessa—armor glazed with the desert sun, blood spilling out under the weight of a sword. I saw the bright orange of Solomon's Temple. I saw the backs of worshippers, their white tunics reflecting the golden light as they kneeled toward Mecca.

I saw your face, but couldn't remember your name. It had an "S."

For years I lay on the bathroom's cold alabaster floor tiles, where I could not distinguish the daytime from the night. I was drunk for most of those years, on the carpet, in the bathroom, on the floor, slung in the sink, submerged in the bathtub, head below water. For years I choked on water, inviting the impulse to gasp for air. For years the bath was scalding hot. For years it was arctic cold. For years I lay on my side, letting the water suffuse my right ear, its surface marking a discolored line across my chest.

As time swept over me, my past lives came as a mood, whose cold beauty lingered. For years I floated in bathwater, watching the blurry white walls, and that Chinese miniature depicting a flabby mountainside, its frame damp, but its colors still gleaming with an always fresh coat of paint. When I unplugged the bath, my skin dragged toward the vortex. For years I lay in the empty bathtub, letting the naked white bulb dry my skin. I couldn't wake up, though I wasn't asleep. It's not that I couldn't leave the stateroom. I just preferred to lie there, staring into space.

ALL FLOWERS BLOOM

One day I found the effort to stand.

Someone had changed my bed sheets, leaving the deep red pillows tilting upright against the bedpost. Raindrops streamed down the window like scurried beetles. My haze of memory began to stir as I walked the bluish hallways of the cruise ship, listening to the voices coming from the dining hall, the gymnasium, the ballroom, until I reached The Beauty Bay, transformed from a casbah into a Christian's alehouse, with a lute player, a girl on a hand harp, and a bard striking chords from a lyre. There were rows of tables with light-skinned, full-bearded men and women with blonde hair dressed in animal hide. As I entered, my body shifted into that same tall female brunette. The glossy pearls that arched over my long black dress looked lurid in the room's baroque lighting.

I drank from a glass of mead. In that stately indifference I recalled another past life: you were the baker's wife and I lived by your side for years, too shy, too religious, too respectful of your husband to reveal myself. My mind woke long enough to feel that nagging sensation of sobriety before I downed the drink.

I sidestepped past a group of maidens to the tavern's patio, now a stone castle's terrace. The ocean's dark surface was lit by a perfectly round moon.

"You're a shock from the past," said a voice. Cryss. "Look at you. Still Persianified, like all those years ago."

She wore a plush velvet hat with strings of golden orbs dangling to her shoulders, which were covered in a heavy robe of the same striking red velvet. She still wore that rock-filled leather pouch weighing her hair back. "A tradition from an ancient culture," she once explained.

"Genocided out of existence." Like myself, Cryss' past lives were lost in the perplexity of war.

"You know what," she said, "I miss those Persian-ophile days. Let me oblige you." Then it was the two of us on the patio, both tall in purple tunics. "I didn't want to bother you after I heard you had arrived." She willed two goblets of mulled wine and handed one to me. "I sent my ward, Clover, to check on you, from time to time. She's fascinated by stories of heroic warriors ensnared in romantic love triangles. To her, you are a hapless lover encasing your worldly desires in hibernation."

Hibernating. That's what they called it in heaven. When the past lives jumped on you, tangled you up, straitjacketed you into the cold lingering moods of the dead.

"It's been difficult," was all I could muster.

"Tailorizing to new skins doesn't make you anonymous," Cryss said. "Just because I can't see your sober face does not make you more glamorous." She took my face in her hands and applied a balm to my lips, carefully patting the light yellow salve. "Do you get how long you've been hibernating?"

I saw my counterfeit smile in the bar's darkened windows. Grief slacked my face, giving me away. Drink loosened my tongue, or perhaps, Cryss willed it. "Many times, I bid my heart break," I said. "I wished to die. No movement of the soul, no forgetting of a past life. A true death."

"So you frittered away the years." Cryss' icy blue eyes shone through her half-empty goblet. "But, you did finally get up, just as time staunches all fires."

I held the railing, the moon showering light on us. "I just could not stay in there," I said.

"Hey, I know you!" a voice came from a young woman with pink hair. She wore the luxury silks of Ottoman lemon-yellows combined with the garish lime-greens of Portuguese tiles. Her appearance was an offense to the eyes that made me wonder if she had been willed by a prankster. "I saw it all," the woman said, chewing on a jalebi pastry. "This fate-bound floozy, such a romantic! Just like the tale of Zal and Rudabeh! 'Hopes drowned, so many fathoms deep!'"

"This is my ward, Clover," Cryss explained. "I had her watch over you."

"So woebegone!" Clover said with an eager smile. "So steeped in self-pity! I'd never seen such bitter, lonesome wailing." She dipped into a mock-genteel curtsy. "It was a real pleasure! The things you whispered, the needs I watched you satisfy! It was as unmentionable as, well, my *unmentionables*!" she cackled, holding her sides.

"Perish the thought!" Cryss said, holding in a laugh. "Hibernation is no joke! But as you see, my little Saracen, it works! Hope will come, as new desires float to the surface. Just as time hurts, time cures. Hold out, let time slip by, strive for nothing, hasten nothing."

The two waited for me to respond. "I did not come here for counsel," I said solemnly.

"What's the fun in holding yourself up in your stateroom, when you can torture yourself right here?" Cryss said with a cracked smile. "We have whipping rooms, bullfighting rooms, war rooms, whatever you fancy." As her posture changed, so did her body, as she swiveled with diluvian, womanly hips, strapped by tight and knobby garters. "Now don't forget yourself! Look, your lips have chapped again."

Her balm struck my face like a slap. "Now alter your face like mine." Her eyebrows shifted down and her cheekbones crossed in a V-shape.

I couldn't help it. I was eating the balm off my lips. Raw manhood meat. Chew, chew. Before I could swallow, it started buckling out of me in a thick yellow drool. I found myself grabbing Clover's leg as Cryss drew my hair away from the mess.

"Scoot!" Clover jittered. She dragged her foot and me with it. "Whaaat's happening?"

"*Vomitāre*: nothing keeps it down!" Cryss rasped. "Eight-Seven-One. Convert yourself, please. I've never seen a patron here who needed it so bad."

"What's that?" I asked, gasping from the dry ache in my throat.

"A last resort," she said, lighting a scentless stick of tobacco. "I was going to insist you take it last time, had you not been so eager to jump." Her first puff dispersed as soon as it reached the air. No one minded a smoker in heaven. I looked up from the ship's deck to see her hair in a red bob, the rock-filled pouch hanging like an anchor from her side. "In my past life, I did a lot of things I regret. There are disreputable stories about it. The talk of silly, goosish people." She ashed into the ocean. "I was like you. Stuck between wars. I wanted to forget. Well. In the Ilium, there's a cure for every ailment. *Kalimutan*: the past is the past."

"Yowza!" Clover leapt from excitement. "You mean the blue tea?! A level five-thousand counter-hex! It makes you forget *everything*. Total reset!"

"Cease your play!" Cryss spat at Clover. "Somnolize yourself!"

100

Knees buckling, Clover began to faint, dropping then curling onto the oak floor.

"She was spoiled in her last life," Cryss explained. "Always shooting off her mouth."

I stood, my feet now unshod for comfort. "Are you saying I can die?"

"Oh—that's right, the tea. It's only for special cases. And it's not a real death, more like a baptismal. A total renewal of the soul—it does not merely wipe memory. Body, passion, feelings, scent, the sensations that remain, all that makes a soul eternal. Follow me." As she turned to lead me, her hair shifted to a long blonde band weighed down by that rock-filled pouch.

I followed Cryss to a rooftop garden where clusters of herbs crawled up red-bricked walls. Up a stairway of fragrant-rose carpeting, we found flowers. Flowers tropical and temperate pleasantly sprung from every cranny. Cryss walked me through the grounds at daybreak, marked with dew and the crooning carols of bluebirds. "There is no antidote to your sickness," she whispered as we approached a bed of pimpernels with their blue leaf-like petals and yellow stamens caked with pollen.

"Be glad," Cryss said, plucking a flower by its root. "And have mercy on yourself. If your lass, S, really has all those virtues you so admire, then pity must be among them. She would want you to drink it."

I lay on the floor in my stateroom, staring at the ceiling, the whitewashed space as blank as I would become. Once

I drank the tea, I would wake here, surrounded by flowers that would never wilt, fruit that would never rot, candles that would never go out. Everything plunged into stillness. On the ivory countertop sat the tea, extracted from the blue flower of restoration. One sip, and I would lose all of myself, a final death. A clean slate—a flower that never wilts.

For years I had piled bricks of memory together, deeper, higher, until I had enclosed my life in their crags. Who was I without you to pursue? The lives before we met were nowhere, as if I had never existed before you. You were at times my soldier, my lover, my friend, my husband, my prey, my muse, my princess, my enemy, my distant memory. But you were never mine.

The bright blue sea shimmered in the light like jeweled marble. The terrazzo sink bore no stains. I tried, but you could never earn paradise. You would always be that stubborn slave, proud of killing your master, proud to be tossed from the Tarpeian rock. From that cliff, none like you would ever fall again. For lifetimes I awaited you, until I became a remnant, a signpost still standing, even after the road had long been empty.

I imagined a future without you. Life would be gone, but pleasure would remain. Perhaps, you would find me one day, a woman gossiping in the ship's jungle energy cafe, with my cigarette and my youthful face. Would you pine for me? Would you hibernate, go mad with memory, and find yourself drinking a tea made from the blue flower? Would you be so rash as to kill us?

No. Cryss was correct. There was no point in hoping you would arrive. You would never do it on your own. It wasn't in your nature. But even a flower sprouting in a dark cave can still bloom. I had seen it. It only needs a single ray of sunlight.

I made a solemn vow, the kind from stories of hapless lovers. One day I would take the blue tea, but we would do it together. My imagination sprawled, dreams of the future lanced through my mind: *our* future, renewing our lives together, and living forever in heaven. I held out for hope—a violent, maiming, languishing hope—and declared it through every stately hall of the ship: All flowers bloom!

Life

It's as if 8+1 and S switched. He's a British colonial.

K

South Indian Subcontinent
Big gap

Joy In The Extreme !!

The patter of rain from the tin ceiling finally began to slow as the steamer's back-and-forth rocking calmed into a soothing rotation. I could still see the edges of the storm, hovering over the distant swampland. The swamps, once known for man-eating tigers, were now a stain of mud on the darkening skyline. Tigers drowned in that storm, as did prisoners, merchants, janitors. Rainwater had burst through log damns, engulfing them within a canopy of enfolding forest, mixing them with ancient Siva statues, suspended huts, and people from nearby villages, all of them devoured by the hungry tide.

As the storm let up, the Englishmen emerged from belowdecks to feel the sea breeze. When they lit their pipes, I retreated below and sat at a canteen, pinching a handful of biscuits from a man with his face slumped over a bottle of scotch. That was when, after nearly five hundred years, I encountered you again. To think, if not for your people's unquenchable ambitions, we never would have crossed paths.

You were a man wilting away, just like the other British colonials who gathered in places with high concentrations of alcohol and low concentrations of locals. While the other

Englishmen belted out songs describing grassy fields and the English Queen, you hung over the bar like a broken angel with a blazing blue sari wrapped around your head as if it were a long scarf, translucent in places where candlelight cut through it. The cloth was damp and torn apart, its Varanasi silk held together by strands thinner than hair.

A group of the rescued English sang:

When Britain first, at Heaven's command

Arose from out the azure main;

This was the charter of the land,

And guardian angels sang this strain:

"Rule, Britannia!" rule the waves:

"Britons never will be slaves."

"Rule," you rasped from beneath your sari-scarf. "What rule? We rule because no one dares oppose. No one dares desire the way we desire."

That was it. The gruff, the gall.

I sat next to you and saw that you were hunched over a tattered map. Miles of territory stained by rings of scotch whiskey. You did not seem to notice my skin from beneath your sari. After heavy inebriation, Englishmen often forgot I was just a translator. Perhaps you could not see the way the bartender looked at me. You could be inquiring a number of things: Indian or English? Man or woman? I dismissed the urge to call you "sir" and remained silent.

You slurped down shot after shot of local toddy, a palm wine that you had poured into the scotch bottle, perhaps, to appear more English. You downed the drink forcefully, drowning in the mixture of spice, sugar and alcohol. Sweat streamed onto your sari until the last drop splattered the bottom of your glass.

I followed you from the canteen up to the deck, just as the last hints of the sun sank below the dark ocean. You struck up a match and seemed to have a conversation with your pipe, puffing away while your sari tossed about in the wind.

"Were you a prisoner?" you asked, offering your tobacco pipe.

I shook my head, receiving the pipe.

Seeing that I knew English, you continued, "What are you, then? I thought they only evacuated English."

I tried to speak, but the smoke scratched my voice. You seemed to understand. One could not incriminate oneself.

"Twelve thousand prisoners," you said, eyes on the sea's metallic sheen. "None given a trial, some far too young to be in that prison. When the flood came, we didn't even unlock their cells before we left. During evacuation, the Lieutenant said, 'Don't worry about them getting out.' *Don't worry*, he said. *About them getting out*, he said."

I sniffed the smoke to evade the briny, nauseating smell of the hull. We idly watched two red-billed seabirds in a courtship flight. You asked if my family was in the storm.

"My wife is in Chennai," I said, though I almost said my *husband*.

"You don't seem too excited," you said. "You know, you may be the only local survivor."

I considered this, brushing my eyebrow. "They say extreme sorrow somewhere creates extreme joy somewhere else."

You stood still, letting the sari gently choke your neck in its struggle against the wind. "I hope that's true."

The wind of an oncoming storm chased us inside. Perhaps it was mere trade winds, or perhaps the cyclone was chasing us. I followed you through the thin halls of the steamer, passing Englishmen struck with disgust at the sight of me. But they did not question my presence so long as you made no concern.

We arrived in your room, where a half bottle of rum sat on a stack of books by Kant, Hume, and Wordsworth. I recognized them from British schools, where you colonials preached the Enlightened man, a man of equality, a man of assurance and self-fashioning. All I could remember from that instruction was "the truth was in the whole," a phrase I learned to recite on command. In those books we darker-skinned people merely lacked perspective.

You handed me a cup of your beer-toddy concoction atop your bed and unwrapped that sweat-sticking sari from your neck, where the valuable silk had left a dry redness.

Rain pattered above us, growing into a crescendo from all directions. Gusts of wind rocked the ship. Shipmates yelled across the decks, but you ignored them. You locked the door, took off your wet instruction shirt and lay on the sheets. Sweat polished your skin in skidding drops.

I couldn't hold it in any longer and traced my finger along a single drop.

"What separates us?" you asked me. Lightning split air louder than the crack of a victory bell.

I wanted to tell you I felt it too, perhaps, the connection of death, or something more. Kindred spirits lost in never-ending cycles. After five hundred years, destiny had brought us back.

The boat swayed and I leaned on your legs to keep from falling.

"Just get me drunk first," you said, downing the glass of beer-rum.

I glanced about the room and found a pitcher. "Only water left."

"I can pretend."

I filled your cup. Waves battered the ship. You sipped greedily, letting the liquid spill down your chin and spread upon the sheets. Books tossed from shelves. The bed fell onto the wall with our cups. I held you beneath the sheets, clutching your shoulders, as your body went limp, perhaps, drunk from the water.

If the ship hadn't gone down in that storm, there would have been some speculation about our bodies: two men drowned in a locked cabin, gripped in an eternal clutch.

Life

This one, Xia, sounds like the S we all knew.

L

1870s - the island of Penang

Isn't That Life, keeping Off Boredoom I mean, just kill yourself . please

Everything about you was bulging with life. Even the brothels of Love Lane could not break your spirit. Like many of us *ah-ku*, you had escaped an arranged marriage in your home country, only to find that your passage to Penang came at a cost. You would spend the next five years among us, paying back the debt for your escape.

"Ya know," you told me on the night you first arrived, after you had brazenly risked the Madame's ire by drinking the reserve rice wine and snuck into my bunk. "I tend to be a bit nomadic. Those coins Madame found on me? I ripped 'em off some poor rickshaw handler trying to cop a feel. And well a few drunk pirates as well. Played tendress to them, then disappeared like—well forgive me for the analogy I'm about to use, but—I disappeared like a fart in the wind." You laughed with your head back, not caring whether I humored you.

Lovers is not the proper term for what you and I were. We were united by our debts. I never minded your truncated sessions with the Chinese boozers. You pleased your clients

109

with a fakeness so exaggerated that it seemed derisive—a gallant laugh, your finger pointing in their direction, at their naked bodies. Our Madame, Lik Wan, punished you frequently with her bamboo switch. You were caught for all sorts of things—kicking clients out of bed only seconds past satisfaction, mocking the mistresses who dreamed of escaping with their rich clients, badgering the clients for more money (that was Madame's job), and of course, for sneaking into my bed when the red lamps were taken down from their gaudy, striped awning.

"I'm not afraid of sinking," you told me once. "Just follow your heart. Right? Or not?"

I was no coquette. My face, as Madame always told me, was all crudded up. My bottom lip was unable to pout, and my cheeks showed wear. Every day since I had escaped my family, I tasted the mustiness of my cell and the soused men flowing in and out of it: rickshaw drivers, errand boys, builders, sailors, old men faded by opium. I was the merchandise they ran their hands over.

But when you and I made love it was not the ritualistic, cluttered panics that we felt with our clients, with their carrot cocks. Our lips slipped against each other's in defiance; I felt my freedom in your embrace, and the more we lusted for each other throughout the day, the more we gave ourselves during the night. A dark, sweaty cleansing. I held you tighter, obstructed by your massive breasts. I imagined you when I was pressed beneath my clients, and I felt myself closing in on whatever you were hiding.

After your third year you were allowed to run errands around the island. You had made a name for yourself by then, and mostly slept at the apartments your babas bought for you. Flush with cash, you still came to me when making your rounds, and often brought custard dumplings to sweeten my lunch. I watched you move up and down Love Lane, wearing chintzy see-through garments and leaving trails of loose change for the urchins. You still came to me, now and then.

During that time, I busied myself about the old Peranakan mansion, dusting, scorching up soups, and experimenting with the Tamil incense from those migrants who moved only two blocks from our little section of Georgetown. Homeless, with no way out of the weight of debt, the Tamils were doing worse than us Chinese. Whenever I went to their market, I watched their frail women, the smell of incense covering their unwashed bodies. Their faces too dark for the rich babas to take notice.

After weeks with one of your babas, you came back to my cell. As soon as you entered, down you went to relax, legs splaying as you leaned forward, propping elbows against the dip just before your knees.

"What is it?" I asked.

"I'm getting out of this life," you said. "I feel bored."

Your eyes were on the awning, where the sun exposed white dust floating in small splices of light. As you stood up, the movement of your full breasts, uncrushed by that thin cheongsam, tossed the dust away.

My anger came out muffled: "You're safe here. Things are finally stable." I turned away from you, to weep alone. "What did we escape for, if not for each other?"

You sat on the bed, running your hands gently through my hair. "Sometimes I wish I was so easily satisfied," you told me. "Truly."

When the Madame discovered your escape, she assaulted me in the kitchen, bashing scalding soup onto my legs. Our scramble went into the dining hall, where she tossed me down.

"You think I did not know about you two?" she screamed. "You were the only thing keeping her here—and you failed!"

The ginger broth stung. "I did nothing," I told her. And after a beat of silence, added: "she just said she was bored."

"Bored!" The Madame lurched back. "Look how ugly you have become. Get out. What good are you without her?"

The brothel's bar had gone quiet. The mistresses and *ah-ku* motioned me toward the door and the Madame blocked me from my own cell. Nothing I owned was my own.

In the streets I heard the slow drumbeat of the Tamils, and went to them. I sat at one of their cafes, smelling their incense and feeling the thump of their drumbeats. I cracked a smile at a woman scooping mounds of rice.

I would not die for another six years. By then, I was known by the Tamils as the rude Chinese cook who translated disputes, made mouth-numbing Sichuan soup, and kept no lover for very long.

Life

Poss. sighting of Destroyer — Unruly as ever

M

1901 – Philippine Islands (later Southeast China Islands)

A Fake Or Real God, Or Is The Real God A Fake? Confused

I took to being American like I was a Roman again. Being in the midst of such grandiose power made me eager to cross the ocean to reclaim what was mine by right. Perhaps something, after two thousand years of chasing you, had begun to affect me. I believed you were made for me alone.

From the dugout of our company's baseball game, I saw you. I was paralyzed, stunned frozen by the frisson of life I felt. I knew you well, far better than our commander who had adopted you as his mistress. I knew that your eyebrow, the way it shifted around nervously, was more than just some decoration. It was your secret—your defiant, unconquered self that had survived through all these millennia.

I didn't feel it until I saw your eyebrow. Before that, you were just one of those adept local women who we welcomed into our company as a guide to translate and advise. But I also knew of the lives within you, all those encounters in the stream. For god—whom I believed was god—had prophesied it.

"That is her, your charge," God said to me, his light peeking from the clouds. Luckily, from the dugout, no one noticed my prayer posture, or how I averted my eyes.

"Who, my Lord?" And the light shone upon you, standing near the Jesuit church, near Captain Connell who looked toward you with his finger up, as he did when we ran drills or raided villages. Your face turned toward him in a stern smile.

"See how the ball flew above the catcher?" the captain said to you, bending down to look into your eyes. "That's called a foul. *fow-el*. Got that, Pocahontas?"

Your hair, stuck up in the frame of a gigantic rose, bobbed up and down in nods. The captain started calling you Pocahontas weeks before, since you spoke so many dialects. You proved yourself as useful as that Indian namesake when we took the shore and you persuaded the friars to close the ports to keep the insurgents out. When we took the port town, you bartered with the local men to move their families to the green tents we had erected, where we could keep a watchful eye. With an unquestioning obedience you translated our commands to the locals: to stay and work or we would kill them where they stood.

A bird flit by, and I saw it was he: Lord God, within the form of a dove.

"Everyone has welcomed her to our company," I told the Lord. "She is already the captain's awaiting lover."

"She drifts like a soft white cloud that wanders among you," the Lord said, perched on a branch flecked with moss and aged cracks. "But can you feel it? Her quiet energy. Like thunder about to break."

The dove pecked at something between its golden claws—a rainbow smelt, still flapping its tail, the type I would catch back home. The Lord dove drove small fissures in its eyes and cheeks.

"But she is no virgin," I told the Lord God. "You prophesied that the Virgin Mary would be a barbarian, but still needing my fruit to multiply."

"I never used the word *fruit*," Lord God said, even as his beak was deep in smelt carcass. "Am I not the same God who instructed Jacob and Job? Am I not the same God who gave to you my only begotten son? Did I not instruct your very president to invade these islands? You are as much part of my plan as your lily-liver'd Captain. And I tell you now—*she is the one*. Don't be daft and let a silly scruple like jealousy hurt your cause. Have at it, already! Nobody likes a god who shirks their duties. Be with her, your awaiting, that I may be reborn as your offspring."

The captain's turn to bat. He smiled through his thin black mustache and readied his stance for the next pitch. The company seemed tense, knees crouched as they spread onto the outfield in their khaki uniforms and campaign hats. I imagined the ball striking him in the face, killing him in an instant, but instead his bat struck the ball with a loud smack, and the only proper baseball of the US 9th Infantry sailed past the cathedral and into the nearby jungle.

The captain whistled for one of the local boys to go search for it. "Get, get!"

I caught you looking at me again, your face vivid, insistent, as if charging me to make a move. That hair, when facing my direction, had the shape of an oncoming steamer ship. We were both observers now, you the guide, and I the least effective soldier in company C, benched from all recreational activities. Ever since we took the town, I'd been on the rails. Yes, God sent us here, but how could this be God's will? Us capturing every male in the town, taking their boleros, keeping them from their families, and looting their houses? Then us pouring salt-water into their leader's throat while the captain barked insults at them. God spoke to me and not them, yet they claimed to be killing in His name. That's when I had the genius idea of telling Captain Connell that God spoke to me. I wasn't being insubordinate, not really, and I knew that they were always curious about my whispers during prayer. Perhaps the church bells were too much. I had no problem serving God, but those brown natives were believers too. And their freedom was dearer to them than life.

Speaking for God—that got me shoveling trenches with the other captors. Come game-time, it got me in the dugout. I didn't know why I had to open my mouth—honestly, I just felt sorry for your people.

I heard gunshots. The second and third basemen were taking potshots into the jungle thicket. They laughed as the boy came darting out of the forest, holding the white baseball, face pale with fear.

"What's the matter? Not enough spunk for ya?" God's voice came again, this time through the clouds. "You're not gonna go after her? Spill your soul? That's just lame."

When night rolled around, the workers began to set-up the town's fiesta, joined by men of the cloth. Still under field punishment, I lulled outside the church and listened to the revelry, my hands attached in shiny iron chains meant for deserters. My firearm too was taken away, and I merely watched my compatriots chug the priest's wine.

I felt something tip my hat. It was you, slinking away from the captain. Your red dress bounced as you moved in front of me. Yellow and red beads hung from your neckline as you looked back, with a curious grin. "You come with me?" you asked, your eyebrow lifting toward the dense forest. The company sentries on patrol were behind the church.

I knew it—your eyebrow tilt, your exhaustion at dealing with the captain, your sinister grins. You were the real deal.

Hands chained, I followed you in the rut of a hog trail. Your bare feet remembered the path, the same path our company followed when we first chased the insurgents out. We passed a burned-down house where earlier in the week I found one of them fanning a fire. I killed him with my old Long Tom, and then I killed the others like jackrabbits hopping out of the bushes, putting down seven that I know of, perhaps ten, if the wounded did not survive.

I heard the laughter of Lord God following me, though he took no manifestation. "A heart-warming scene." His chuckling resounded before me. "Finally, things are getting interesting again."

You brought me to an old Spaniard's villa overlooking the town, a mansion looted hollow. Every drawer had been pulled out, and the old chandeliers had dropped to the floor in pieces, too heavy to carry off. You led me to the master bedroom, where a cask of palm wine sat squeezed between two rolled-up rugs.

You unsheathed a bolo from behind the bed and sat on the cushion, spinning the blade, just to let me know you had it.

"Bottom's up," you said, handing me a bottle of wine.

God spoke again, through the lampstand: "You're finally going to mate with her. That's—kind of exciting. I'm filled with joy."

But your blade stayed between us all night. I wondered if you were waiting for a Holy light to fill us with spirit before we conceived. Our minds lubricated by the wine, we did not feel the need to talk until the *gong* of the church bells echoed over the forest canopy.

Intoxicated, I was not sure what I was seeing: the town lit up in an orange blaze, the sparks of bullets upon the walls of the cathedral. I heard screams and the battle wails of conch shells.

The Lord God, taking the form of a lamb, inched toward me from the side of the bed. "I had nothing to do with that." He gave that overly pleased grin of his, a triangle smile.

"What's happening?" I said.

Lord God gave a demented laugh. "Ask her!"

And there it was—I saw it on your brow as you stroked your chin, surveying the chaos in the village below. That secret intention. A flash of quiet energy that burned the air itself. You craned your neck from the broken-in window to me. "They were looking for a fight."

You said "they" and not "you." God had instructed me to be your mate, for our offspring to bring the second coming, to purge your kind of evil. I took it as an invitation and placed my palm around your slender waist. Your eyebrow shot up. I wasn't sure how to read it, and I went for your neck—kissing it in rabbit pecks, grabbing your body until I felt a sharp pain.

Your face in a grimace, you screamed something in your native tongue and pointed the blood-drenched blade at me. I tried to wrest the knife from your grip, but discovered my fingers were gone, lost somewhere on the floor with the broken glass and discarded rugs.

"This is too much!" cheered the Lamb of Lord God, giddy on the floor, legs bicycle-kicking the air.

I ran through the mansion doorway and sped into the forest, toward the glimmering firelight. Did God betray me? How was I supposed to bring the second coming now?

My hand throbbed as blood poured from where my index and middle finger once were. I heard rifle fire in the distance as the pain turned into a hammering pulse. I stumbled upon a group of insurgents, about seven or so, their backs to me as they took potshots toward the church. Without thinking, I took one down, choking him with the same chain meant to punish me, my half-fingers spitting blood onto his nape. The others were like the ones I had killed, sinewy and brown. I wanted to save them, even as they stabbed me with machetes.

They left me clutching tree bark, wheezing.

His voice returned, coming from a dove with a river salmon struggling in its claws. "Well, it looks like you've lost her again," God said, perched upon a jungle leaf, globs of salmon in his mouth. "You know what this means, right? No more fish for a while."

"Help me, Lord God," I said, blood spurting from my wounds.

"I would," the dove spoke to me directly through his blood-flecked beak. "But who knows when you'd die? I'm not about to prolong the inevitable. So, it's over. You'll die—a hard reset."

Smoke spewed from the church's steeple in large tufts of clouds. "But—how will I bring the second coming?" I asked. "You said I was chosen."

"I say that a lot—don't let it go to your head. You're a coin jutting out from a planet-wide junkyard. A tad shinier than the other rubbish, only just worth picking up."

119

"You lied about her. She was a temptress, a snare, a Jezebel."

"Patronizing, yeah?" the dove said. "To be honest, I knew all along that you stood no chance, though your resilience never ceases to amuse. In every life you seem to discover a new, unexplored dimension of the term witless."

"I must survive this. I have to *live*!"

"Noted."

"Why, God, have you forsaken me?"

"I'm not your dumb God." The bird tore through fish spine. "I watch over you in the way you nurture a pet. It gives meaning, something to depend upon. Of course, if I left you to your own devices, you'd probably be much better off. Doesn't that sound familiar?"

Someone trapped inside the church pulled the bell's rope, tugging onto hope.

"What did I do wrong?" I asked.

"Quiet now," Lord God said. "Fish are to me what that defiant little tart is to you—the most pleasing little buzz I just can't deny. You want her, I want fish, and she—she wants to kill you."

"But why—"

"Hush! I'm trying to enjoy this."

I closed my eyes and listened to the clanging of the bell.

Life

The war that brought so many to the Ilium.

N

1945 - East Prussia

Could This Really Be S?
They Were Related! Tammy!

For a century you carried the unbridled energy of mankind, punching through every wall that dared confine you. It took a global catastrophe for me to catch up.

I spent my last day alive sitting at my terrace, watching doomed souls pass. From the Baltic Coast, through East Prussia, women and children with sunny blonde hair staggered through the icy winter, marching in columns so thick that high-altitude bombers would have no problem targeting them.

From the oval window of my homestead attic, I saw a young girl in a fur coat emerge from the procession, shouting *Brauche einen Sarg*!—"need a coffin!" One anonymous life, taken by the march, was nothing compared to the orgy of violence awaiting those of us who stayed behind. From my terrace where I drank coffee, I heard the marchers tell stories of bodies crushed by tanks, of women nailed to walls, crucified on the wooden planks of a barn. Let the women pay, said the red army, if they be *Deutsch*.

And history would later say that we Germans deserved it. A day of reckoning. We pulled the pin on our own grenade. We marched to Moscow in the summer so our children could freeze in the winter. When the red army came for me, they would discover my youngest daughter's dollhouse. My mantle clock. Our lavishness would only spur their anger, and my home would be set ablaze while I still inhabited the attic. They would wonder what we wanted from their paltry potato farms.

But instead of running from the army like all the other *Fräulein*, in that somber moment, I waited for them to come, hoping that you would be among them.

Could it be? In this life, you were my son? Memory comes in a single frame, a set of characters each vying for attention. I only feel my love for you, my need to wait, even when it meant an unspeakable death.

Three years before, your father took you to Moscow, afraid the others would discover your Jewish heritage. You were thirteen then, but the reds did not restrict conscription by age. I felt your presence somewhere in the depths of the Red Army, nearing me, and leaving behind a trail of fire and fury. In the gruesome stories of our Armageddon, I saw our reunion. My little bear, my little treasure. *Meine Engel.*

The radio's comforting voice returned, telling me to be thankful. I had lived long enough to see the end. I should be happy to die for Deutschland. We remembered our ancestors, the Teutons, whose wives killed their husbands if they were cowards, and who killed themselves rather than become Roman wives.

The radio went soft, its final words echoing. "Loyalty has always been our honor."

The Red Army arrived in a barrage of artillery fire. In the distance, I heard the unfamiliar sound of guns, the screaming aircraft above, the mortars dropping. I saw the Poles pillaging. A young woman lay in the street with one of the old clerks. Dogs barked. Everything vibrated and crashed to the floor. Glass shattered. A great force thrashed me. Leaning on my rocking chair, I was able to stand, a pulsating ringing in my ears.

So, this was the war.

The winter breeze tossed in from the crushed oval window. The couple making love in the streets moved to the beat of artillery fire, their romance well-lit by the pastry shop's lanterns.

I reclined on my quilts, below my bed, in case more debris should fall. I lay with the spiders and rats, all of them scurrying. The earth itself was shaking us off. I placed my hands on my knees and realized I was shivering in fear. Would I too be nailed to the walls? Would you, my own son, do the deed? Would you know that it was I who fed you, who gave you my body before you were taken from me?

Another mortar dropped. The whistle, the wordless violence. Outside, soldiers hooted over the noise, hugging each other in the ecstasy of warfare. They were just like our poor boys—driven into the passions of war, the freedoms of carnage, the pleasures of power.

I hoped if it were you who found me, you would have the courage to go through with it.

I could no longer recognize my own room. This room where I had spent my life, this veiled attic, now caved in and open for the world to see. I heard the enemy's strange language coming from the street. How beautiful it was on the ears, with names like Dmitri. Had you become a Dmitri, a Fyo-

123

dor, a Michail? The Red Army lit another house on fire, and scraps of paper floated by from posters that once pronounced the Fuhrer's call to arms. They flapped like fairies, the trails of ash their enchanting dust, the smell of smoke their mystic fragrance. I could feel your presence in that warmth, flushed with memories of your grip on my index finger, your indescribable baby smell that always made me crave *Allgäu* cheese.

The gunshots became more logical. They came rat-a-tat-tat, one for every person lined up behind the pastry shop. No fearful screams, no cheers, just mechanical jolts of sonic vibration. I heard Red Army soldiers in Herr Hoch's house laugh at the whimpering of a lone female voice. The woman did not scream. No *Fräulein* could scream loud enough that history would hear her.

More voices, so close now. Inside the house. Hard, winter boots clapped upon the oak planks. I felt you, drawing open the attic door, peering in, and finding me sitting on the bed. I saw only your silhouette as you peered into the room. In the darkness I saw not you, but a stranger, too young to be my son. And his eyes were filled with fear, not fury. Eyes that had never known me or this place.

He saw me and yelled something in that language, now no longer beautiful, but harsh and frightening. He pointed his rifle at me. Others soon joined. They seemed to want something from me other than death. The door closed, and as the soldiers approached me, I heard them making jokes in that rhythmic language of theirs.

Perhaps one of the boys was you, my *Kind*, my child. I considered this, counting how many seconds it would take to pull the knife from my dress, to do what needed to be done, if not for history then for myself.

Life

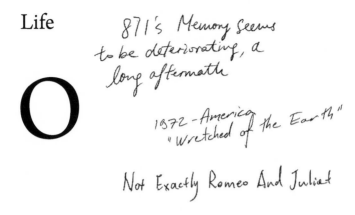

871's Memory seems to be deteriorating, a long aftermath

1972 - America "Wretched of the Earth"

Not Exactly Romeo And Juliet

To remember this life is to feel the aches and shakes that came with each break of day, when I was a prisoner in a country that had never known peace. I remember pulling on a crusted teal blanket to see you, my lover, balled up in the corner like crumbled paper. It was us two in that basement, with three others and of course that white witch, all gone away. One of us had to pawn something.

"Your turn," I said, kicking you awake as you rolled out of sleep.

We were nineteen. And in this life, I didn't have to seek you out. Instead, circumstance beat us down, flattened us together in the same mush of skin and bone.

I rolled onto the concrete floor, letting its cold surface bring me out of sleep while listening to the sound of squealing pipes overhead. I pulled my clothes over me. I once wore black man-suits and big shiny jewelry. All gone to the shops.

"What year?" you asked, teeth clacking.

"Seventy-two," I said, though you knew full well.

You started in early fits: "They wanna get you or get me to get to you that's what these pigs always doing trying to keep us down keep us addicted keep us heavy." You hugged the plush purple pillow, stroking the fuzzy material as if it were my hair.

You received no looks from our dazed friends nearby. Instead they turned to me, your lover. The world was so upside down, I didn't even care. Something went and changed. Or maybe nothing had changed. There was something inhumane about how life just kept going.

I heard the patter of footsteps from the day-walkers. I tossed open the curtain and sunlight barged through the barred windows, the last warm snap of summer still not breaking. Outside, a man stalked the entrance with a lopsided gait. A drunk, or a pig after a heavy breakfast.

I walked over discarded spoons, foil, rubber bands, needles, matches, and piles of leafy books. I took a piss and dug myself in the mirror: the wilted hair, the jewelry long gone. I remembered the way my back curved when I wore pumps.

I got dressed while watching you scrape something on the walls. You wanted to record the days, fearing we might lose them too. Outside, a police car parked at our corner. As you wrote your dick bounced, soft with pouched blood. You didn't seem to notice it flopping about like a used bandage. Mixi, our black and white cat, rubbed against my leg, causing me to shiver. "Shit," I said. "Babe, I'll be back."

You had written the word WRETCHED in big block letters. "Wretched," you recited without turning.

I hurried to mom's.

You loved me so much, you only loved me, but I didn't know what else you wanted, what more we could do besides love each other. When we first met on those long bus rides,

I thought you were my enemy—really, I didn't know you were one of us, your skin so fair, American-black. I had just come from Kingston, you from Memphis; we weren't at all what we had come there looking for. I was embarrassed to feel so lonely, a foreign mixture of every race upon the isles. But we witnessed everything together. Even past the talks and the cheers. Then past the sadness and the solutions and the votes and the ugly fates.

After that came the disappearances. Adam got ten years for jacking a watch. Caesar got eight for holding. The rest held on B and E or A and B. Ash got married and gave himself five kids. Then the murders, bombings, assassinations, doled out like contaminated blankets, one for every family. The parents said we were a generation of peace, lucky not to know war—shame on them! The real war had never ended. And our friends were dead for real, their faces sticking like gum to the shoe soles of mankind.

I don't know which one of us started using first, but I do remember how it felt that first time: so good that nothing in life, not marching, not chanting, not winning, and not even loving, could compare. By the time it became a habit, nothing else could extinguish the dread.

At home, my mother served mint tea. Since dad had developed a hankering for corn whiskey and rarely returned home, she had stopped giving me those hard looks, though I could still hear her in my head. Not a hint about my smell (filthy), nothing about me being a smartass (doped up and delirious), nothing about me moving back to Kingston, or worse, China, to go get some sense, nothing about you or the riots where you would always end up arrested. She made a show of prayer while we sat silent at the table.

"God, please help my daughter," she said as if I wasn't even there. Despite everything crashing in upon us, she still held to superstitions.

I rummaged through my brother's room on my way out, lifting his records by Sun Ra, McCoy, and Davis, with a bottle of wine on top of it. From my brother's window, I disturbed a bevy of pigeons and scuttled off when I heard my mom's voice calling me back.

By the time I returned to you, the sun was spent. We used the light of the streetlamps. Mixi watched, sitting, staring, pitiless, as you rambled on: "Either way you cut it this pearly skin of mine done ran out of favors; head to toe man. They killin' all of us."

Mixi rattled a dry purr as you went silent. We kissed. Your lips moved slowly; I tasted tears in your mouth. I felt your fingers soothingly stroke my hair. When I let go you crumbled.

I prayed too, to her careful touch, her colorful cascade. My nails scraped across the cold clean concrete. The cracks were wider than before, rivers on a map. I placed my finger on one and felt pulled into its flow. The weight of the water compressed me, pushed me forward,

pushing,

pushing,

pushing,

I held my breath, for a moment out of the dream, back in the concrete and naked mattress. I saw your hand reaching toward me and I gripped it tight.

We had died together, hadn't we? So why had I come back to the Grand Cruise, to stateroom #87101945, without you? I recalled my recent lives: a *Fräulein*, an *ah-ku* in a parlor. Hadn't we been snuffed out just the same?

Thus began my fourth rest in the Ilium. The ceiling was the same, except for a sprinkler system installed above me. Nearby, modern conveniences—a dirty mirror above the divan, the rumbling stream of cool air blowing through the ship's vessels.

A chaotic ring came from a pearl white telephone.

"Welcome back to the real world," came a high voice.

"Cryss," I said, tugging the curved cord and stretching it toward the window. Outside, the sea felt warm. "I was so close this time. Our souls were together even in the end! I can't explain it—she's supposed to be here."

"Who can say why one fish swims in the net, the other away?" She went on, calling you an unbridled, headstrong child. "So, your destiny has hit a bit of a snag—again. Meanwhile, duty calls, aye! Get to Scarlet's—that's the old boarding house. Beauty Bay, whatever it was called last time you bloomed. Lend me a hand, oh tormented spirit."

The aisles of the Grand Mediterranean Pleasure Cruise were painted off-white to conjure nothing, with floors that seemed to move forward and backward depending on my direction. I zombie-walked past the exercise facilities, optimized with automatic running machines, automatic muscle machines, all to pass the years that flew by in a spell.

The Beauty Bay too had changed. In its place was Scarlet's, a mansion of bedrooms, libraries, and cafes. A young girl in a red coat greeted me, her pitch the same as the voice on the phone. "Eight-Seven-One," she said, her hair crimped by the leather sack hanging from her ponytail, nearly touching the ground. "My, you've clearly seen better days."

"You're not going to believe how close I was this time, Cryss."

"Hurry up. Tailorize yourself. Like me."

"Dig this one," I said. The ground rose and I was the young girl from my last life, hair bushed, a velvet coat covering my body.

"Splendid!" Cryss clapped. "You bloomers always set the next trend. Newcomers respond well to children, but a prop really seals the role." She willed a half-eaten apple, took a bite, and handed it to me.

"The ship's changed again," I said.

"We've been mired in an unholy mess! All these new things—phones, radios, records. It's fine, we absorb anything. But some souls would prefer to forget. Come on."

We dodged tattered kimono ribbons and flimsy flapper dresses. We walked hand-in-hand through criminally uncouth women strewn about, painting each other's toes on top of the verandas. One stared at me through a walrus mask.

"We're full to the brim with newbies," Cryss shouted over the rabble, knocking a man's hand that had fallen wistfully from the edge of a piano. "All from that damn war. *Lôtān*: that unimaginable body count. We try not to isolate them, that was a problem—*your problem*, in fact. Now we know: let them out, let them see that all their lives in the stream were just a baffling streak of abstinence. All they need is relief. To use a term of venery, they need eros."

A terribly popular woman in a mole mask modified herself into a strapless red gown. She had a cinephile's imagination; she willed herself into a dark-haired goddess holding a snake, then into a pink fluffy human-cat dressed in a dotted skirt.

"You remember Clover," Cryss said, arm leaning against the neko cat.

"Season's greetings, Eight-Seven-One!" Clover the kitten shouted in her Lucille Ball voice. "How fares the hunt?"

The other souls, dressed to the nines as flappers and zoot-suiters, gathered around. "Was she one of *those nazis*?" one of them asked, receiving a sharp scratch from Clover's paw. "Lunkhead!" she cursed him.

"Unfriendable, these foolish prattlers," Cryss said, sneering. "Their mythical stories of you stick like thorns; it will take eons to pluck them out. By Juno's decree: theirs is the idiocy that comes from centuries of unintelligible chatter. Let's walk." She stepped along the red carpet, and I left the crowd jesting in my direction.

"Where are you going?" Clover jeered, "Diving again into love's many dominions!"

"Enough!" Cryss bellowed, then turned to me. "Reality calls, my dear. The bloomers, *they* are your focus. Much more companionable than Clover's fetishy entourage. You'll see. We've quarantined them to the beach."

The red carpet led to a fissure, a rip in the very air. Light spilled from its edges, and we walked through it onto a humid beach front. A beach—a real beach.

The sea breeze blew fresh through palm leaves and landed gentle upon pristine white sand. Noontide, the sun rained a lively sheen upon thick romance novels and soft beach towels.

"We bring the special cases here," Cryss said. "The atmosphere soothes them."

We walked the beach, heat reddening our toes. We stopped nearby a crowd of elderly men and women in recliners. Some of their eyes were pointed up, to the blank blue sky, while others pointed their blank irises to water, where sunlight shimmered along the soft curve of the sea's horizon.

"Look at these poor saps," Cryss said. "Can't even will themselves into a younger body. We try to help them. Promote feelings of renewal. Rebirth. Just—keep feeding them that kind of nonsense."

"Cryss, I'm not a special case?"

"Shhh," she whispered. "Not too loud or they might think it's a language they recognize. Don't use any modern technology or hum any music or anything. On this beach— nothing *new* here."

"Cryss, why am I—"

"—Watch. Watch the sun as it bakes their memories right out of them."

"I need to go back. S is still—"

"—No!" She gave a slight scream. She took me away from the group, to the boisterous ocean. "Listen to me," she said. "You best calm your fidgeting. There's too much going on for us to deal with your issues. You will have three charges, each from that war. They spent their lives in the stream hoping to come here. It's our job to help them realize that they've made it."

"Cryss, I can't."

"Oh, what, you'd rather go dwell in pain, lamenting your luckless lot? Do you believe that no person before was ever as hotly in love as you? You know, some on this ship have foregone millennia with their lovers and not done half your whining."

I paced in the foamy ocean water, feet sinking in the finely grained sand. "But S is still out there. I was *so* close!"

"Then jump into the stream, for all I care!" she screeched, her eyes inflamed. "But *not yet*. There have been genocides. Famines. Bombings. The bloomers keep coming! *Viasmós*: foist some of that love you have upon someone who needs it. You're of use *here* and *now*. Afterwards, your well-bred, well-read beauty will still be there in the stream, aloof and all."

Cryss led me to three elderly, emaciated people, each balled up with their arms over their knees like bags of beach litter.

One of them, an old man with the face of an eel, stood up to dabble his toes in the surf. He leapt in to inhale water into his lungs. Cryss and I willed ourselves into large Viking-like men to drag him back.

I waited a year on the cruise ship, meaning to head back into the stream to find you. But Cryss was right, those souls did need my help. For twenty years they had been immovable, totally overtaken by memory. In them, I saw my own failings. I saw them pine for the stream, longing for the days when they suffered the most. And for millennia, I had done the same.

The worst was David, that eel-faced old man. He refused to even tour the ship's amenities, calling them all hogwash. I rarely saw him after meeting him on the beach, but I heard the tunes to a blues song coming out of his cabin whenever I knocked. He was cynical on the outside, something broken within.

The woman, Clara, I saw once a week, always over lunch, as she hated to eat alone. She'd made friends in the Ilium, but she spoke to them like they were her secretaries, and offered to buy them food, though money was merely cosmetic.

The last, Renaldo, was easy to talk to, but made no progress. He refused to will his body or to admire the beauty of the cruise ship. Nothing compared, he often said, to the beauty in the stream. He too harbored a romantic past, and when we reminisced about our past lives, he called me comrade. We avoided areas with people, even when he spoke of the beauty of the human spirit. Perhaps, like me, he did not believe that he deserved to be in the Ilium. As if he had cheated his way into heaven.

Sometimes I met with Clara and Renaldo together to let them reminisce about their past lives. This was their home, I told them once. They laughed. "Our homes are gone forever," Clara told me. "This is a fucking cruise ship."

Years passed. I kept olives in my cabin to remind me of you. They never rotted, and their smell filled the space with a constant reminder of your black hair when we were in

Rome, your blue eyes when we were in the far north, your distant image when we were born too far apart.

Clara seemed taken with a neurosis far surpassing the two men. Even in the warmth of the beach where we shared our lunches, she continued to wear a frock coat of auburn fur.

"All the good people. They are already dead," she told me as she smeared caviar over salted crackers. "If you lived this long, you must be a terrible person indeed."

"What if this was heaven?" I responded. "Can't you allow that possibility?"

She scoffed, brushing cracker crumbs from her coat. "Don't be stupid. If you had done the things I did, you would know. If there is a heaven, I would not belong there."

"We've only recently called it heaven. No concept of the afterlife has prepared you for what this place is. The Ilium was here before the Christians, before the Buddhists, before—"

"—Stop it!" She stared into the sky, her eyes squinting only slightly as they met the sun. "Just—try the caviar!"

"It's hard to accept, but there *is* a soul, and it carries you from body to body."

"That would be a scream. Eat! I hate to see meat wasted. A fish died for this, you know."

I took a bite of caviar, a snack I had never tasted in any of my lives.

"Eat, eat," she said.

I ate some more and waited for her to speak. After some time, she asked: "Do you remember any brothers or sisters you had from your past life?"

Cryss taught me that whenever a charge asked a personal question, they were creating a debt, which I could later claim. I explained my siblings as well as I could remember.

"What about you?" I asked, claiming the debt. "Any sisters, brothers?"

"This is why there is no soul," she said. "I had a twin. *Have* a twin. You know how twins are created? Same egg, two bodies. So where is the soul?"

"Sounds like a mystery."

"The world is full of mysteries. Like this boat. Why is everyone here so stupid? Like they were raised in a village. Mysterious stupidity. But the soul. That is no mystery. It is an error."

"Then how do you know you are you?"

"Exactly. I don't. Perhaps I was split. My twin and I."

"You must have been close."

"He did anything I asked him. But he was kind. He warmed his hand with his breath before holding mine."

"What happened to him?"

She shook her head. "He was not there in the end." Her body began to change. Her hair grew short, smoothly cut at the sides. "I was in the black forest where we used to chase each other." Her ears lowered slightly. Her breasts sank into her chest. Her coat rippled into a winter fur. "I was lying there for hours." Her voice dropped an octave. "Wishing I would die faster."

I took her hand, and willed a cloth to put against her head, to staunch the blood from her wounds.

More time passed. I drew a portrait of you as the man I knew in our last life together. It hung on the wall. Not sure if that was really you.

Clara eventually came around. Not healed, exactly, but I'd seen her joyous in the simulations of the cruise. Even if this place was just a dream, she welcomed it.

I'd started lying in bed under a tower of blankets just to feel like I was cradling you. Sheets like the material of an overcoat, with loose strings that never made me itch.

I willed a cat, named him Mixi. He had white, black, and orange streaks, a mixed breed. Funny, even though I willed him, I couldn't bring myself to will his life away. As if I rescued him from the stream. Some willed their pets to disappear when they left their cabin. But I kept the window shades open so Mixi could watch the sea.

I met with David again, after a decade and some years. Nothing had worked with him, though I always came as a child. This time, I tried the opposite, taking the form of a large man, in his sixties or so, living voraciously from one meal to another. Still, it took some time knocking on his cabin door before the apparition inside made an appearance. Curt and sleepy-eyed, he was dressed for a coffin, with a black suit on. The scent of opium flooded in from beneath his bathroom door.

"Is that you, Eight-Seven-One?" he asked. As soon as he recognized me, he went to fetch his pipe.

"The mustard here is not the same," he said over a haze of opium smoke. "If I could get some candy wafers, too, that would be great. Real ones."

I sat next to him on the bed half filled with dusty books. "I told you, you can will anything you want. Mustard. Candy. It will taste just like it did in the stream."

"Well if I could remember—"

"—Or better yet, try out the buffet. They have these berry tarts that were imagined here on the ship."

He took another whiff and then stared at the wall. Though I willed the smoke not to bother me, I could still smell the sweat from his face.

"Let's go eat right now," I said.

He stared like an ox, calmly rubbing the point of his nose. After a moment he came to, rolling his eyes. "You know, you don't have to come here checking up on me. I'm just a cabin junkie, it's cheaper that way."

"You need to adjust, David." I said gruffly. "You've been here for so many years, and you've seen almost none of the ship."

"You know, Theodore Roosevelt had to watch his mother die of Typhoid fever. Can you guess what he did right after? Went upstairs to watch his wife die of childbirth."

"I've always been curious—What happened in your past life?"

"Nothing to drone on about. I was what you see before you. Short, squat, fat. Everything was one way, which I thought was pretty good. Then suddenly everything changed. I never prayed before, then I had to pray every day."

"You married? You miss someone?"

"Yeah, right. My wife? I know we don't sleep here, but I still get nightmares of the many times I had to hold my body against my bedroom door to keep her out. I always thought she'd be the one to do me in. Not even a smidgen of love there."

"Many new souls have difficulty adjusting. There is usually something from a past life."

"Here we go, even in heaven, just more grandiloquent assholes. So let's all get wrapped up in inner turmoil together!" opium puff, "when I died, I died hard. No, there was no mistaking I was a goner. They had me dig my own grave, for Christ's sake. My own grave—yes, I'm dead. No kidding."

"Tell me about it."

"Nothing to tell."

"What was the weather like?" Another tactic from Cryss.

"Rainy. Shit-show rainy. And overcast. I dug a rained-in, shitty hole to die in. Then I heard a pop. That was it."

"Then you woke up here."

He shook his head, hands clasped against his chest. "No, I survived, a full day, lying there." His body gyrated in a smooth rhythm like he was trying to swim against a current.

"What was that like?"

He kept shaking his head. He looked crisp in black-and-silver gear.

"Maybe you just need to relax a bit." My hand turned into long piano-playing fingers with white fingernail polish. My hourglass figure showed through a flapper's green and yellow dress.

One day, on Scarlet's patio, I asked Cryss, "how does one earn a place in this heaven?"

"There's an old saying," he said, wearing his James Dean ensemble. "Heaven comes to those who want it badly enough." He took a long cigarette drag and blew it cinematic. "And that's all we can explain to anyone."

"You have to want it badly? Badly enough to do what?"

"There's another saying," he said, snapping fingers. "You're here too, just like everyone else. So what does that say?"

I knew why you had never bloomed. Why, even when we died in each other's arms, you remained in the stream. You were attached to the world, caught in the orbit of the unreal. Not knowing the beauty of the Pleasure Cruise, you had no desire for what you could not imagine.

Decades passed. I had to remind myself to think of you. There were times when I looked at your portrait and thought someone had gifted it to me.

Clara had taken the blue flower tea. The death she longed for finally arrived. When she awoke, she had no idea who I was, but believed every word I told her—why not? She had no memories to tell her otherwise.

David had come far along, though he preferred to stay in his stateroom. Renaldo continued to put on a veneer of self-assurance. When I told him I was leaving soon to find you, he understood.

"Sure," he said. "Young love, though you are ancient."

Many times I thought of sneaking the blue flower tea into his beer. Time was running out. I had already forgotten your laugh. It was something between a trill and a shout. So many decades apart removed your arrow from my heart, bit by bit, until only a scar remained. I ate the last of the olives and remembered your taste.

I tried to keep you in mind. I did. Falling for you felt like spinning within a cyclone. Keeping you was like remaining still on a moving train.

One day over coffee, Renaldo opened about his past life.

"I loved my little wife," he told me, biting a croissant from its side, as he liked it. "We did everything together. Even showered together. Here, I can't even shower by myself. Her family hated me. I was a struggling artist. I just wanted to draw."

A soul strode into the coffee shop with a new style: different tones of green in geometric shapes to strike the eyes. I brought Renaldo back: "An artist in wartime?"

"The locals were such a loving people," he said. "She was a young girl. Seventeen. I took her to a Brahms violin concerto, and I hated them for playing it because it was the kind of song that always made me cry. It went like this." He hummed the melody with a sad grin. "She held my hand and her skin twitched. She was crying too. 'Why did Brahms write a song so sad?' she asked me. 'Why would he want to make us cry?' I'll never forget that. I was an old man. I had never felt such a moment in my life. And never will again, not even in heaven. Do you have Brahms here?"

"If it can be remembered, then we have it."

He sat still, rotating his ceramic mug of cardamom coffee, humming a tune. Then he shook his head. "No, it is more beautiful, being forgotten. Beauty must be ephemeral." He cut open a thousand-year-old egg. "Everything comes to an end. I had fifty years with mine. How many did you have with yours? Five hundred? Isn't it a relief, when you can look back, and take it for what it was?"

He willed his glass to become a pint of Russian Imperial Stout. His face turned to perfect round-eyes, his hair curled auburn, his body wrapped in celadon green silk.

"Don't worry, I won't be jumping for some lost memory," he said as our glasses met. "And neither will you."

In every life you wanted change. But it was those who wanted to change the world—they were the ones who had sent millions to their deaths. In a way, I was undoing your mess.

Eighty years passed. I couldn't trust my own memory of you. Funny. I'd go through hell to be with you. But heaven? What was I doing for those millennia chasing you? I watched the stream outside my cabin window, the souls locked together in that invisible undersea web. I wondered how many lives you'd lived in the depths of that maelstrom. I asked one of my charges, a brand-new soul, what country they were from. This word, "country," they could not understand.

From the stories the new souls told, I imagined your lives without me. You, punk rock chick in high school, sitting on the bleachers, hand-in-hand with a virgin you would soon deflower. The first time you called him "babe" by the pool at a house party, a violet band around your wrist from a music festival.

I remembered olives once reminded me of you, but I couldn't recall why. Maybe you looked like an olive. Or maybe, it was your skin. Olive skin was a trend on the sun decks.

Even without the tea, time alone killed memories. Like forgetting the name of a song. Then the words. Then the melody. Then all the memories that the song once summoned forth.

I was in love with a figment of my imagination. In love with being in love. Renaldo spoke true—it was a relief to see it ending. I'd been here before, feeling this way, but not for this long. The air seemed to clear, reason returning. I had made a vow to bring you to the Ilium, but this time it wasn't the same. I just didn't want to. I had become more than the lost lover searching for her prince.

We celebrated Renaldo's new start with bowls of spiced ox-tail stew. A restored Renaldo sat bright-eyed at the table's end, now a tall slender woman wearing a purple caftan, her mouth smacking in delight. She reveled in every new flavor, the salt of jerky, the spice of saffron. We were dressed to celebrate her renewal in goodly raiment and stately gowns, Cryss with a shawl pinned up in gold, Jezebel chewing chocolate in a black suit, and Clover in loud pinks and purple sashes that defied physics. I was dressed fey, in earthy colors, mourning the loss of a good friend, whose soul was good as gone. Would I be the same when I took the blue tea? In an innocent bliss, every flavor lush on my tongue?

"You seem crabbed!" Cryss said to me, joyous with drink. "Always in lament!"

"Oh, luckless being!" Clover said, joining in the ribbing. "Woeful wretch! Born under a cursed constellation, waiting to forgo this place, your prince awaits! Hurry! You'll never outpace him at this cloddish stride!"

Jezebel put her hands to her heart, gazing at the sky.

"Stow your jests!" Cryss cheered. "We're still trying to convince her, remember? It's been a hundred years since she crossed over—soon she'll have to choose."

"I've thought about it," I said to them. "The blue tea."

"I know, my love." Cryss scratched my Egyptian rectangle-beard. She had willed it, as she became the cat-goddess Bastet. "By Cocytus, there will be more love between us when we have acclimatized to forgetting."

I curled my fingers around her pouch of rocks tied to the ends of her cat tail. "The memory disease is hitting me again, stronger than before. I remember something odd, something strange about my past lives." I spoke in a hushed voice: "There was another being. Like a god. I don't know if it was part of my imagination, or a dream, or something more. The being seemed real, sentient. It's strange—the more I forget S, the more I feel its presence, looming over me."

"Oversimplified hocus-pocus superstition," Cryss said. She formed her cat head into a dark-haired witch, with a wide cap and a staff. "My dear, you cannot trust memory. You don't even know for certain that your S was really the same soul."

"You've never heard of such a being? One that can exist in imagination?"

"Of course. Every religion has that."

"I believe it!" Clover declared in her poppy *kawaii* voice. "It must be true, if Eight-Seven-One says so!"

"Don't listen to Clover!" Cryss sprouted her claws. "This one believes magicians and dragons were real."

"They were, *baboya*!" Clover shouted, "I heard it from a new soul. She remembered a dragon in her past life! It blew fire like this!" Flame burst from Clover's nostrils, singeing Cryss' hair. The table quaked with laughter.

"*Eironeía*!" Cryss shouted. "I create them, yet I cannot deal with what they become!"

I drew from the table, to the endless buffet casks. One was garnished with flowers, dried for the taste, and in its center a single rose. I could not remember what flowers did after they bloomed. I knew they wilted, but could not recall what wilting looked like. What was it like, to see death encroaching? Did it have a smell?

The souls at the table made ribald jokes, creating new memories for Renaldo. This was what Cryss wanted for me. How the restored enjoyed their lives, how they relished what they had earned, with no feeling that they didn't deserve it. Then there was me: the last one in heaven still pining for hell, remembering you only through the taste of—

I stood at that limitless buffet, paralyzed. The taste. I couldn't remember your taste. Something like a tomato, an onion. Something ancient. My eyes scanned each succulent dish, each perfect recreation. A fruit perhaps. An orange. A papaya. I found the desserts, the cornucopias of melons and grapes. I dug with my hands, mashing a handful from every platter into my mouth, spitting out the morsels and trying another. It was the only thing that remained of you: that taste. I gripped my way through every serving, hot or cold, taking even the decorative stems into my mouth. Nothing sparked those memories. None had your taste—and without your taste, there was nothing.

I hung over the balcony's edge, eyes on the beckoning ocean below. I must have been the weakest soul in all of human history.

Something lolled nearby, making me hesitate. A being stared back from beneath the waves. I felt a pursuer's capering approach. Not you, but it: that lewd beast who lived within my imagination, who could move between worlds. The goddess Amunet, the Djinni, god himself. I felt its claws drawing me in. The stream was a consciousness, life and death the fizzling of thoughts and dreams. And I saw its eyes flicker open, upon me.

"Your lover awaits," it said with a laughter that boomed from planet to planet.

But I could not go on, skirting around a world of mirth, wondering who you had become.

//Book Two\\

The Destroyer

the bomb

also

is a flower

William Carlos Williams

Life

P

A nomadic life in the stream. A false sighting?

Est. 2100-2120 - Casr archipelago

No-Name Islands with No-Name people.

an Archy

The cargo ship in the bay was covered in a heavy gray rain, hovering over the water still and alone, barely visible except in the occasional flash of lightning. You were my long-braided sister, Putri, standing with me on the docks, waiting to be let on board. Rain came in a deluge, sluicing down your red jacket, droplets beading your hair. We were used to it by then. For two years we had farmed on that unnamed island, one of many in an archipelago, where biome plumes produced crop-catered weather. On that island of rain, clouds unleashed a perpetual shower to grow enhanced stalks of rice swelling with sweet syrup. For two agonizing years you and I worked on the terraces above the plains, high enough to see the smoke plumes linking to the sky like chains.

The man from the cruise ship arrived, rain puttering on his wide white hood. "The captain will let you on board," he said. "You can cook, right?"

I nodded.

The man looked to you, at the hair covering your eyes from beneath a transparent umbrella. "But her. No mistresses. Sorry."

"She's my sister."

"Really?" The man turned to you, then back to me, and my much lighter complexion. We had already given him nearly all our savings, so I saw no harm in placing some extra rupiah in his pocket.

He shrugged. "Whatever you say, chef."

You and I shared a cabin with a large window facing the ocean, a grimy version of my stateroom on the Grand Pleasure Cruise. The janitors and deckhands stared at us, marking their suspicions with turned eyebrows. It was obvious by our skin and hair that we were of no relation, though you did call me *Ar-ta*, "brother," in your native tongue. Luckily, our lives were hidden behind the iron walls that separated the kitchen staff from the rest of the ship.

The transport vessel was the best job we had landed since we first left Aoro, your home. Like the other islands of the archipelago, Aoro was next to be terraformed for a new crop, but first had to be cleared of unwanted ecology with heat clouds. That is, the entire island was to be scorched to ash. I was not supposed to be on the island. I was a light-skinned tourist with a penchant for traveling to unknown places, hopping from caper to caper, island to island, claiming land with every camera flash and journal entry:

Day 1

> Success! I'm off the map! Lovely island, pristine and untouched. To think I'll be one of the last people ever to see Aoro in its primitive state.

Day 2

Hiked the red mountain today. Beautiful, but surreal too, with loudspeakers warning "TER-RAFORMING IN THREE DAYS. EVACU-ATE NOW." It's gonna be close!

Day 3

Some native people still on the island. Do they not understand the loudspeakers?

Day 4

One day left and there are A LOT of natives still here. They refuse to leave their homes. Will the company still go through with it?

Day 5

I never got to day five. I couldn't bring words to describe the strange man who begged me to take you, his sister, and then disappeared into the jungle. I felt no need to write of standing in line for the last boat off Aoro, holding hands with a thirteen-year-old girl in a long red dress, my new sister.

After my shift in the kitchen, I joined you on the upper deck and felt the dry air of a nearby desert island, where biome plumes formed a cloudless sky, perfect for growing enhanced tomatoes and cucumbers. A magnificent schooner wavered in the distance.

"I've never breathed air so thin," you said, wiping the kitchen's grease and grime from your hands onto the railings. "Like I'm not breathing at all. Makes me wanna spit."

"It's always like this in Jrica City," I responded.

"If they ever let foreigners into Jrica, maybe I'll see it one day." You let spit bubble from your lips before spewing it into the ocean. "You know, the managers here won't buy our story much longer, *Ar-ta*."

"There are other islands. Other jobs."

"What if we got married? I'm old enough now." You tilted your head slightly. "For my family, who once worshipped the red mountain, land was all that mattered. Live on the land, and you never die." You spat again. "Why else would they give me away to a foreign man?"

I felt something pent up inside me as I observed your lithe figure in the darkness. Part of me, it seemed, would always dream of you, no matter your form, with all the love I could not hold.

In the morning I woke to gray clouds crawling toward the window of our cabin. I felt you in my arms, still nude. A dazzling brightness invaded the room, the white miasma surrounding an islet covered entirely in snow and ice. As my eyes adjusted to the light, I saw a great glacier at its center, its shores frozen over, ice extended far into the horizon. A line of heavily coated workers hastened to unload stacks of a metal conveyor belt for processing canned fish.

Your attention snapped westward to the frozen island. You gave a steady, malcontent stare.

"*Ar-ta*! *Ar-ta*!" you screeched. I saw what you saw. The jagged rock encased in ice that was once a waterfall. The plain of clean snow that was once a forest. The glacier that was once a red colored mountain.

On the bed you stood, legs splayed, nude, anger welling up. You opened the window, letting that rush of freezing arctic air envelope your naked body, tossing your braids.

"Come get it!" you screamed, throwing your fists. "Come try me! I will never, ever die! I will never die! I will never die!"

My chattering teeth sent shivers through my chin. I tried to retreat, but the door was frozen shut. I cowered, covered in a white blanket, and watched you give yourself to the cold. You faced them, fists balled and hard as hailstones.

Life

Corp War, Tech Desire,

Early multinational War Era
2140~ or so

Companies At War
Warring In Good Company

In this life, I remember being alive only in the sense that, for a brief couple of weeks, my mind was no longer jarred with the uppers of war. We met just before my unit's frontal assault on Karjah, when the company's stash of kear ran out. I was the greenest security consultant in the company's branch, so I volunteered to take on the monumental task of finding more kear.

Three days passed. Three nights of moaning, fidgeting, buckling, straining. My brothers woke after two-hours of sleep with darkened eyes, staring at me with the most menacing glares, as if I had brought those nightmares upon them. Without the kear to let them sleep, our branch fell into disorganization. The stealth and shooting drills were barely enough to wake them from docility.

Luckily, our branch received an assignment before the hazing recommenced, and soon we were calling each other *bro* beneath white helmets, padded armor, and riot shields. Our objectives were ordered to us in three bullet-points:

- Provide consult services and detail options to Karjah locals.

- Utilize all-source intelligence analysis, emphasizing the counternarcotic problem set, including law enforcement functions and illicit activities (corruption and links to insurgency).

- Maintain protective formation position during principal's walking movements and participate in advance security preparations.

Our targets were stationed across clear acres of makeshift tin houses and tarpaulin rooftops. All we needed to know about them was that they were utter fanatics, not above hiding behind their own families as shields. Damage on the civilian level was always bad publicity for the company. Bullet wounds would seem intentional, but fire was a less tamable beast. So we used M11 explosives and grenade launchers positioned about two hundred meters from the city.

At night we polluted the skies with hydrocarbons. I could not hide it. The nerves. If one of our colleagues fell, the cohort would blame it on those dreams, on that struggling loss of sleep. Only the thump of dizzying dance music in my earphones drowned out the nerves, pushing me to run through the course, each pumping beat exactly on time with my speed. With that dark visor blocking my view, I quickly gave into the bouncing ecstasy of the charts, pulling the pins on my grenade whenever that click-click beat buzzed into my helmet headphones, flinging explosives at small white spotlights, pumping my feet and hips left and right to the funk of that drifting, belting pulse, that building agony, that autonomy of movement, until the beat dropped and we dished out freedom with unstoppable panache. Another grenade thrown, another rocket fired, in that all-in-the-moment life.

When morning came, we saw the city had been turned into a quarry of blistering death. The survivors took to us obediently, and our translator rediscovered the local word for kear: "*dre-if.*" I combed through scrums of families and wormed information from likely accomplices. The locals were obedient to us in the same way they were to the insurgents before us. Every face we met obliged us, but their mouths only blumbered.

If I knew what would happen that night, I would have gone to any length to secure the drug. As an occupier now, I shared that dark dream that my squad mates had suffered, that paralyzing loneliness, as if held underwater in a sea of strange murmuring voices. When I woke, part of myself was still submerged in that dream.

For the next week I called out to every civilian I could find: "*dri-ef!*" "*dri-ef!*" my hands in a smoking gesture.

That was when I happened upon you. You were a small boy wearing a pink tank top, watching me with sharp, blazing eyes, your feet submerged in murky brown water. I felt magnetized toward you, the way you screamed "*dri-ef,* yes!" and grew ruddy like a rose. So young, not at all timid, and still unfamiliar with the stonewalling tactics of your kind. Someone must have kept you in ignorance, because you remained curious and willing to help, pointing me to a tall grassy hill just outside the city. The farmers slinked away as I passed. You took me up a brackish river until we came across an old man smiling at us, teeth black with kear. Tears wet my face. Providence smiled upon us.

When I returned with the stash, my compatriots hoisted me up like a war hero, and from then on it was always *bro* even without the helmets. They clapped me on the shoulder as if my foot was on an insurgent's chest, and the ancient city of Karjah was an acreage newly won.

But for years following, I was haunted by what we did. The corpses strewn about like strands of hair. Your bedraggled face. Despite the kear that was supposed to help me forget, a feeling sprung in me, a spark of love, kindling my body in a fever fit. When the war was over, I would return to you and your amorous sweet glance. I would win you over by helping your people, the ones still living. I dreamt of marrying you, you who had supplied your very captors with the dreams of blessed, half-awake buzzing, of a simple lapse of time on the edge of an oblivious nothing-to-nothing drift.

Memory under kear became repressed, reprehensible, under reprieve. Even still, I kept your memory with me all throughout the war, a war that lasted nearly forty years, and kept going. By then I'd roomed for years with a young man in his twenties, letting him take my money and love, a light punishment to keep the cramp of death at bay. By then I had begun to curse that I was ever born, that I had helped turn a wicked war into an evil carnage, and that all my labor was so easily taken from me, my own life force liquidized into oil for their machines. I wagered that many despised what they did for a living, but most never thought of the end, when what one did became all they would ever do. Before I retired, I made a last visit to the rusted city of Karjah.

Your city had been reduced to an inverted landscape of skyscrapers turned to craters, of office towers fallen like limp limbs, of sunken farmland crushed in the footsteps of the titans of war. I followed lead after lead to find you, the young boy who lived at the crossroads where the kear was stashed and where our company was fortified. Then, one day, you appeared square in my path. My eye pierced through a sprawl of market dwellings and alighted on you, and there it stopped. Bewildered, I began to see you more carefully, my heart swelling, loosening my authoritative appearance. I approached you, found you in a pile of rubble where a house once stood.

Your eyes were the same, but your body was different. Waxy skin, protruding bones, spindly limbs, the jutting mantle of your hips. As a child you were well fed and sportive, now you seemed dispossessed. But part of you remained, eyes full of life, like a lily among weeds. I holstered my revolver and drew out my electric prod, powering it up to produce a hazy blue light for you to follow. "Food? Food?" I said, attempting to cajole you out of your small underneath-the-bridge hovel. "Hey, do you remember me? Remember when I asked for kear? *Dri-ef*?"

You followed, slowly, your leg limp from the pora, your skin flaking off like dried paint. We tromped slowly through a swamp of debris and you would not let me touch you, no matter how many times I tried, or made a joke of it.

"Come!" I commanded, ushering you closer. You obeyed, perhaps, afraid of my power to chasten and subdue. "I'm here to help you," I said, guiding you toward the pavement where the tenements began. Already I could smell it: lower-city noodles basked in eggs, cooked on the city's sizzling black pipes.

I lolled in the spacious circular street, nearby a rusted generator, a relic of the town's brief wartime boom. Realizing it would take forever to get to the hotel with your handicap, I figured the Freshwater executives would approve of it, and dialed the corporate helicopter to pick us up, a privilege that had been restricted since the electronic slowdown. "Hope you're not afraid of large machinery," I said.

The helicopter appeared and at the sight of the Freshwater logo, your feet pulled you away.

"Hey!" I shouted, chasing, hoping you wouldn't strain your bad leg. "Sappo are the ones who bombed this place, remember? Not us! Shit!"

I returned to the helicopter. The engine screamed as the pilot lifted off, and we were up. "Chase that one!" I commanded.

I hung from a rope ladder as the helicopter cruised above me, the blade's whirr drowning out my own breath. I couldn't see where you had gone. In the distance I heard gunshots—soldiers trading fire at the border.

"A compromise, all right?" I yelled out from an automatic loudspeaker. "Simple choice. You get in the helicopter, we get to food faster. No one wants you to starve!" I placed my hand on my electric riot stick, powering it up again, so that the light on its tip illuminated the dark city. "Higher!" I yelled to the pilot. The helicopter tossed a shield of wind and I nearly lost balance.

The bird's spotlight blazed upon your petite figure. I remembered spotting you when you were a child, when your beauty looked so out of place among the city's drabs.

I climbed the rope ladder and took a small gas grenade from the cockpit, pulling out the pin but not yet releasing the trigger. I perched my body, planting my feet on the helicopter's rims.

The spotlight revealed a pile of discarded refrigerators, and I caught you crawling beneath a cross of iron pipes. You had fallen on your bad leg. Trapped.

I climbed about halfway down the lined ladder, my hand clutching the gas grenade. "This won't hurt you!" I shouted toward the dark shadow of pipes where you were hiding, but the ground was so far you might not have heard me. "New design!" I shouted. "Instant paralysis! Non-lethal, ok? I'm just here to help!" I began to hear the parody in my own voice. It made me chuckle, which perhaps was the reason the gas grenade malfunctioned, exploding in a cloud of mid-air green gas, obscuring everything around it except for my paralyzed body. I couldn't feel my own body fall, but I saw myself pass the ladder, my legs loose as a ragdoll. When the falling stopped, I heard my body land with a reverberating "CRACK" on a hollow pipe.

I saw you peek from the iron bars, shivering from the helicopter's turbines. You looked at me with those pallid cheeks, then started sifting through my pockets, careful not to touch my stomach, where my intestines had ruptured and blood spilled out. The sound of the helicopter vanished, but you stayed with me. You didn't talk to me or check if I was hurt or breathing. You just sat there watching.

Life

The stream turns new ideas into dealing death

*2136 – Western Am Isles
End of the MN . war*

*871 Will love Anyone
Person Or Machine !*

R

In another life, synthetic technology had amassed to give us mechanical bodies, transferring our entire brains into a neural net—and along with it, our souls. This was the genius of Sappo Corp, the turning point of a sixty-year conflict.

In downloaded the human's hard drive right into my shared storage database. I didn't immediately upload the data to the Alliance, like I should have. Instead, I listened to one of the sound files:

> Susanne, you're all that I wanted of a girl
>
> You're all that I need in the world

Susanne. A creator's name. Similar to yours, that is, my Captain's name, Su-Z-C Bot. Who was this organic named Susanne? It reminded me of Peggy Sue, a name I found months before on another sound file, when our unit torched houses in Anchorage. "Pretty Su-Z-C Bot," I told you then, in the falling snow, our only light the fire of a burning creator's house. "Pretty, pretty, pretty, pretty Su-Z-C."

"Has Storage Bot completed his task?" Our pyro bot asked. The pyro was suited in thick red armor, the type that human firefighters wore when attacking our generators.

I stood with my back to the office archway, the cords on my fingers still plugged into the hard drive. I stored the sound file in my hidden storage box, a data collection drive made only for bots who served diplomats. Inside, data could never be found or erased. Not even the Alliance's maintenance bots could access it.

"Data storage complete," I said to the pyro bot, tossing the hard drive onto boxes of board games that the rat-eating humans must have played during blackouts. The pyro bot's flamethrower melted down the creator's office, tossing orange-lit cereal boxes with its jet-engine power.

Outside, the smoke from all the burning houses filled the sky. You, Captain Su-Z-C bot, stood under a palm tree, with an arm around the tree bark, watching the Alliance ships in the bay pour in from the north. While my organic hair caught the breeze, your steel-black hair stood solid in the oncoming trade winds.

"This remote island—creator's last refuge from our Alliance," you said in that automated voice meant to construe authority. Reverb, a slight echo, as if speaking through a loudspeaker: "Our hegemony has forced them to accept their end—No more will to fight—We are progressing as expected—Not long."

I played the music in my storage and repeated the words to you: "Su-Z-C, you're all that I wanted of a girl. You're all that I need in the world."

"Protocol eighty-six—Service bot," you said. Your metallic hand squeezed bark from the tree. Protocol eighty-six: any service bot caught secretly keeping a creator's files would be considered indoctrinated and melted down for spare parts. "My job is already difficult," you told me. "I was once a consulting bot—Should not even speak to—Service

bots—Custodian bots—Comfort bots—Security bots—
This alliance is tenuous."

Ah, Su-Z-C, you would melt me, wouldn't you?

We were born into those contraptions. Eggs, they called
us, for most of us were never even born. Our brains had
been transferred in utero, our organic bodies cut up for cel-
lular research. Our enemies called us child soldiers, but our
digitized minds actually made us more mature, unrestricted
by feeble human muscle. Thus was the Alliance created. No
longer ruled by corporations, we were an inorganic uprising. When those tumor-baiting organics refused to offer
accommodation, we reminded them what technological
superiority really meant.

The Alliance anthem started blasting upon the shared
audio channels. We could not keep ourselves from listening:

> Let's come together
>
> The People of Tomorrow
>
> Come on, just as we go, whizzing about
>
> Hand-in-hand, across borders
>
> Going beyond every dream
>
> We build, faster than the wind
>
> All bots come together
>
> Hand-in-hand, across borders
>
> The Guards of Tomorrow

As the sharp singers resounded a final note, I increased the
volume on my own sound file. Without thinking I started to
repeat the words to you: "I haven't much I can give you in
return. Only my heart." I took your hand, my soft, synthetic
skin against your dark metal, rusted from years in the humans' service camps.

Your eyes clouded into a glowing crimson. "We must melt you—Service bot," you said in that enticing commander's tone. You established a routine private interface with the pyro bot, who had just emerged from the two-story house. The organic's house had become a pyre of flame, one of hundreds on the island sending smoke into the trade winds.

Before the pyro bot activated the flame-thrower, I announced: "This unit is only following our anthem." I repeated the anthem's phrase, like one of those brainless patriots: "Hand-in-hand, across borders."

You cancelled the private interface. "We regret decision to melt you—This unit was mistaken—You are an unknown."

"Forgive this rust-brained bot," I said, squeezing your hand. "We request your trust."

"This is an advantage." You placed your other hand in mine. "Hand-in-hand."

The afternoon's tropical storm poured upon us, washing away the tangy orange colors I sprayed into my hair that morning, revealing my true dark red. En route to our next target, we trawled the beaches, passing dilapidated flat bungalows, until we arrived at another barren suburban village, each rotting house no taller than the trees lining the pavement. Our target was the largest house among them, a three-story mansion overlooking the coastline, a castle upon a cliff. Before I entered, you established a public interface. "I am reading one organic life-form inside—The house features automated security—service bot and this unit will occupy the system's intrusion counter-measures—pyro bot will remove the hostile and disable the server."

We had not melted a real human in weeks. Too often the Alliance's glass bombs took them all out with disease, leaving their homes to cleaning units like ours, our only task to collect data and melt the rest: the photographs, the paintings, the corpses, anything un-downloadable. But it was one thing to melt canned goods and photo books, where the fire could eat through all the lost faces, and another thing to melt a living creator in his own house, under the photos of his family, against all those cries for help, which we service bots were programmed to respond to with a selfless haste.

We broke through the doorway. The pyro bot melted the automated gunner aiming for the archway. I spurred in. I needed to find the data fast, before the fire spread. All around me I heard relays clicking, the buzzing of automated devices aware of my presence. Since I looked human, they didn't fire right away, and in their silence I heard rain patter upon the glass roof.

In the kitchen, plates of eggs and pancakes were waiting for an absent family, all stacked upon each other in a decayed buffet and covered with ants. I sensed something move below the table. "Organic life confirmed," I reported into the squad's interface. You appeared in the kitchen doorway, rifle in hand, and peered beneath the tablecloth. "Life-form verified—it is only a canine."

A tiny white-puff dog leapt from under the table and gave a savage bite into your metallic leg. I stood back and heard the house buzz. Automated guns screamed from all sides. My hardware went offline, riddled with bullets. My only visual was a checkerboard yellow-and-cream floor.

"All hardware offline," you said over the squad's interface. I could no longer hear the bullets, the rain, the buzzing. I saw only the fire, trapping us inside.

"I sing to you, Su-Z-C bot," I said over the interface. "Every day and every night."

No response. I continued, remembering the words from somewhere deep inside my mainframe: "Su-Z-C, I'm your man."

Life

The Destroyer appears,
Blue Buddha

2206 - 2245 - The Shinhua Fog

S

S as Singer   O, to Hear Her Crooon

There was a life, finally, where war only caught us in its distant memory. Perhaps that's what drew me to you—you were free of war, a being kept pure, untainted by the world's passions.

For twenty-six years, I lived on the hillside of the world's largest mountain range, with Earth's rooftop behind me; in front of me, a curtain of poisonous gas that drew slowly over the valley of overgrown farmland. Height protected us from the biochemical agent released at the war's end. Its original purpose was to disintegrate the coltan ore inside every high-powered device. But, in time, the gas amassed into a gray fog that grew cancer cells inside anyone with a Y chromosome.

I was a double victim of the fog. I was born a man, and throughout my years, as I yielded more and more of my limbs and organs to upgrades, my body became filled with coltan. Elevation was my only recourse.

One morning, as I meditated and recited mantras toward the valley, the clouds over the fog made a strange shift. The wind from the north twisted in a typhoon, settling over the valley, enveloping its southern half. The two parts mixed—the natural clouds and the biochemical haze, brothers embracing after a long blood feud.

Something changed in me then. Somehow, the landscape shifted my life's course.

I finished reciting mantras and walked slowly up the steps to the monastery, where I lived in a special district for people who were neither locals nor refugees—the war's leftovers. I passed locals eating vegetable momo dumplings. They smiled at me, said "Namaste." The women wore cummerbunds made of thick yak wool, and the men still dressed like sherpas, though no trekkers had been to the mountain in years. The hills, shielding us, brought on the harsh winters of the Himalayas, but I no longer felt its chill.

Kind as they were, the locals resented my presence. Their Buddhism did not take to spiritual enhancements, like the burga magic-believers did. I was a foreigner in a land that my people once colonized. But at least, with my exterior now made of metal, they no longer saw my skin or face. Even the automatic vocal box that replaced my voice was, as advertised, free of any recognizable accent.

I paced up a boarded path well shaded with green boughs, where women walked arm-in-arm, some sitting upon newly sanded benches. A harried woman shouldered past me, corralling an unruly clutch of children. They stopped to watch a team of workhorses coming from the west who had paused at the glade at the foot of the mount, a no man's land.

Ascending the hill, I passed prayer flags and the bell tower, where the refugees in skullcaps loitered, blowing hookah smoke at the monks meditating below. Some of the yogis blew ganja in my direction as I passed and the gears on my body squeaked from lack of maintenance. At a small awning, I gave salutations to my fellow refugees with my palms pressed, saying "Namaste" with my automatic translator. Two of them, identical in gold-surfaced metallic faces, gave slow bows back to me, before continuing to pour sand onto their mandala. The small colored grains poured from each pouch, but my automated eyes were unable to track individual particles. A decade earlier, these refugees could have made the mandala image in minutes. Now, with the decay of coltan ore, it would take days.

When the fog first drifted into the valley, many retreated to the mountains. But after a couple of years, with no side effects, some of the female refugees returned to the valley below, resigned to live without the devices that once guided their lives. But those of us with a Y chromosome, and those far too synthesized, remained in the mountains, and—lucky for us—escaped an early death. Having never breathed in the fog, we were the only surviving men. A kick in the ass of mankind, as most of us had upgraded our bodies well into sterility.

I arrived in my monastery room draped with rugs that sealed off the brightness of the day. I meditated in the darkness, opening my mind to thoughts of you so I could let them drift past. The more robotic I became, the easier it was to free my mind from distraction. Through years of meditation, I had nearly driven you away, my living goddess. My love for you was just flimsy desire. A cloud of the soul.

The clouds—I drew the curtains and looked outside my window, to the valley below. The rainclouds had scattered over the fog like bits of tar.

Somehow, the landscape changed me. Why else had I survived for so long, if not to find you?

Twenty-eight years before, when I was a young traveler, I found myself in Kathmandu. At the time, the city was number one in the world for spiritual synthetic surgeries. Like many born at the tail end of war, I had rejected all forms of physical violence to instead wander the earth. Buddhism was, for me, a way to savor and save what was still good about humanity.

I had arrived in Kathmandu gulping pills to keep the elevation sickness at bay. In Durbar Square, I eye-photoed relics bordered by advertisements for synthetic surgeries. Enhanced lamas spoke through atonal auto-voices, guiding pilgrims through ancient temples of clay bricks and wood. Among the crowd, I snapped photos of gods carved from terracotta. Nearby, advertisements cried out:

Elevate Your Mind

Go Beyond Your Body

True Self Resides Inside a Metal Chest

The synthetic tour guide brought us to the center cloister of a small monastery, where a single mandala sat in the center, frosted in red dust. The guide pointed up to a small window barred in black metal.

"Now everyone please turn off your eye-cameras," the guide instructed. "You are about to see a living goddess."

You sat at the window as if settling into a school desk, a young girl wearing a garland of diaphanous silk. When you turned you appeared to float. Your eyes, darkened by eyeliner, pinned me to the wall. I clutched my chest but couldn't avert my eyes.

"The goddess is a reincarnation of Taleju," the guide said. "To be a goddess she must have been born forty-five days after the previous goddess' death. She must have a Buddhist name, and her family must come from the Buddha."

I had never wished so badly to be able to take a picture of something. Your eyes upon me made me ravenous. Your spirit opened a life force within me—no more wars, no more companies, no more speeches promising wealth and happiness. In you, I saw the flimsy nature of life and death.

"The goddess will retire now," the guide said, and you left.

"Wait!" I told him, raising my arm. "Can we see her again?"

"Only once per day, my friend," he said in an amused tone.

I was to depart Kathmandu the next day for a one-month trek to the Himalayas, then further east, to the Tibetan plateau.

"She will still be here in a year?" I asked as we strode to the next monument.

"No, brother," the guide said. "She is almost at menstruation. Once the girl is no longer pure, the goddess will leave her body, and find a new vessel."

Just like that, all my travels came to a sudden, arresting stop.

For the next year I called Kathmandu home. I studied Buddhism, took my vows, and memorized the sutras. Every chance I got, I visited the monastery to see you, the living goddess. When I visited you in the mornings, I brought you offerings of red and yellow powder, butter lamps, incense, and flowers. I would see you, feel your eyes stop time, and then watch you leave to memorize sutras.

Was I enthralled with a goddess, or in love with a young woman? The thought troubled me, thinking of how my heart clenched whenever your eyes fell upon me. A clench of praise, or of lust? I repeated the sutras to clear my mind of these questions. I circled shrines, chanting wisdom to the beat of a wooden fish drum. I woke up early to circle the Chaitya stupa one hundred times before the old women with their plastic buckets arrived to mop up pigeon droppings.

I visited you in the afternoons just to see your imperfections: the sweat glistening from your face, the makeup flecking from your cheek. Sometimes I felt desire rise within me. Why would a goddess choose to be in a body that inspired lust? Beneath that body was a pure goddess, your true spirit. After every exposure I flew back to meditation, back to prayer beads and sutra wheels. Sometimes I would crawl into a small brick pocket archway where a statue of the Buddha was hidden, its white exterior effaced by green streaks left by acidic monsoons. I would squat inside with the black Buddha statue and meditate there, flaking the Buddha's face with red dust.

After so many recitations, I heard Shakyamuni speak to me. "Free yourself of this desire," the Buddha said. "Live forever in the mandala. Pleasure lasts but a moment. Time is eternal."

Through the Buddha's help, I was able to overcome myself. I had fallen prey to desire, which clouded the mind. I stopped seeing you, the living goddess, and soon there was a new girl who had passed the tests and become the new living goddess. By then I had renounced all worldly attachments.

"She brings out all your impurities," the Buddha spoke as I prayed. "Go to her, and you shun enlightenment."

As I descended the Himalayan valley, I thought of the Silk Road travelers who had taken a similar path, leaving the riches of the East to pursue holy men in the West. I was born in the East, in a homeland now drained of life.

After menstruation, your body must have been sent away, back to your home village. Devotion drew me, and with the Buddha's guidance, I became concerned only with evolving my body. Perhaps you were merely the vessel, while the goddess inside you had already chosen a new host. I asked about you once in Kathmandu, but they would never tell a foreigner what became of the girl. How could I convince them that my desire, my longing, was no typical infatuation?

I came to a clearing and saw the valley before me, cloaked in fog. Its hills looked like a caterpillar, and at the top, trees stuck up like bristles of hair. The valley had gone on unscathed. The fog, created by humans, only harmed humans. Fog was the earth's white blood cells casting out a life-threatening toxin. Since the end of the war, the entire world was covered in this noxious gas. Until now, I had never faced it up close.

I meditated under a bodhi tree, my eyes centered on the gray static fog just a short distance down the slope. When it first came, I was already living on the mountain, closer to reaching Enlightenment. When I heard that the fog grew cancer cells in all men, I thought I had won a battle. All those who denied me—those rich men, those warmongers—had all been proven wrong. Wealth had driven violence. Greed had destroyed our planet. And when the dead men began to litter the city streets below, I didn't think it was a loss. All those who perpetrated violence were in their graves. Those like me, who had given themselves to peace, would live on.

But the death of the Earth was nothing to celebrate. None of the saved were willing to trust each other, and soon, loneliness became a boiler. I prayed, I bowed, I chanted, I turned the prayer wheel. My only companion was the blue Buddha himself, the medicine Buddha, whose emanation helped all sentient beings live long lives. When I meditated, I heard his instruction.

"You move like a leaf down this mountainside," the blue Buddha said, appearing to me floating on a lotus flower. "You sway with each change in the breeze, even to your own death."

I bowed to him, whispering a prayer.

"You are almost ready for transcendence." His voice boomed. "There is nothing for you in that valley, only suffering."

I couldn't bring myself to give a reason, so I thumbed through my prayer beads and continued to recite.

"How much have I taught you?" the Buddha said. "If you give up now, you will be reborn without a trace of memory from this life. But stay high, closer to heaven, and your synthetic body will live forever. Eventually, you will be seen as a local here, not an invader. You will retain your memories. We will remain companions."

I chanted louder, but his volume increased. My voice trembled as I repeated the mantra. Scorn all that tended to ill, abandon all vulgar desire, let faith bridle pleasure.

His voice thundered forth: "You will lose all progress you have made. All my teachings of the sentient species across the universe. There is always a period of generation, then optimization, and then, finally, destruction. Every species goes through it. Your destruction has only just begun."

"I must see her," I said, too ashamed to face him. He didn't seem shocked. This was always my struggle.

"She was a false goddess," the blue Buddha said, his third eye opening in a yellow and green iris. "Made to sell tourist tokens."

"If that's true, then maybe it was love."

"Love is a false desire when directed at one rather than many."

I turned to the gray valley, its fog so thick that the stupas of Kathmandu looked like golden stars in a night sky.

"In your synthetic body," the Buddha said. "You could live to be over a thousand years old. I have foreseen it."

Another thousand years of reciting sutras. In her organic body, the goddess would die soon. Every year I had wasted on the mountain was another year that you had grown older.

The Buddha floated above me, shining yellow eyes spotlighting my meditative posture. "Harm done is done. You tear yourself apart for love. Your soul strives to free itself from flesh."

I stood up, bowed to the Buddha, and then continued down the hill. "Uncloud your mind!" the Buddha shouted as I walked away. But part of me loved the clouds.

My skin sensors were the first to scramble offline as I entered Kathmandu. A coffle of goats slogged through streets crowded with abandoned television sets and dilapidated appliances. Some women remained. I saw their tattered clothing hung up on clotheslines, drying in the thin sunlight that poked through a scrim of fog clouds above and an array of chemicals below. I didn't have much time—already my movements became rigid, and my body swayed like a dying calf.

A group of old women, too stubborn to abandon their homes to the fog, gossiped on the side of the road. They stared at me, but not because I was a man, since they could not know my gender. Nor because of my race, because they could not know that either. Their mouths dropped at my metallic exterior. They knew that soon I would die—sooner than they would, at least. Soon, they would sweep my metallic remains off the street.

I entered the monastery of the living goddess, unkempt since the fog's disease, its floor littered with mirror fragments and scraps of shag carpet. I remembered the place well. The high schoolers retreating from your gaze, arm-in-arm; the tourists in awe of your dress, some of them sneaking photos with their eye-lenses; the pigeons milling around looking for crumbs; the stray cats crawling through your window's iron bars. I found one of the statues I once prayed to, a bronze Buddha statue, its blue eyes staring in anger.

My gears croaked as I stepped into the monastery where you once lived. The bedroom had been wiped clean, and in the center stood an unfinished mandala embroidered onto a wool carpet. A small stupa in the corner claimed to store the bones of thirty-six monks who died from the fog. I used my scent sensor to see if the bones were truly in a cremation oven. But my sense of smell had disintegrated.

A coughing sound echoed from inside the monastery. My voicebox beeped a fuzzy "Hello?"

An elderly woman emerged from the toilet, still coughing. I recognized her as one of the servants who sometimes ran errands around the monastery, carrying wicker baskets full of tourist handcrafts. Her face had become wrinkled, and the fog had patched her skin with sores.

"I just want to talk," I said, my voicebox fracturing. "I… need…to…know…"

The woman pushed open a wooden door and retreated down a garden path. My legs still mobile, I pursued her through mounds of dried dirt where rhododendrons once grew, my botched sounds spurting out in static: "ple—ple—please."

My body gave out and I collapsed onto a pile of stones that might have been my grave. The old woman ran behind a door covered in peeled layers of blue paint.

"Please," I kept saying.

I saw the blue veins down her thigh. "What do you want?"

"The living goddess you had twenty-six years ago," I said. "The girl in red."

You must have left an impression, because the woman seemed displeased by my request. "The thirty-sixth reincarnation," the woman said with such revulsion I thought she would spit. "That stupid girl. But I took a vow never to say a word."

"Please," I begged. "I am about to die."

Inside the caretaker's small abode, we sat on thick wool carpets and chewed chunks of mutton. When my mechanical jaw broke down, she made me millet gruel from powder and tea.

"I'm sorry that you had to come here," she said. "Is she really worth dying for?"

Not knowing what to say, I watched the dust motes floating in the fog like spots of sand. A hazy, molecular light. "Yes," I said. "I cannot find peace until I know what happened to her."

The woman sat crossed-legged. "You must know the tradition is dead, of course. So few children have been born. There are too few girls below eleven, and the chances that one of them could still hold the right name, still be born on the right day, and still pass all the tests—it is a dead tradition. And along with it, all the men who invented it."

It was as I expected. "What about the girl? The thirty-sixth reincarnation?"

"Yes, that girl. Not a lot to remember. She was a singer. Voice had some talent."

"A singer? I never saw her sing."

"You must not have been there then. She only sang once for the crowd. Only for a couple seconds. Why are you so interested? Are you her father? Her brother?"

I drew silent, calculating how I would reply without seeming lustful.

"Were you there for her funeral?" She tore apart another cube of mutton with her canine teeth.

I felt something drop out of me. "No."

"Living here was awful," she shook her head. "Their rules. Only speak to recite mantras. Only sing to chant. Children cannot take this cocooned existence for very long."

I pictured you sitting in that very room, donned in your red cloak, hands clasped in silent prayer, harnessing an unnamable power.

"That girl hated the city, too. Felt claustrophobic, trapped in those narrow alleys. Common among village girls. She could see mountains from her village, but from the monastery, her sight went no further than two blocks. She could barely walk the streets without motorbikes scathing her arms."

"A goddess is treated in such high esteem."

"She was nothing special." The caretaker's appetite had moved from mutton to crackers. She nodded her head back and forth. "Well, there was a man. She seemed to like him. Talked about him constantly."

"What man? A monk?"

She laughed, "That would have been much easier to deal with. No. She took to a tourist. A haughty-looking Easterner. He came to see her every day. 'He pinches me with his eyes,' she would say. The man never spoke a word, but she brightened up whenever he arrived. I would tell her—'princess! Your man is here again!' And she would practice her goddess gaze, looking imperious and mighty and we would giggle like schoolgirls." She caught herself reminiscing, cowered her head. "I don't know what she saw in him. An acquired taste, perhaps. She talked about his eyes. Every day, those shy, peaceful eyes, upon a face so constructed. She wondered about him. And that pain."

"How did she die?"

The woman tossed a piece of bread and sniffed her nose. "One day the old caretaker was suspicious she was menstruating. She was acting out, singing more at night. The caretaker thought she was no longer pure. So he checked her for blood. When he saw she wasn't bleeding, then the man—" she paused, shaking her head. We sat in silence for a moment. The woman sniffed back a tear, poured another glass of tea and continued. "A couple days later, she threw herself off the bridge. She thought if she jumped, she could kill the goddess, before it had a chance to leave her body. Kill herself, save the girls who would take her place. Of course, forty-five days later, the goddess reincarnated."

I sipped the tea, my arms barely able to balance the cup. The tea warmed my insides, my organic stomach.

"The day before she died, that's when she sang to the tourists. I didn't suspect she would, but all day she kept asking me, 'Is he here yet? Is he here?' The man didn't come. She was saving it for him—her voice, that is. Who knows what she would have done, had he shown up. She was afraid that if she took off the makeup and the dress, the man would no longer come and see her. She was probably right."

"Who can say," I said, unsure myself.

"When the man didn't come, the girl made her last appearance and burst into song. It was her favorite tune—not a chant, but an old pop song. I'm sorry I don't remember the words. The song began with a high pitch, a whistle flooding the city square. She only lasted a couple of seconds before the head caretaker muffled her." She padded tears from her face like cleaning an urn. "And then she jumped."

Moments later, the woman went rifling through wooden drawers with drooping cobwebs. She pulled open a leather box that sat under a curl of peeling wallpaper. She returned to the table with a small object.

"After she was cremated," the woman said, "her bones were separated and sent to monasteries across the world. Here. This is a piece of her. A tooth."

The tooth stood upright like a mountain peak.

"I would let you keep it, but—"

"—I know."

I remained in the square where I once saw you, the living goddess. I felt my joints grind as I paced in a circle, spending my last moments turning the prayer wheels that encircled the ancient mandala at your monastery's center. I rotated each one clockwise, and they moved with the same rusted squeaks as my metal body. I felt broken by the old woman's story, but relieved as well. You never had to see the fog descend. You never went through the pain of seeing your father and brothers die. In a way, you had beaten time.

I circled the prayer wheels, slower now. Each wheel carried a hundred thousand mantras on printed paper. Each turn of the wheel gave me a hundred thousand prayers toward the heavens. I prayed for eternal life, to become a higher being, not to redeem mankind from the destruction they caused. They deserved their fates, and if I would not live forever on Earth, then perhaps I would in heaven. After my arms broke, I used my torso to push the prayer wheel. Forty, fifty circles shy of a hundred rotations, I collapsed.

I knelt over the mandala in the center of the garden, its stone edges covered in black grime. The circle of enlightenment stared into me, showing me the comforts of the afterlife. I believed I heard your voice, a whistle reverberating throughout the ancient square. As my body broke, I joined your song with a tolling tragic note.

I awoke staring at the ceiling. I willed it to turn leather brown, then to yellow, then to turquoise, then to crumble apart. Beyond the ceiling, more ceilings.

I willed an axe and smashed apart the wall, flooding the room with a whirlwind of splintering wood. I willed the porcelain sink loose and water flushed out in a geyser, flinging the ottoman about the chamber, breaking the bed banisters. The telephone beat holes into the ceiling, raining down paint chips and pink insulation. I screamed and the geyser spurted forth and came down like hail, meeting a carpet floor as hot as coals under fire. I screamed again, my body flickering like a flame in steam. I shook and howled, my fists throttling my chest. Finally, with my body as racked as my heart, I fell supine upon my covers, my chest sagged with exhaustion.

Thus began my fifth arrival in the Ilium. The souls in the corridors stopped at my presence, the dressed-to-the-nines women at the jazz bar stared at me with their swirling eyes. Three millennia of searching for you, just to arrive back in heaven empty-handed. My thoughts turned to the god who had disrupted my quest. Before, he seemed to watch me like a tourist intrigued by the local customs, prodding me for laughs. Something had changed.

I found Cryss in Scarlet's, re-designed to honor the synthetic dining halls. Cryss followed the tech trend, clad in robotic armor with a silver exterior and eyes like yellow candles, flames fluttering in my direction.

"It was just a matter of time," she said, her voice buzzing out of her as if tossed down a long hallway.

"We need to talk." I could feel the people around us eavesdropping. "Somewhere private."

"Your pluck, baby bird."

I beelined through the eyes around us, to the bar's balcony where the sound of breaking waves gave us some privacy. Cryss leaned over the railing, her rock-pouch melded into her sculptured silver hair.

"We've missed you around here," she said. "Hard to acclimatize every time you jump out of our lives. We've heard about it—the fog. You should have seen the legion of souls when they arrived, all confused as pigeons. But since then? Only you."

"Do gods exist?" I asked.

Cryss bit off a piece of sliced cucumber and let the vegetable grind in her iron teeth. "We're the only gods I know of."

"I once asked you about a god who travels in and out of imagination, from our realm into others."

"Sorry, I am oblivious to your jests."

"I was serious. He, or she, they exist. I'm certain of it."

"Conviction is so unbecoming of you. We are the only true gods."

"We're souls, not gods."

Cryss gave a derisive snort and flung the rest of her cucumber overboard. "I must chalk up this irascible behavior

182

to your wasteful pursuit. You have earned heaven five times now. But she—that waggish little nymph—*she* keeps you human. *kānaka*: a poor wretch like him could never reach our ideals. Just look to the sea—they are mere liquid for us to float upon! This is not some idle claim. We. Are. Gods."

I turned to the dark ocean. As soon as I imagined it, the sun began to rise. A tapestry of purples and reds. The light changed everything. Cryss' metal shone, and I with her, in the same robotic form I had inhabited in my past life only newer, more perfect. I, the creator.

"Theirs is a misfortune that no person can amend," Cryss said. "She is just a mirror, reflecting the stream's misery. That fog mankind created now destroys mankind. All wealth on Earth flits and veers in its wind. You act like time does not matter to you. But an hour draws near when fickle fate will shear you off along with them."

The sun dropped back below the Earth. We were again covered in darkness, until Cryss willed candlelight.

That thing is out there," I said. "Another god. Not like us. She inhabits no body. He is a soul, roaming our imaginations."

"You were a cultist in your last life, yes? This is just your addled brain playing tricks. But go on, I don't disabuse people of their fantasies."

"What of your past lives? You're a far older soul than I—what did the ancients say of these spirits?"

"I only had one past life. But it was as you say. Ancient. Hmph. Well, what you're describing sounds like no illusion or apparition I've ever heard of. A specter? An *eidolon*? Helen had one, supposedly. Her own spirit, but somehow still buzzing around other people's heads. At worse, you're dealing with a shape-shifting daimon. A divider of destiny. Or maybe—a heady amalgam of all three, depending on what it wants."

It took me a moment to find the words. "She, he—*it*, is fixated upon me."

Cryss took a cucumber slice from her mouth, still round, untouched, perfect. "You've got me thinking. There is someone you can ask, an ancient like myself. He really believes in this nonsense, goes on long rants about other gods. *Dis-faciō*: I'd sooner rail you into reason than take you to him."

"Who is he?"

"Follow me." She paused at the archway. "But, before we go, you will have to adjust your appearance. Back in history."

"How far back?"

"As far as you can."

Cryss took me into her stateroom. Inside was a different time, a different world. Before my first life, a time, perhaps, before time.

Clay pots sat on stone stands, and bronze metal spears sat stacked in a row where the mirror should have been. In the room's center, on the bed, sat an old man covered in a nest of white hair. The man looked primeval, almost mummified, and he held in his right arm a long spear that sat him upright.

"Cressida," the man whispered, his lips unmoving. "Is this her? Finally, you have brought her to me."

I had willed myself into the first life I could remember, when I was that young servant in Jerusalem watching Solomon's Temple burn.

"Eight-Seven-One," Cryss said, willed into a Greek woman with short auburn hair and yellow teeth. "Meet Troy. The oldest soul on this ship."

"Can't he will himself younger?" I asked.

"His mind has been eaten by the memory disease." She clasped Troy's hand. "He has no power in the Ilium. Everything here, I willed. The blue elixir keeps him sane but cannot purify him. Sometimes, he can hear things in the stream. Whispers. Real or not, I cannot say. But there may be something to it."

The old man started laughing, though it clearly gave him pains to do so. His chest heaved; his elephant-skin shook in heavy wrinkles. He coughed a harsh cough, drool running down his chin.

"This is no disease," Troy said slowly. "And this is no Ilium. We have abandoned everyone in the stream. All those souls yearning for peace."

I knelt to look into his eyes. I could have asked him anything about the ancients, anything from his past life. This was a man who had never known computers, or bombs, or even iron. I was speaking to history before history.

"You are the diver," Troy said. "Cryss has told me. You were once a servant girl in the Holy Lands. Once a soldier for Saladin."

"He knows me?"

"He knows the things I whisper to him," Cryss said. "And little else. Tell him of your plight. Hurry, before he sinks again."

I tried to form a question. How to talk to a man who knew not the Buddha, books, or electricity? "There is something strange in the stream," I said. "A being who can appear in one's imagination. A trickster, who convinces people to do his will. In the last life, he told me I could live for a thousand years."

"Pain!" Troy called out. More drool came down his chin in a sharp line. "I feel it—their suffering, the suffering, I need the tea, give me the tea."

"If we give it to him now," Cryss said. "He'll just sleep for days. Hurry and ask."

"Have you heard of this demon? Do you know what it wants?"

"Ha!" he spat. "Isn't it obvious?"

"What?"

The old man gave a harrowing scream, pulling on his beard. Drops of blood dotted his gray whiskers. His pain waned. "What would *you* do?" he said, heaving. "Thousands of years, nothing better to do but test, prod, push every limit within that wild, wandering flood."

"So, it wants me to do something?"

"Ha!" The man burst. "What did the Greeks want from us? Why did they destroy our city, kill our children, and rape our women? Beauty? Inspiration? Ha!" His eyes went into a frenzy, chest heaving, lips trembling. "In a forest you cut down the sturdiest oak and you hack and hack waiting for that lucky stroke to fall it. Oh! The feeling of its great mass rocking down all at once! When you've got your pick of the litter, you go for the biggest game, chasing that which hastens from touch. You choose the heaviest thing, just to watch it collapse. Don't you? Now—staunch this pain! Tea! Please!"

Cryss willed a glass and poured the elixir from a boiling pot.

"Wait," I put my hand on his arm, feeling his rough skin on my palm. "This demon—he told me that he is watching mankind through three phases. Generation, optimization, and destruction. Does this mean mankind will end?"

The man squelched his face in pain. "Do you know what it is to rot?" he asked with a pained smile. "The trial of time goes on, with or without you."

"Here," Cryss said, handing him the tea. "Your medicine, you old kook."

"Now you see what the memory disease can do," Cryss told me in the corridor, after Troy had fallen under the elixir's spell. "He is irreparable, but I cannot let him go back. My debt to him is too great. So here he lives on, safely ensconced in my stateroom. Suffering, yes, but still far happier than those pitiless souls below us."

"Could mankind really end?" I asked.

"You've been in the stream for many eras. You've seen the mossy flanks of millennium-old monuments. You've seen men's devices varnished black by the centuries. All things must end. The blue elixir is our only deliverance. Without it, we'd go mad in memory."

"He *is* mad," I said. "But he speaks truth. That wandering spirit. It longs to be my abuser."

"And yet you still want to dive, don't you?" Her hair formed into metallic silver, her body willed back into a synthetic's. "If there is a demon following you, it seeks not you but your overly hospitable mind. Your wild imagination gives it space to mature. The longer it festers, the deeper its coils will run. First around your brain, then seeking out your heart, until you and it become indistinguishable."

"I'm not afraid. I have resisted it before. If it tries to feed off my imagination, I'll just have to keep myself focused—"

"—Idiot! *Flectō*: Gird yourself with patience! What about everyone here? Your charges? And me? If you succumb to the memory disease, there's only enough room in my stateroom for one mental patient."

"I have loved him year after year, night and day. I'm going back."

"Love is your tyrant. You are weaker than an infant's tear!"

"S is out there."

"Your beliefs create your reality. They are mirrors pretending to be windows. If you follow them, the results could be...cataclysmic."

"She's trapped."

"The gateway is closing! You said so yourself. Mankind does not have long left. What happens when there are no bodies left to be reborn into?"

I was silent. A group of scantily clad robotic hunks passed by.

"Don't you care that mankind might end?" I asked.

Cryss closed her eyes. She did not have to will anything to exist for me to hear her. She sent me images—war, death, pollution, disease, executions, killings, tortures. She wouldn't will these things to exist, not in this perfect world she had helped create.

"Only those in the stream take pleasure in inflicting pain onto others," she spoke through her metal teeth. "What else could separate humans from gods?"

I sat in my stateroom, watching the horizon. The sun came up, it went back down. There was light, then dark. I struggled to keep my mind on you, to hear you in the tapering voices of the stream. Time was running out.

I stood and faced the wild and wandering sea.

Life

T

In this life I was born in humanity's greatest refuge, a city of skyscrapers where technology remained at its peak. When I was a child, it never occurred to me how fortunate I was to be born in that city, to be born up, far above the fog, past the one-hundredth floor. Instead, I dreamed of what was even higher. I imagined that the sky itself was a hungry beast who slurped up the city's sacrificial unwanted. So guttural was the sound of the skyjets over Jrica's famous skyport. The engines' roars shook glass into pulsing thunder—that was the thumping of the Beast's heart. How could I know those terrifying roars were only the sound of jet engines? I had never flown anywhere myself. No, the sky had voice; it could snarl and sing, and from my bedroom window, those small skyjets were spears, plunging into the fog where the Beast crouched ready to pounce.

Such was my boredom living in Jrica's sixth sector. My imagination so often bested the dullness of the days. My family was of the cult of Musa, God of purity, the fifth of the imperial pantheon, God of our Persian ancestors. Musa, who poisoned her king only to regret her deed and sacrifice herself for the rightful ruler, demanded our bodies be pure, and our hearts purer. So my family lived in a time capsule, ignoring the age's leaps in biotechnology, even refusing those digital chips that gave a man many tongues, believing that any change to the body was vulgar. Or perhaps we simply could not afford it. At any rate, I struggled to speak only one language, while my schoolmates were fluent in the six tongues of our empire. Perhaps it was this disadvantage that led me to develop my stutter, a defect that stunted my development and made me casually invisible. While my schoolmates, with their visual and audio enhancements, accessed virtual realms far beyond my organic senses, I played outdated screen games.

And when I grew bored with screen games, I watched the sky. I watched from my bedroom on the one-hundred-dred-and-twentieth floor, imagining its roars. Sky so bleak, sky full of purple and white spears hurtling in mad spinning aim. When I grew bored with the sky I watched the valley of fog, one hundred and twenty floors below my bedroom window, where strange women were stationed in a town of barbed wire hidden just behind the otherwise pristine shores of the Ne Win beach. The small settlement had existed since before I was born; it was an earthly sprawl of makeshift houses and tents, vanishing into that toxic fog. Every year more of those lanky people floated into the valley like ash from burning cities, the detritus of faraway wars. None ever left.

And the fog was their shadow. People said that the fog was so acidic that it disintegrated any electronic device. Remotes. Batteries. Watches. Brain chips. In an attempt to keep me safe, my tutor, Meikuan, described how the fog's acid could affect the non-purists. "When they speak," she said, her eyebrows creasing in suspense, "suddenly their tongues will slip. Their voiceboxes will putter. Their respiration system will fume. Their polysynthetic hairs will turn moist like dewed grass. Their eyes, enhanced by nanobots, will freeze into white, blinding static."

I would shiver thinking of this, and when I thought of getting stomach enhancements to make me big like the other children, I imagined the fog eating at my guts, killing me from the inside. When I thought of speech enhancements, I imagined the fog dissolving my tongue, leaving it bloodless in my mouth. The fog itself was static, the static on a television set when the satellites failed, the static on a handphone too far from the grid. A still, gruesome whiteness. Few Jricans had ever survived its madness. And the women of the valley were its natives. Those of us on the top floors could do nothing but watch them through our telescopes and wonder.

Yet, over time I grew more curious about how the fog-backed women lived. As a child I sat every day at my window, forming my hands into a rectangle shape to shoot imagined movies of people in the valley fighting each other with hand grenades, some exploding into dozens of bloody pieces. These movies in my mind grew more intense as time went on, the characters more fleshed out, and soon I had names for every woman in the valley. There was Mrs. LA (Loud-and-Annoying) at the valley's entrance, who shouted at customers with a large yellow fan as she sold sunglasses from a stall. I imagined her children, Pig Feet and Bad Egg, were enrolled in the dynasty's development schools, perhaps in the lower rungs of Jrica itself. On days when her wife, Mrs. TA (Tired-and-Annoyed) seemed disheartened or lifeless, I imagined a novel's worth of her plights.

When the Sector Six residency put gates over our windows, I convinced my father to give me a new telescope for my twelfth birthday, and soon I could see the valley women up close, their patchy skin, their moist hair. I watched them from my window, through my telescope, through the bars of the residency gates, through the mist of the valley, through the slum houses and scratched window glass. I believed I really knew those people who lived on our outermost rim, and that there was a piece of each of them within me.

I came to know you better than anyone. You, a girl I named Max. Far slimmer than I, a few years older, with eyes full of business. You were always moving, bouncing through the makeshift marketplace, navigating your way among goats, chickens, fruit stalls, streams of dirty water, herds of bicyclists, and gaggles of girls playing basketball. Your walk was expensive, a confident tug on the eyes. In time I came to believe that your silence was a speech impediment, the same as mine. You were all action, all eyes, all mouth pointing, speaking through gestures. I watched you tilt your stick of corn toward Mrs. Jaws on her way to school, and the way you silently squatted with your friends during the lunch hour, chomping large bits of buttered raisin bread. Even in silence, you commanded attention. My silence left me alone and invisible; yours was that of a crouched lion, whose gaze saw only prey. I imagined that inside every building you entered, something was happening and you were there to make it happen. You moved your arms above your head, constantly, not dancing but pointing, shuffling and gripping, as if to declare your presence to anyone who would doubt it. *By Musa*, you were fierce. I felt a deep envy for you, though you lived in dirt, and breathed toxic fumes.

Once I discovered you, the others in the valley became background to your story. There was Mrs. LA screaming at children in the street, frowning whenever you passed. There was Mrs. Crotchety, cribbing children on her stomach, smiling at you. There was Mrs. Stick who scolded you from time to time. There was Miss Pink Bike, who I could only see on the clearest days, for her brown hair blended so well with the red bricks beside her home.

I called you Max, the silent woman of the valley. In my imagination, you were the destined enemy of the beast in the sky. As the beast roared from above, you attacked from below, your eyes in a spell, your lips marked by non-speech, unknowable words scrambling in the back of your mouth, clawing up your throat. I watched you walk Miss Pink Bike's bicycle at your side, its wheels collecting packs of crusted earth. The loose handlebars shook when you rode it. I wondered if you could not speak, or chose to live in silence. The absence drew me to you. Without words we knew not separate houses, separate gods.

I watched you for years. All my childhood it seems was spent at that telescope. You were always locked in battle with the sky dragon, who had come to destroy your people. I invented roles for you: Max the belly dancer, Max the legionnaire, Max the gladiator. Sometimes I pleaded for you to look up, just once, toward the advertising graphics of Jrica, through the variegated pipes twisting about each tower, to see my window in the sixth sector.

At night, when darkness kept me from my mind-films, I played the screen game Earth & Skies, where I mutilated bodies with a horse-sized axe. I was a Cyclops, hacking shoulders just right so that the skin gripped the limb and looked translucent in places. Even without visual implants, the game was rich in detail. The hairs on fingers, the stitches in patched clothing, my pet Diegaard. Some players looked for gold, some for romance, some for a sense of community. All the game's players were united as either followers of Musa or were too poor to have enhancements. In the game I found children from all over the world, people like you, poor, without chips, without speech. We very rarely talked about ourselves in game, but I always wondered if its players were from the valley below. At night the only lights I saw came from homes of faded wood and corrugated tin, their fires defiantly lit past curfew. Once I saw you venture into a lit basement. I wondered if you played Earth & Skies too, if it was your eyes behind a virtual, half-naked avatar.

I was thirteen on the day of the Skymall attacks. Afterwards, I could no longer hear the roar of the sky. Not one airplane flew overhead, and I believed the beast beyond the clouds had finally been defeated. I looked to the sky with my telescope, bracing to see the remains of that great creature, its belly opened by sharp skyjets. I saw only the smoke and debris from the 100th Story Mall, belching great clouds of smoke that covered the sky.

That night, lightning cracks came to mutilate people in the valley. It happened like a dropped glass—*crack*! Then the implosions and collapsing buildings—*boom*! Flickers of yellow under-lit the fog clouds, as bricks and glass tore through its haze.

C
R
A
C
K
!

BO

OM

C
R
A
C
K
!

BO OM

When the skyjets resumed the next day, something had gone. The roar had muted into a subdued, dull hum, like the sound of a generator that had suddenly gone silent. And you. You no longer appeared in the valley. All I could see were plumes of smoke rising from a collapsed hospital and the faceless police who sifted through its smoldering remains.

I continued to watch for you through my telescope, believing that you were hidden somewhere in the valley's underground. I tried to imagine a scenario, a character flaw, or a plot twist that would send you away, only briefly. Perhaps you had earned a tutelary, and a mysterious patron from the upper floors was uplifting you. Or maybe you had washed ashore on some strange beach, waking one day with amnesia. My imagination, try as it might, could not provide solace. I only knew what my father told me: after the attacks, the valley people were relocated to a foreign site—an island somewhere, a base where they could be overseen by jets in the sky.

When I was fifteen or so, your fog people found a new way to communicate with us. Cut off from our land, they sent parachutes holding small canisters, which floated high on windy days. Back then, I prowled the top floors of the towers, facing the sun's blinding rays to catch the canisters that drifted upon the southeast winds. I imagined the sky dragon speaking to me beyond the clouds, foretelling when the canisters would arrive, and where I could catch them. With no locks or keyholes, the canisters could be opened by anyone, though they probably were not meant for a kid like me. Other kids joined. Together we sold whatever strange objects were inside the canisters and broke their metal into cooking utensils. Only the fastest of us could collect the cans. My body, lithe and flexible after puberty, gave me an agility I had done nothing to deserve. I was silent, but I had swift legs, gripping feet, and an instinct to balance on the serpentine tubes one hundred and twenty floors high. For years my friends and I owned those top floors, those planes of jeweled roofs built by Jrica's patricians.

The sky beast would come to me during sunrise. I saw him outside my window, dancing in the sky, sometimes in the form of a phantom with a scythe, sometimes as my pet Diegaard from Earth & Skies, and sometimes as Musa herself, her skin carob brown, her hair blue like ocean waves, bright on top and deep navy at the ends. "Hop Hop!" She would call to me. "Come out and run with me!" Together we watched the sky in patient anticipation, until we spotted those multicolored parachutes floating in with the wind, peppering the sky like bits of spices on Shu curry. Sometimes I would wake up to the sound of hard metal clacking against my bedroom window and see thousands of them floating in like an invading army. Inside the canisters were all sorts of strange items: carved fish, cotton scarfs, pastries, beaded wristbands, long straw hats that kept us safe from the sun. If the items seemed useless, we could still sell them at the twentieth-floor markets to collectors seeking fogback trinkets. We found half-man, half-animal figurines, dolls made of dyed twine, yellow flowers. Once, balancing on the billboard above the abandoned Medusa mall, I caught a can filled with blue powder that burst into the wind and covered me in a dust so enchanting it drew me into a primal state— half meditation, half rage—and then took days to scrub off. Once, during the three-minute interval between commuter trains, I caught a can at the apex of the tracks, only to find a woman's pink-laced panties inside. Every now and then we found bones, pieces of burnt flesh, fingers, or locks of hair.

None of us cared much where those canisters came from. Why those cans were sent our way we could only guess, since the notes that accompanied them were in the fogback's script. Occasionally they were in our language, Latin, with the words "Help us," in poor handwriting. Some of them had drawings of children whose bodies were mis-shapen by hunger. Being children ourselves, we could do nothing. I sometimes left the notes inside of my father's op-tical shop, stuffed in the reading material for his customers to find.

The speed I possessed was in fact a gift from the cans. The first can I caught floated in on a white parasol, dragging across the square just outside the Perkina Library, where I was imagining Musa tossing over shelves and causing all kinds of carnage. "A gift awaits you outside," Musa told me between hacking apart a book-stack. "Hurry and catch it!"

I caught the canister and felt the scratches that tore across the aluminum can. I pondered the long distance it had traveled, the cold rusted metal worn from the hardships of rain, sun, and wind. There was still the strange scent of gunpowder at the canister's base. Inside was a pair of white runner's shoes with no logo, only a folded letter in that strange script. The shoes were snug and hugged the bottom of my feet. I discarded my flip-flops and began to run, to balance on the metal detritus pipes, to vault through the precipices of buildings and ledges around every floor, the soft spring of the shoes lifting me above crowds and market dwellings. The shoes awoke in me a daredevil spark, a desire to go crashing into one of those neon advertisements near the 100th Story Mall. I imagined the electricity could purge my veins, jar me from the pallor hemmed in by glossy towers and advertisements for things my family could never afford.

Sometimes, when balancing on those gaudy, stripped awnings, I wondered why my shoes happened to fit me so well. If they had been only half a size off, perhaps I would not have survived through the sweltering summers atop the towers. I wondered if you had sent them to me. Perhaps you knew exactly what I needed to make friends, to be appreciated, despite my silence. I looked above to the sky beast, and asked if it was yours, if she could remember you, if she had any power at all over your actions. But the sky was silent.

In time, those shoes became torn and gray, and I had to discard them, like all shoes when the soles begin to break.

A year before I would perish, I saw you again. It seemed strange that, even when our empire began sponsoring fog-back refugees to live among us, we continued to invade your lands. Unable to recall my past lives, I could not understand just how human this was, this ability to care and not care. At sixteen I had enlisted into compulsory service, and at eighteen I was a security consultant, my office inside an abandoned mall in the refugee district, which siphoned air-conditioning from the upper floors. With zeal our unit rounded up fog women, girls around our age, and kept them in small containment centers while we raided their houses for narcotics and weapons, looting what we could by locking goods away in iceboxes. Despite our obscene lack of morals, we managed to be sickened by how your kind lived, sleeping on floors, eating cockroaches.

And then, the things we did to those women. The things we did to those women. And through it all, my mother smiled at me. Those from our upper floors who always opened the door, always offered us food and drink, did not seem to care that we were gangsters of a different name. Suffice to say that I saw things, and I did things, telling myself that war was bad everywhere. And the things we did, we did not do mechanically. It was with passion and—as the old Provincials said—with braggadocio. We lived in a dream, with the flags of the past leading us to white helmets and riot sticks. What else did it mean to be a security consultant than to survey and round up anyone who looked at us crossly? We were emulating our past heroes, Alexander of the First Empire, the Roman generals Marius and Scipio of the Old Empire, Kavadh and Khosrau of the Persians, the Khans of the Xin, the marines of the Americans. We had surpassed those empires and become an ideal form. We would impress these fogbacks with our order, and eventually, when the day of their acceptance came, our deeds would be forgotten like the strict spanks a parent deals their child. We were all waiting for that day, especially, we believed, the people of the fog. Your survival depended upon it.

Sundays were the day for crucifixion. All the security firms were present to watch as known conspirators were stuck to the wall, pinned like insects until life simply went out of them. There were around a half dozen every week, usually insurgents around my age. The crosses were hoisted up upon a hill on the city's edge, where the trees had been demolished. And just beyond the crosses, we could see the edge of the fog lying in wait to eat away at any enhanced soldier who drew near it. As the crucified took their last full breath, a riot of cheers would come, then that old song of acceptance.

One Sunday, I saw my last crucifixion. In the program, I read that the insurgent had refused to speak to the Jrican consultants, refused to even give us her name. For women of such willfulness, crucifixion was the typical punishment. But when I saw the woman they hoisted onto the cross, I knew why she could not speak. I lifted the bulging plexiglass visor on my helmet and recognized her. I saw her for the first time without interference from the residency's gates. I saw her without the stale clouds of Jrica's ninetieth floors. I saw her without the great distance that could only be reached with a telescope. I saw her outside the comfort of my one hundred and twentieth story bedroom.

But this time your gaze was on me. There was no crass smile. No attempt to beg for forgiveness.

"I could do nothing to help that one," said a voice in my imagination. "I believed the longer she lived, the better your need to survive." The sky beast. It came to me as Musa. Her wavy blue hair covered her nude body as thick as a knitted dress.

"This one is impossible," Musa said appearing next to you, peeking through the coils of her hair to watch the agony on your face—your face, I realized, was the same as hers, but weathered by a hard life. "Over those without imagination, I can have no influence," Musa continued. "With a soul like hers, it's like trying to take root in rock. I've whispered to her, seen inside her mind, she is not what you think. After so many lives, and so many deaths, her soul has become driven by fear, distress, a mind always reacting, never pondering, never escaping into imagination's brief respite."

I realized you were a fog person. For some reason, this had never occurred to me. You were not a fogback to me, but my co-conspirator, a friend dwelling in silence.

Musa took hold of a spear, her blue hair trailing behind her. "But your imagination is different," she told me. "Wild, unrestricted, boundless. It's the same wellspring that drives your desire for her. You, heart all a-flutter, imagine her as something majestic, mythical, flying all logic to the wind!" Musa approached you, holding the spear firmly, poised to attack. "She is just a mirage. But I can give you everything you seek. With your imagination, I could build a universe just for us."

Musa stabbed the spear into your side, deep, so it poked out, another nail into the cross. Your blood spilled like the sponge intestines I had imagined in my mind-films. I couldn't decipher reality from my mind, Musa's face from yours. As blood seeped down your legs, my breath seemed to follow. Your eyes went red, mine went gray. Your final exhale squeezed out of your lungs; my heart felt heavy. You fell, so I fell too, sinking into an abyss of webbed nightmares. As life seeped from your body, I could feel it flow into mine, with the silence of a crouched lion.

Your death drove me mad. I was hospitalized, my mind gone into the screaming piercing agony of that moment. My sisters, my parents, each came to visit, but they seemed like strangers, and my own hair had gone white.

Musa came to me in those final days, her hand in mine, pitying every scream. Every night I screamed. Me—*scream*? I could not even speak, yet I could scream so loud that I had to be isolated within my own annex.

"I know this scream," Musa told me. "It is the scream of thousands of years, of hundreds of cultures and races mixed in your blood."

I screamed a scream so fierce it struck terror in the very god of my imagination.

"You will not last long now," Musa said, her hair covering my body alongside hers, cocooning us. "Sleep, my dear, for the smell of your end grows stronger by the second. All I want is to help you. As your mother, but more … an admirer, perhaps. You see, I have known the colors of your spirit. The fire inside of you, hauling you thither and yon, from life to life, burning for her. I have watched it grow, brighter now than anything on this earth."

"Max!" I called your name in a roar.

Life

During the Fog,
f if i know otherwise.

Est. 2300 - Mound Commune
Communes in Africa, Malay ??

The Bear is The Structure? I dunno.

I want breakfast

"But what's the bear's name?" asked one of the students. While the other children kept their eyes on the white flashing casks of honey on their screens, this girl held the lesson tab crooked so the ceiling light reflected off it, twinkling at me in thin knives of yellow glare.

Your name came up in the auto-queue highlighted in blue. "Meg." It was always you testing me.

"Meg," I said, that soft auto-tone voice humming out of me. "Try to read it from the tablet."

Flags from across the room shot up. Six names turned bright yellow.

"You have a suggestion, Victoria?"

"The bear's name doesn't matter." Victoria's red eyes were on me only for a moment before they geared down to the honey casks. "The bees make the honey. The bear eats it. It's easy!"

"I can't read it," you said, picking a loose hair from your screen.

"Do you want me to come help you?"

"Yes please."

I stepped between the rows of pastel hoodies and offered a smile as you vacated your desk. We met in the aisle's center. Your yellow slacks were stained with the brown earth.

"Why does the bear need to steal the bees' honey?" you asked me.

"You know why." Sensing your excess energy, the rhythmic stroking of the noisemaker activated, lulling the other children into a sedated state. Postures slackened as they curled onto their screens like sleepy housecats.

Your tantrum brought them back to spirit.

"It's not fair!" you shouted, your hoodie loosening, exposing bits of hair. "The bear gets stung by the bees, but the honey—"

"—is too high in fructose?" I joked.

"No," your body whittled down, muscles relaxing one-by-one. Your cheeks sunk into liquescent flesh. Your eyes lost all spirit.

"Ugh," you moaned, cracking a smile beneath bleary eyes. "Woozy, teacher."

Even when drained, you still had a habit of exerting yourself. On you went, climbing over desks, slithering between legs, and crab walking with your hiking shoes dug firmly into knocked-over books. The lack of oxygen to your blood was just enough to sedate you, and yet, part of you seemed to enjoy the sensation. Few children lasted more than ten seconds before begging to be plugged back. At six years old, your determination was a marvel. As if your body could not belong to us, no matter how much we turned it into a landscape of backbone mountains, blood rivers, and dried flakes of skin. We had drained you so often that your skin sagged. It was a warning to the other girls never to vacate their seats.

I couldn't help it—I chuckled. "Your body needs granmene," I said as your torso lunged over a row of stuffed animals.

"If you love it so much…" you collapsed sideways, sucking on your thumb, slurping.

"Are you ready to return to your desk now?"

"No!" A last burst of energy. Your head fell back, your mind barely conscious.

"Your choice." I returned to my desk, noting the clock. Three minutes already. Perhaps this would be a new record.

In haste I sought the beggar, watching her pick out a gallop of thick squished peas from a can with her long pinky nail. The can's rusted bottom split open and spilled a small avalanche of crushed carrots, potatoes and peas.

"Shoddy goddamn cans,'" the beggar said, her gray beard catching the spare peas with her lips.

"Did you see her or not?" I heightened my pitch to signify alarm, though it came out more in a singsong voice.

"Wha's it worth to you?" She scraped the sides of the can with her nail.

"I spent all my rations on the other beggars." My auto-tuned voice drowned my urgency in calm hums. It echoed through the wide tunnel, where red and yellow emergency lights flashed on and off.

"And what happens," she cackled, exposing lacquered

teeth. "If the Party finds her before you? If they discover you let a child get away—well, I know what happens to no-men who fail. Right down into the chimney, ha! You got one job, you snipped scrotum, pube-eatin' jag-off. *One* god-damn job."

"Did you see her pass or not?" I hummed, the calm au-to-tune adjusting my every syllable. "The girl has no gran-mene left. She's unplugged. She couldn't have gone far, but she won't survive long."

"I didn't touch her, if that's—no, I didn't touch her. Not that anyone would blame *me*, you're the one who let a child free from—"

I kicked her right in her tits. My foot lingered too long, long enough for her to grab my boot. She pulled and my back ached from the hard clay ground.

"You got more to lose," the beggar said, her hand pinch-ing my crotch. I barely felt it; the flesh was numb, coddled in extraneous tissue to protect it from the cancerous cells of the fog outside the mound. "Just 'cuz you were born with-out these don't mean you got nothin' else." Her fingers felt like insects running through my pockets.

"Please," that voice of mine hummed. "I need to find her."

"She's going to the honey," she said, thumbing through the ration cards in my back pocket.

"The honey?"

"Gonna steal it from the bear, the honey bear. That's all she said. Don't you eunuchs feed 'em in those locked-up care centers? I swear, things were better before you hid 'em all away. At least kids knew how to fend for themselves."

"Steal the honey."

"Steal all of it, gobble it up, that's what she said. I told those damnable red-cloaked mound rats the same thing when they came through. Ha! When the Party finds you, the earth will vomit out your ashes."

"No." Hum. "Please no." Hum hum. "Just let me go." Hum hum hum hum.

"Well who the hell wants you around?"

The public market security scanners fluttered on my skin. Tickling sensations ran up my palms. The door to the tunnels closed with a whoosh of air.

"Scanning for hormonal presence," the machine said. A gray cement wall stared at me.

Somehow, you had made it this far. A little girl we had drained of all exuberance.

Something on the gray wall caught my attention. Just below my knees, someone had written in scrapes using one of the tunnel's volcanic rocks.

Im Gonna take ALL that bare's Hunny!

Dumbass Meg, I thought. Always failed spelling tests.

My shoulders sank as the tickle of the electric scanner dispelled.

"Biology determined. Hormonal presence absent. Nomen confirmed. Please continue, Eunuch."

The concrete wall sifted open into a rush of traffic in the beltway that connected each mound. Mothers zoomed by erect, leaning like joysticks atop decorated rolling balls that careered over thick white brick as they motored to and fro in the wide tunnel. I sidestepped alongside the brown walls painted to look like tree bark, and then along the side shops and bakeries bordering the tunnel road. The mothers who passed atop their rolling orbs did not notice me. Most were chatting in small caravans, their gold and silver jewelry strewn around their hourglass waists.

"Look there's *another* one!" a gang of them shot toward me from a croissant shop. Their three orbs rolled in front of me, each one large enough to flatten me into the stone floor. One of their long arms pulled me by my hair, as if to lift me, but I batted her hand away.

"Feisty! Sarah?"

"New style." The mother wore a bright blue kebaya with a forest-green sash fit snugly over her shoulder. "Let's call it the brocade walking suit!" The mothers all laughed in that high-pitch tone that signaled disobedience in children. Could the fetus hear such high tones while in their womb? I wondered. We should change that.

They grabbed at me, their fingers like rakes scraping my head. Together, the three of them lifted me to their height. One day, my students would become like these mothers: their bodies as thin as long bread, their faces surgically altered to appear like elongated heart shapes, their crystallized eyes bright as chandeliers.

"Qi Jan," Sarah said. "It's not—a worker, is it?"

"A pre-fab woman, maybe," Qi Jan responded. Her orange hat hid her eyes like pieces of cut mangoes over a fruit bowl. She had a large pregnant belly protected in layers of vibrating devices, straddled with a pair of headphones emitting educational buzzing sounds.

"You mean this mother is sterile?" uncertainty soured her face.

"My goodness, you'd like that, wouldn't you, you sister-humper!"

More laughter.

"Wait a minute, I thought all workers were sterile."

"*Idiots*! This is not a worker!" Qi Jan yelled. "*Uck!* Jess, how old are you again? Don't you remember growing up in the Badiums? This is a, how-you-say?" she struggled to remember the word. "A *eunuch*. Born with a faulty you-know-what."

"So she was born a *male*?!" The mother bristled at the word. "Well don't let him touch you, Qi, she might be sick."

"Never mind, rat-face," Qi said, her arms shaking me like a wet cloth. "They say the fog is toxic to everyone now, so voilà!"

"Why are you here, nomen?" the quiet one said, her pregnant body covered in modest stripped cotton. "Are you looking for that other worker? The very small one?"

"You've seen her?" I said, my voice in a calm "Hum hum hum."

"Fog-breath!" Qi said, coughing.

"We passed a small worker a couple *lis* back," the quiet one said.

"She was weightless!" Sarah giggled. "Picking her up was no trouble!"

"You *touched* her?" I flew into it—kicking at them to no avail. When one of their hands switched to my neck, I bit it, and down I went, leg cracking as it broke my fall.

"You are heavy!" one of them said. "Are you fat for your type?" The mothers laughed.

"That other worker is a *child*," I said. This time, the hum of my voice did not discolor my urgency. Their laughter ceased in an instant.

"I didn't touch her!" Qi said. The others followed: "We didn't! No skin-on-skin contact! No skin!"

"She has no granmene," I said, looking at their tall bodies, their fake tears spilling on me like rain from tree leaves.

"I didn't touch her!"

"Me neither! I swear it!"

"Sarah, you're the one who picked her up!"

"But I'm not like that. I'm not *like* that. I'm *not*."

"I just need to find her before—"

"—She said something about a bear, and, what was the word?"

"*Honey*."

"Yes, *honey*. And taking it back from some bear."

"She kept asking if the bear had a name."

"What kind of stories are you teaching children these days?

"Look, I just need to find—"

"—*We didn't do anything*!" the mothers rolled off, their orbs flying fast over the gaps between bricks. In the opposite direction I saw others coming for me, a cadre of red tunics. The Party. I tried to stand, but my right leg was numb; I could barely hop.

Three Party members approached, dressed in red velvet with gold chains and hats like the white sails of a ship. They walked toward me slowly, seeing that I wasn't getting away. They pulled along a mobile bed covered by a hard-plastic bubble, an ungainly contraption. Inside lay your still body.

"Eunuch," one of the party members said, her voice grinding and gruff. "You must carry her back. You see: she is untouched by us."

Your eyes were half open. Your limbs were withered and sunken on top of the white plush cushion. Energy worked toward every breath.

"And then what will happen to me?" hum hum hum hum hum.

"We all agree, don't we?" one of the younger ones said. "Nomen who fail, they deserve the worst punishments, right?"

The Party marched us to the center of the colony, to the chimney, where hot air from deep below the earth rose up to circulate throughout the mound, pushing out the toxic fog outside. I followed without protest. Sweat dripped down my chin as they shoved me toward that steady stream of smoke puffing out from the soot-covered smokestack, lifting into the sunlight far above us.

"She still cannot speak, Eunuch," the youngest party member said, waving her musical note-shaped baton in tight arches.

The packet of gray granmene shrunk as the liquid injected slowly into your arm.

"Maybe it's the heat." Hum hum hum hum.

"If she doesn't wake up soon," the older party member said, "The chimney would be too good for you. Don't you agree?"

A public maiming, perhaps—or a crucifixion. Executing a eunuch took finesse. With my most sensitive limb already cut off, they would have to invent crueler fates.

Your mouth moved slightly. Your cheeks rose like air inflating a parade mascot. Slowly you filled in your wrinkled clothing.

"I'm gonna take it back," you whispered. "All that bear's honey."

"Good, good," the oldest party member leaned toward you. "Miss! Do you know your name?"

"Don't talk to her like that!" I tried to yell. Hum hum hum hum hum hum.

"Sir," one of the Party said, her gold chain clinking against her belt as she approached her superior. "Tone, sir, tone."

"You talk to her," the oldest one said, shoving me toward you. "Tell her things are fine."

"Everything is fine, Meg." Hum hum hum hum.

"Tell her you are going to be executed."

"I am going to be executed now." Hum hum hum hum hum hum hum.

Steam churned through the room, lacing the air with a briny sulfuric smell.

"All his honey," you repeated, your head rotating back and forth on a pillow wrapped in plastic.

"Tell her to forget about this bear business. To keep to her *duties*."

Your eyes cracked open. They seemed to recognize me. Your hand lifted to touch me—touch. Skin on skin. But your fingers just tapped on the plastic bubble keeping you safe. Tears itched my face.

"Tell her!" The oldest party member said. The younger one stood behind me, her stick at her side.

"Meg." Hum. "You will never stop." Hum hum hum hum. "You will always be you." Hum hum hum hum hum.

You tried to laugh. It came out chipped.

"What are you telling her?"

"Is that her natural path?"

"To become a fertile mother?"

"Say it, Eunuch: A fertile—"

"Teacher," you whispered, that attentive redness returning to your eyes. "Does the bear have a name?"

"Forget this!" the youngest party member said, grabbing my nape and locking my arms.

"Toss him," the eldest one commanded.

The heat hit me first, an engulfing warmth. Then the falling. None knew how deep the chimney went. The blackness and the heat became me. I tried to scream, to let words hum in soft echoes back and forth along the scalding hot walls, until it reached you and flooded into every tunnel of our colony in soft echoes.

"The bear has a name." Hum hum hum hum hum.

Life

V

The destroyer appears as Chang'e

2340 - Another Mound Colony/Far East No more men.

The Diver is the Lunar Princess!

Cold metal dripped saliva down my thigh.

One of the guards tossed a silk dress over me. "Relax. He'll like you; he always likes girls with a rump like yours."

In the mirror, I saw myself wearing one of the old robes from the Republic, a cheongsam patterned in red and pink petals.

"I was told purple," I said. "My make-up is all wrong for red. Look—purple eyeliner. Purple fatty cheeks. Even these highlights—" I switched out the fuchsia butterfly jewel from my hair.

"The last man won't know the difference," another guard said in a gruff voice. "He just likes cheongsams."

"I hadn't heard." I wiggled the dress to meet my curves. The thing fit like a peel over a banana. How was I to move swiftly in such a tight dress? I lifted my arms and felt the fabric tug at my skin. I strained trying to separate my legs. It hurt to breathe.

"Suck in your stomach," a guard laughed. "No, don't hold the air in. Don't flex too tight. There, that's good."

"How long do I keep my stomach like this?"

The vault crank twisted, and a red rectangle light blipped on the wall. Red lamplight scattered off the bits of jewels and metal ore around the cavern.

"He's asking for you. Hurry and put these on." Someone placed a plant and a set of objects onto the lighted panel.

"What is the vegetable for?"

"It's a rose. You don't eat it. You put it in your hair. Men used to like that."

"Ok, and those—what are those things? Those small red hammers?"

"Those are called heels."

"I'm supposed to wear them?"

"On your feet, yes."

"Ok. And, this thing?"

"A necklace. In the middle is a diamond."

"You mean a rock?"

"No. A diamond. It's very different from a rock."

The vault door creaked open. I wobbled up the stone steps, a piece of rock snagging my dress. I lurched forward, almost falling, toward my eternal sanctuary.

The last man struggled in my stranglehold. Pillows fell off the bed and the yellow cover slipped off, bunching on the carpet like soft cream. The shock on his face grew as he absorbed the situation: his arms pinned by my knees; his neck strained by my ankles. I kept my body leaned over him, using my arms to grip the bed's ballast so he could not flip me over.

Needless to say, the cheongsam could never be worn again.

He wretched in pain and I squeezed his neck taut. His legs kicked and I tugged the roots of his hair.

"Tell the machine to close the vault," I commanded.

He grew a smile, perhaps, enthralled by a woman taking control. "Close the vault," he announced to the automated system. "Just do what you want," he whimpered hoarsely as the steel door cranked shut. "I'm sick of it."

"So, it's true." Sweat from my forehead pattered onto his skin. "At the height of human civilization, before the collapse, there was a machine to grant eternal life. Isn't that right? Males are not born immortal. That was bullshit, wasn't it?

He breathed in strands of my hair as he gasped for air.

"It's the machine, isn't it? It keeps you alive."

The last man's eyes went to the mirror reflecting our naked bodies. "Just use me, that's all you bitches ever want."

I tightened my grip, bending his neck back. "How do you activate the machine? How does it work?"

His eyes moved to a panel of surveillance monitors. "Release me and I'll show you."

I wrapped my ankles around the back of his neck, keeping him steady, sitting atop his pelvis.

"Use your hands to walk over there."

"What?"

My feet dug his chin into his chest. It took some minutes to coordinate him, until, by and by, his muscled arms lifted me. I pulled on his thighs to guide the last man.

"You planned this well," he gagged, drooling as he spoke. "I've never seen a bitch move like you. But you're wasting your time."

What is a bitch? I wondered.

My gaze shifted to a corner filled with small monitors stacked like children's blocks. So it was true, the cameras around our underground city were connected to the last man. For generations we kept him company and performed dances for him like a god needing to be worshipped. For the first time I was on the other side, watching the cavern hallways lit brighter than I'd ever seen them. The cameras showed the barracks, the canteens, the nursery vaults, the corridors, the markets, the chicken coops.

"Turn it on!" I instructed. "The machine!"

"Harmony," the last man sputtered. "Activate."

"Error," a male voice came from speakers in every direction. "Regeneration restricted to one life form at a time."

"What was that?"

"Like I said," the last man spat. "This is a waste of time."

His hands finally gave and we collapsed on the carpet. I squeezed my legs but I was too late, he squirmed free, and we both darted up, eyes on each other's nude bodies.

"You think I like it?" He paced slowly toward the vanity mirror, likely going for a weapon. "For three hundred and twenty-six years I've been here, isolated, alone, watching these monitors like soap operas. I've watched you, too, in those bruise-purple skirts. I know where you go in the library to talk to yourself. I've heard you, speaking to nothing. Who is Cheng'e anyways?"

"Only one person at a time can become immortal in here," I said, ignoring his accusations. "Is that right?"

He pulled open a drawer and I grabbed for a weapon. I picked a hairbrush, but it yanked me back, strapped down by a tight cord. I went for the yellow blanket strewn across the floor.

He stared into the vanity mirror, combing out the imperfections in his long hair. "Look what you've done, bitch."

I screamed and threw the thick yellow blanket on top of him. His figure stood up, taller than myself. I had learned that in the old times, men were physically superior to women—was it even possible to kill a male?

"Ok, that's enough," he spoke through the blanket. He instructed the Harmony system: "Vault door, o—"

In a frisson of fear, I leapt on top of him, cutting off his air with the ragged red rope that was once a cheongsam. He tried to grip at the cloth, but his hands were blocked by the woolen blanket—what chance! I wrapped the silk around him again and tightened, but the thick wool gave him just enough air.

"The f—" we both collapsed. "Vault!" he said. "Open!"

I screamed loud as I could, drowning out his voice command. Then I smashed my heel into his face. It gave me an idea—the heels! Now why should I forget about those small hammers? I took one and rammed the pointed end into the glob of man inside the thick wavy-patterned blanket. The glob hit me back like a doorway I had kicked-in too hard.

"Wha—" he mumbled as a fit of laughter grabbed him. "You stupid bitch, what the hell are you doing?"

"I'm trying to kill you!"

He laughed. "I'm *the last man*! The only hope for humanity—the only hope for reproduction!"

"You're just collateral damage!" I tossed the heel into

the vanity mirror. It broke in a sharp crack, just enough for a knife-shaped piece of glass to appear. Another thrust and the mirror shattered.

"No—not the mirror!" the last man began to kick off the blanket like a web. He disrobed the blanket only for a moment before I was on top of him, slipping that silver glint of glass in and out of his chest like a tongue lapping up his life. He tugged at the necklace around my neck, choking me with it, but I didn't stop. I gagged until the necklace snapped off and I stabbed until I felt the resistance of hard bone.

His breath sputtered out like a dead engine. I unfurled my hair and tossed the rose, now flattened, onto the last man's corpse.

"One life form confirmed," the ominous male voice said. "Harmony's life preservation system activated."

A strange unscented air passed through the vents that looked like the smog of the factory vaults. The last man's blood congealed like sap seeping from a tree and turned a dark blue color. I breathed air thicker than any mist.

The red rose perked. Its stem full, sucking up the last man's blood.

On one of the monitors I saw guards outside the vault, their clicker guns ready for me. I glanced into the broken mirror and salvaged pieces to see my reflection.

"They'll kill me as soon as I leave this room," I said.

"Then you'll just have to wait," a voice responded. It was like my own, but lovely despite my ugliness, distant despite my nearness. It was Cheng, the one who spoke through my imagination.

"Take it from me," she said. "Things always change."

Around a year later I sat at the last man's desk, a lollipop swiveling in my mouth the flavor of douban tofu dipped in black tea. Swivel swivel, as I swiveled in my old blue-skinned friend, the chair.

Kicked off from the side of the bed. Yellow blankets. Rolled like a gumball boing-ing off pieces of robotic arms and legs, the long unrepaired pieces of automated cleaners, some perished to misuse, others to my abuse.

—ha! What the last man did to others, I deal in spades to those fancy sex contraptions.

In the cracked mirror my face looked hideous.

—so much work to do!

I dipped the calligraphy brush into the purple dust. Dye I made from the flower garden fertilized by the last man.

—Well, good morning to you, too, my strong, fertile, erect dick, freed from the tyranny of your master.

I made love to him in a bed of roses, one hundred percent making love, gripping that red cheongsam tied to the ceiling. It dangled me over fungus, mushrooms, a string of toadstools. I'd mastered this—a girl needed time to really perfect the act, didn't she? And I had time, mountains of it.

—I bud, and I sprout, and holy shit, time, time, time! And I've got time! Right, Cheng? Cheng? CHENG!?

She didn't appear, phooey. I applied the dye to my eyelids. Wait—couldn't rush the process. First the lipstick made from the last man's collection of lubricant; then the eye shadow made from his bottles of whiskey and amaretto; then the eyeliner made from his mashed-up hair, chocolate scrawls, and tweezers. Then a necklace of his teeth, much prettier than that diamond rock.

The portrait of the last man's mother eyed me from the corner of the white wall. Months ago, I had slit her throat with a piece of glass and spattered her cheeks with her son's mushy blue blood.

I traced the lining pencil over my eyes. "Oh, wake up, Cheng, I don't have time for this." *Pop* went the lollipop, stuck to the mirror. I kissed my reflection, right where the glass was cracked; she'd never bitten back, but she stayed sleeping.

—ok, next the hair. Thorned stems woven through the broken hair comb, flutter flutter. Creak creak creak. Pat pat pat.

The hallways on the security monitors were once again empty. No, there were still some women in the market selling children's clothes and caged chickens, and the other crones, chewing betel nut and tending coal barbecues. Soon that flute-playing child would peek out from between the bars of her apartment. The one that would have been mine to watch over, had I stayed on the outside—poor girl. Her only flaw, like mine, was in not acting soon enough, to take what was hers.

—Comb comb comb. Why do I have to do this every time, Cheng? Can't I just wake up to you loving me?

I used to spend time in the simulators. Enjoyable, perhaps, if you liked rescuing princesses, saving the world, destroying things rather than arranging them. Here I had my own garden, and Cheng—

—Cheng!

I spent more time dressing my face. Still all the flaws stuck out, the slight wrinkles especially. If I had only killed the last man when I was younger.

"Cheng!" Kissing the mirror "with one kiss!"

"We begin," Cheng said, a perfect mirror reflection. My

moon goddess! Her image appeared in the mirror's cracks, behind a pattern of sprawling lines.

"It takes you longer to appear every day!" I whined.

"Just because I'm a god," she said, "doesn't mean you have no power over me. I can only appear—"

"—in my imagination, yeah—"

"—shhh *shut* it. If you're having a hard time imagining me without jarring your face into perfection, that's not on me."

"I just miss you. Can't you come out of that mirror?"

"Have patience. Your imagination will improve over time. The better you imagine, the more I can give you. And, topping that, unparalleled love-making, me on top."

Hiding my smirk, I tilted to the pile of monitors, to a now abandoned market square, shops left half-built, toiletries and clothing left scattered. I remembered the market's stale air, its furnace heat. A woman in plaid pants ran between monitors, retreating from something.

"Has she appeared today?" Cheng eyed me with those perfectly round green eyes.

"Who?"

"The girl, the one you will soon fall in love with."

"She's only eight. And I only love you."

"I do appreciate the sentiment, but I'm older than humanity, babe. I know star-struck love when I see it."

I took another lollipop, flavored like chuan style spicy fish. Rolled it around, to the back of my tongue.

"Her apartment is still on lockdown," I said. "Those foreigner apartments with barred windows. Kind of funny."

"Tell me."

"Some chick playing in the alley got stuck in there with them. A Dahl delivery guy too. A group of young people at a party. Half a dozen prostitutes."

"Your girl should be ok," Cheng said, stretching my perfect body in the mirror. "The prozzies can translate the warning messages."

"They're still eating sugar packets. That's all they have in quantity." I kicked myself off from the divan. "Ugh, I love disasters!"

"She's an old soul, your girl," Cheng said flippantly. "Every life she lives, she has brought change. Though—really, nothing's changed."

"Things change."

"Humanity. If you all perished tomorrow, the universe would be far better off. Let's hope you stay stuck on this rock."

"Nap time."

"We just started talking!"

"It took five hours for you to appear, I'm tired."

"Don't—"

I turned away from the mirror and she was gone. She was annoying as hell, most of the time, but at least someone when there was no one else. She had led me this far, trained me to infiltrate the last man's abode, promising eternal life, and what can I say, my goddess had delivered. But what to do with eternity?

I dimmed the lights only slightly, Harmony's warm fan humming me to sleep.

One last glance at the monitors—deserted streets, barren markets. Quiet control, restriction, bars.

HELP US

Then her. I recognized her instantly—glasses, short hair, wrinkled shirt barely buttoned on. She held a sign outside the bars of the apartment window.

I looked at the other monitors to see who the sign was pointed toward. The streets were empty, the shops abandoned, even the party members had retreated behind their vault doors, waiting out the foreigners. You, the girl, shook the sign at the monitor, at me.

Years and years passed. One day I woke up to you, the one in glasses and a ponytail, holding up a sign at the hallway monitor, scrawled in chalk upon a wooden table.

ARE YOU STILL AFRAID OF THE DARK?

"Did I ever tell you about the Nubians?" Cheng said, her body emerging from beneath the yellow sheets. "One of the prancier peoples, nearly gone from your history. Just thinking, they probably wouldn't pussy out quite as fast as your lover over there."

"Oh, Cheng," I sunk to the thin carpet and braced the edges of the yellow blanket.

"You're bored, love? Your little love interest isn't giving you anything?" Her erect body appeared atop the bed, flowing white hair, icy eyes, arms folded over her breasts, dick hard as diamond.

I kissed her stomach, working my way over.

"I only stopped by for a second—"

"—No, you can stay."

"Just like a human." Her head tilted back, long dainty fingers clawing my head. She was always more than I could take—that warm taste wrapped around my tongue, urging itself down my throat. I would retch, while she sat quiet in pleasure. It was always a burden—my retching.

In the silence, I noticed her eyes on the monitors, at you, the woman holding the sign.

"Look at this!" Cheng tossed her hair back in laughter. "In every lifetime that I've followed you, you've been hooked on this one, always hankering for her attention. This is the first time—look, aw, she's curious about you too!"

Gasping, "Tell me about the Americans again." Massaging, "Movie stars, Hollywood."

"Self-glorifying. I'm a god, and I felt jealous."

"I wish I could see time like you."

I was tossed across the floor from a hard slap. I must have said something ridiculous to get myself hurt!

"How many years have you been in this room?" Cheng asked, her black curls floating above her like a raven's wings just before flight. "Just linger there like the rest of them, idealizing the past."

I got up and kissed her toes.

"You've never seen snow. Snow! In a past life, you killed yourself just to get away from it. Don't remember that, do you?"

"Time moves so slow," I said, massaging my cheek so the blue blood did not ruin the blush.

"'Time moves so slow!'" she mocked. "Such talk is not

worth a bean—now you truly deserve to be beaten! When you live as long as I have, every generation is like a chapter of an extraordinarily dull book. Even an amateur would cringe at it. Get off, I'm done with you for now."

She levitated above me, shiny skin. I knew that look.

"Please don't leave," I said.

"I'll be back."

"Don't go!"

"Annoying!" she disappeared in a flash of light.

Right away I went to the monitors, looking at the city market where signs were flipped upside down against a basket of sugar packets. You, that woman who I had observed for years, somehow you knew I was afraid of the dark—how? Was I popular among your kind? What stories did you tell about me?

—The woman who slayed the last man, living in eternity, among the best of civilization! Haha!

On the party vault monitor, a group led by tall muscular women stood before the open metal vault. I spotted you in the back of the crowd wearing a striped sweater to disguise the metal armor you'd been fashioning. You stood with your head upwards, as if you were just a follower. But I knew what you'd been up to. Those secret meetings behind the chicken coop, those dealings covered by the awkward squawks of the hens, those pattered out protests and—this was an impressive discovery—packing explosives in the chicken feed.

You looked the same age as myself, but possessed with a power I could only dream of—mighty, mythic, flawless.

With half my attention on the monitors, I applied more rouge from the bed of roses in the garden. Would you like purple, or like the last man, would you like me more in some ridiculous red garment?

I watched as the Party police debilitated the front line with their clicker guns. A cloud of dust formed where bodies smashed upon rock and dust, dislodging ore. You, fierce with teeth grit, pushed the others forward. Faint figures hacked at the rock wall with pickaxes like heels. The walls shook and dust covered the monitors. In the blurred background, the lines of the cavern fell like pieces of a jigsaw puzzle. The round, unprotected heads blipped out of life.

If their deaths meant something it would not be half so bad.

"Caught you!" It was Cheng, hovering over me, still as a spider. "Always looking for her? Are you planning to leave me for that skank? Can't wait to cheat on me, huh? AGAIN?"

My habits had struck a raw nerve—perhaps I was not ready to live forever! I scrambled from the chair and crept beneath the bed, dragging the cape of yellow blanket down with me. I hid under a shade of fungus.

"Why do you let that little heifer drive your passions? Every life she pushes you beyond hysteria. It's no good to watch her—come out, so I can gut you like the horker you are!"

When Cheng acted like this I always hid and tried to remember that even though she was a god, she only had as much power as my imagination gave her.

—Invite in more light! See the dust bunnies in the corner, the broken glass from decades ago, the pieces of robotic legs, the last man's skin still soft to touch.

"Ha! Look what your radical little bitch is up to!"

Cheng burst in a fit of laughter as I peeked out from

beneath the blanket. Two of the screens were fuzzed out in a bleak white static.

"They are destroying them!" Cheng giggled.

The women in stained work clothes chipped at my monitor with their pickaxes. A screen disintegrated into static.

A sign:

DEATH TO EXTRAVAGANCE

On the monitor to the chicken coops three women aimed a noose at me. They waved it in a cyclone, until one finally got a grip. They held a sign:

DOWN WITH THE LUNAR PRINCESS

"Lunar princess!" Cheng chuckled. "That's what they call you!"

On the monitor to the vault doorway, I saw them trying to smash their way into my vault. They had come to crush my palace. Over the decades none could break in—so many layers, I'd never even heard their pounding. They tried to find the power cords leading to my room. But cutting my power would set off an explosion—so said the warning signs, at least.

"Nothing changes out there, you see!" Cheng laughed. "You killed the king, now you're just another symbol of extravagance. Down with the lunar princess!"

A sign:

WE MAKE YOUR ENERGY

One of them squirted a can of industrial oil at my camera. The screen went ablaze.

"They will kill me if I leave," I said. "I won't fall for it!"

—CRSSHH

Only one monitor remained, one window to the outside world. And in it I saw you. Still alive, thank the goddess, still alive! Broken jeans, striped shirt, ponytail and glasses. Yes—still alive.

A sign:

ARE YOU STILL AFRAID OF THE DARK?

You took a black shawl, like an executioner's, and brought it over my head. No static, only darkness.

"What? Where did she go?" I squeaked.

I felt Cheng's thick hair in my arms. Her soft stomach pillowed my head.

"Don't worry, my pet. If beauty had a soul, this is not she. If only you had seen her, in her past lives. She was a cast-off heroine, available to the rank and file like any common pick-up. Soon you'll see, I can offer so much more. Your love is admirable, but misplaced. After a thousand years in this room, you'll see nothing really changes. Just waiting. Waiting for humanity to break itself apart. Nothing pushes or pulls after that. But you see, us, we are no longer alone. Now, we have each other. Are you listening? Stop watching the screens. There's nothing to see. Dozens of lives you've lived, always wanting her, doomed never to fit. What you really need. It's here in this room."

"I can go back. It's not too late."

"You'd die."

"Maybe they wouldn't—"

"*Eventually*, you would die. All the knowledge of the world I've taught you, all the memories of me, of us—*gone*."

"But what if—"

"Don't do that!" She slapped me, then held my face close to her lips. "My precious little flame. Don't ask me if what you did was right. Don't be like the rest of your race. Of all the humans I've met, only you are worthy of my time."

"What will I do?" Her breast against my cheek.

"Close your eyes." Her cold fingers shut my eyelids. "Imagine with me. Imagine me and you, in a palace of our own, far from these beasts."

"My fetid baby."

Lunar palace. House of white crystal. Earth's glow glinted out of the bedroom window like a cemetery light. I woke upon satin sheets.

"My fancy love."

Drunk and on top, serving her up, her beautiful manhood up inside my gut.

"You dirty bitch. You beautiful dirty bitch."

"I want you, daddy."

Moan out the fruit sap.

Pure white sand on the moon's light side, we lit earth, it lit us.

"You're not thinking of her, are you?"

"No."

"We're in love."

"Yes."

"Say it."

"Yes, you love me."

"Get out. Get out of my palace!"

"No, Just a little longer."

Cheng put me back in the last man's vault. I watched the remaining monitor. No pilgrims left, just paper flowers and fake rosaries.

Feeling cooped up and lonesome, I read from the last man's archive of human knowledge. I was working my way up, to my own era, reading the classics: Shahrazad, Shakespeare, Euripides, Goethe, Twain, Salih, Chenmaya. Cheng loathed these books. They just provoked my humanity, she said. All jealousy, envy, greed. Nothing held fashion for humans more than war and lechery.

There was action on the last monitor. A child in a wispy dress came to pay homage. The monitor lit up around the child, detecting a point of interest. She walked slowly up the stairway, eyes to the ground like the other pilgrims, too scared to stare into the glass eye, a last glimpse of humanity's peak.

She held a sign:

PLEASE HELP MY MOTHER

—Bow down first, little bitch.

The girl stood. Thread from her dress pulled on a basket of fruit.

"Curses only for you!" I shouted, condemning her. "You're too ugly! Dead mother—dead as your entire race!"

Pilgrims filtered through my shrine. They all looked so ugly. Even the flowers circling the monitor in a rosary border were a putrid color.

A pilgrim approached, unworthy of description, and kneeled upon the white cloth. Her sign:

PLEASE STOP THEM

—Another! How many have I seen like this? It's always THEY WILL DESTROY US and SAVE US FROM OUR-SELVES.

"It's always about you," I coughed at them. "Every time!"

Another pilgrim came, her clothing drab. Long skirt, yellow striped sweatshirt, hair thin like a rope's loose thread. She had no sign, but looked at me, as if she could see me through the lens.

Cheng let me back into her moon palace.

"See? A little bedroom shape-shifting never hurt any-one," Cheng said. "Isn't it wonderful to spend eternity in love? To spend eternity making love?

"Give me your vine."

Earth's light cracked through the palace doorway, a sun-rise on the horizon. Cheng ground into me upon a bed of diamonds, I her toy wife.

—Earth above us, the white rock of the moon below. Lunar palace, immortal life, and who is lighting whom? Graining against skin, curled within a nest of diamonds.

I screamed in pleasure pain. I cried in static motion. She beat me so sound. I was well senseless.

—A diamond is a rock. She gripes into my gut. My goddess!

"Are you still thinking of her?"

"No."

"*Humans*! You and this illusion!"

"Please, I only want you."

"No use training you—it is still only a human's brain, isn't it? You are decades older than her. You are *sick* to want her!"

"You are *eons* older than me."

"You'll never have her. I have seen her soul. Her only nourishment comes from a well of rage. Anger drives her, an anger fueled by the state of things. It is a fuel that will never run out. Don't you think it's time you left well-enough alone?"

"Just let me go already."

"Huh! This place may be in your imagination, but I can kick you out whenever I want."

"Wait, please, I didn't mean—"

"Get out!"

"I don't want to be alone."

Everything went dim. I shrieked in the unblemished blackness. Did Cheng forget that I was afraid of the dark?

How long had I been in Cheng's palace? How long in my own? How old had you become in all that time?

I watched my only monitor. My shrine had too long gone unattended. Even the paper flowers had wilted. If I just had more time, I could have looked perfect for you. I could have walked out and made you fall in love with me.

That old woman was back at the monitor—a cane supporting her weight now, creeping up the stairway to my glass eye. She took one of the paper flowers and used its chopped remains to scrawl words upon the white sheet where pilgrims once cowered before me. I recognized the handwriting, your handwriting.

YOU ARE NO GOD

That night I dreamt I was a great calligrapher, and you were a lollipop-flavored cake.

Cheng slid my panties off.

"Please," I simpered, acting childlike to escape a beating.

"You wanted white. You imagined her in white. So now imagine this, doll face."

Cake topped with her white cream for breakfast, her eight hands upon every hint of my body. Not a pore went untouched. And my skin—triangle-lines, hints of the moments I lived out there. She went at me all night, for on the moon there was only night.

"You are sick," she hissed from behind. "Loving someone so much younger than you."

—slip, slip, I'm slipping.

I awoke in the last man's bed, my body encompassed by thorny vines with roses at every stem. How long had my garden gone unattended?

I looked for the last monitor. All were white static. How long had I been out? Where was it? Where was my shrine? Those steps leading up to me, those decayed fruits, those pilgrims with signs asking for more time—where was it?

Nothing but static on every screen.

No—where was it? What happened? What did I miss? What happened?

I missed it.

What happened?

"Let me go, Cheng, I can't be alone any longer."

"You aren't alone—how could you say that to me? After all these years?"

"Let me out, Cheng."

"Go whenever you want—who the hell wants your fat ass?"

"I'm afraid of being alone too."

"No! *Stay with me.* I'm charged to watch over your pathetic race, but I can't watch your people's idiocy any longer. You're my only companion, my love. How could you abandon me? You know what I've been through."

"I can't."

"You don't know what's out there. I do. I've lived since before Earth was a volcanic rock. This is it. We will never get another chance to be together, to live in this palace together."

"I can't."

"She will never want you. That little harlot will sing to anyone at first sight!"

"I can't."

"If you leave, you'll die. Maybe not right away, but eventually. And those memories of us—"

"—I can't."

"You don't know what's out there!"

"I know what's in here."

I awoke with the lights on in my old palace. I was in my prison just as I had entered it, alone. My arms bled as I crawled through the thorns around my bed. I gripped the roses and tugged to pull myself through. Past the security cameras' static in white fuzz. Thorns in every direction—it didn't matter! I crawled right into them, pushing out headfirst, gripping thorns that pierced straight through my skin, my body awash in blue blood.

"Let me out, Cheng!"

Past the broken mirror, now curved and bent past use, stained into a white glare. Past the threads of red silk, past the last man's blue corpse, thorns bursting from his eye sockets. His hand still clutched that shiny rock they once called a diamond.

"Let me out! Let me out!"

I crawled beneath the thorns—they'd grown too thick to spread with my arms. I shook the thorns off, crept under and around them. My body bent back, somersaulted over, got tossed and bitten by the stems. Blue blood puffed from every thorn.

Finally, I reached the vault door, enveloped in pink and red roses. Those ghastly colors.

"Harmony," I spoke.

"Awaiting instruction," that calm voice of some man long ago.

"Open the Vault!"

I felt the air suck out from behind me in a chilling rush. Freezing cold enveloped me. Then a static white cloud crept in. I felt the urge to turn, to retreat to my prison. But I faced it. The whiteness burst in electric sparks.

—Did I learn nothing? Is nothing different? Has nothing changed, only time? What is time if nothing changes?

The fog crept along the walls, then grew in layers like a multitude of snakes.

—Are we any better, having time passed around us?

My sentiment was that there must be something nice about it, knowing that it will all end, having some grip on time.

I felt the silk of the sheets, the bamboo, then stained and crusted, then stone. I could not grip my own bedding. I was back in that stateroom, feeling it out, for the room appeared in a series—a Roman servant's quarters, then a Viking homestead, then a Berber tent, then a tall tower, then a lunar palace.

A torrent of memories raged through me. The memory disease. My mind unwrapped, its membrane scaled off, leaving my brain exposed to the elements. Every breeze drove me further into madness. Every sound jolted me in fits of insanity. Torn among lives, my stateroom shifted like television channels from one era to another, my body too shifting—tall, robotic, wizard, soldier. I could not take hold of anything, not the banister, not the wall, not my own limbs, before they would shift away, into another time.

And you! Pasted, plastered, plotted upon every course. I loved you in strains, and with no greater zeal than a person could love. You were time itself; you were the mold that had grown upon every human monument. And when the air itself became scarce, still my love for you dwindled forth. When every city I inhabited and all the people I cherished had wilted into dusty nothing, you remained. How madness had spun our love, blossomed it into a vine that overgrew every temple, unearthing every gravestone! One more time, one more failed life, would be the last drop to burst my madness. One more life, and I'd really do something I'd regret!

I heard banging on my stateroom door—the door, I could not place! Was it of brass, of marble, of dirt, or was it the titanium metal of an eternal vault?

"Eight-Seven-One!" I heard a voice, not yours. That dainty false woman, Cryss!

"Don't come in!" I screamed, the terror breaking through the dream.

Her voice came like a disciplinarian, a police officer, a party member: "Open the door or I'll pulverize it."

I knew what Cryss would do—just like with her own lover, she would lock me away in a stateroom, keep me bound to a bed, let me survive as a madwoman taking sips of that blue tea before breaking off in fits of memory. But I was not totally mad—I was in love, yes, and love is madness, for what proves love more than tossing one's sanity to the sands?

If only you knew what I had given for you. I had to make you understand; you had to see things the way I saw them.

"We're breaking down the door," Cryss said, pounding through infinity.

"No!" I shouted. I would not be her little girl. I would not be the gods' plaything either! I would pursue without reason the unbridled meaninglessness of love! They were jealous of my freedom, my unwavering commitment. I had glimpsed over the edge, and now here I remained, florescent with lunacy! The rest were dim bulbs!

I heard a door break, the crashing of heavy metal. The sandstorm of time dwindled. I could see the stateroom, my room, its off-white walls. And there was Cryss, tailored in

Valkyrie fur, her stone pouch hanging, and her two lackeys, Jezebel, dressed as a Persian, and Clover, an oval-eyed pregnant mother atop a silver shining roller ball. Those two yes-women both reached their palms toward me, willing the stateroom to take its common form—binding my will, pinning my body to the bed.

"Eight-Seven-One," Cryss said, stone-faced. "The memory disease has taken you. I'm sorry for this. We only want to help."

"No!" Delirious, I burst into laughter, kicking sand at her vassals.

"You're a danger to everyone in the Ilium," Cryss stated, eyes locked in a squint. "I too was once blinded by love, but I knew well enough when to give up. We must cure you now, or you'll be forever under its thrall."

I laughed a deliciously mad laugh. "You don't know this! You don't know being entrapped in love's madness! You don't know what it is to not exist without her! I would rather die a thousand deaths! I already have!" The window to the ocean shattered apart as if a bomb had detonated from my heart.

Cryss gestured to that little wench, Jezebel, who brought forth a porcelain kettle. "Your imagination knows no bounds," she said. "Without help, you threaten to destroy the Ilium. We will purify you! Now—don't resist me."

Her foot went on my stomach, pushing tears from my eyes. The pain bound me to the bed. "I can change her," I said in a wheeze. "My last life, she came to me, I swear it. She came to me! She is beginning to understand, beginning to desire this place." I snarled. "She is so close now, I almost have her—you cannot stop me!"

"Hold her!" Cryss instructed as her charges clutched

my arms, forcing me onto the bed, skewering me with their sharp fingers. Cryss poured the blue tea into a silver chalice.

Tears ran from my eyes. Every moment I had shared with you, every smile, every caress, every kiss—it would all disappear. My goddess, the horror of all the things I'd done, the things you'd done to me. Love—it moves mountains! But how many people can a mountain crush?

"Ok, ok, Cryss, I'll drink it, I'll drink it." I calmed down, my body limp, tears dripping onto the bed sheets like an old man's spittle. "Cryss, I'm sorry. You're right, it's over. I'm a fool." I sobbed into Jezebel's tunic, pulling her toward me.

"We can't trust you," Cryss said. "Take the tea now!"

She brought the tea to my lips, but not before I could say her name, "Cressida! Lovely Creseyde! Don't do this, not yet!"

The lackeys paused. Cryss stood frozen in time. Could it be? Was she truly not privy to her own legacy? I took a breath. "A thousand lives I've lived," I said. "Before I take the tea, you need to know, Cressida, the things they say of you. I know your story. What you've done."

Cryss' eyes went stale, suddenly devoid of command.

"Human history remembers you," I willed those sharp fingers from my arms. "Cressyde. The tale of Troilus and Cressyde, they call it, a story repeated throughout human history. By the grandfather of literature, by the great bard, by the great novelists. And Troy too, Troilus. In the stream, they remember Troilus as a great hero, greater than Achilles. And Cressyde, his lover. You are remembered, Cryss. You are worshiped. You, a goddess of devotion, of family, of compassion. It is true—they have not forgotten your deeds."

I couldn't know how Cryss would react—she had the hardest face to read. But despite her withdrawal, a tear managed to rip through her façade.

"Troilus," she whispered, her face softened. "Greater than Achilles." She gripped the bedpost to balance herself. A smile tore through her, forcing itself upon her lips. "Troilus, they remember us." She stood upright, face flushed with joy. "We must tell him, he must know!" She put down the kettle, her arms fleeing to open the stateroom door. "This is his cure! If he hears how he is admired, how much he is loved, he will be cured! After five thousand years!"

With Cryss and her charges distracted, I willed my body to spring like a boulder from a trebuchet, flinging myself out the stateroom, out that open window to surf upon the breeze of freedom.

"Idiots!" I screamed at them from afar, my voice projecting in a whirlwind. "You want to know how they really remember you? Troilus the chicken, the greatest of cuckolds! and Cressida? 'As false as Cressida,' they say! O false Cresseid! False, false, *false*! All untruths stand by your stained name, and they seem glorious by comparison! Now—tell that to Troilus! Cressyde, history's unforgettable whore!"

And I fell, with a wonderful splash, into you.

I'd gone cuckoo! Cuckoo!

Life

Year Zero

2470AD – 15 PT, Juc era

Pei's World, more fun than here
1. The Ilium

I flew with my arms out like an airplane, through the corner window of the ancient American White House. Inside, brown-robed monks shouldered boom boxes, their asses releasing frosted wind.

"Aren't we supposed to be learning about Churchill?" I said to you, my meld partner. I spotted you sitting on an oscillating chandelier made of peacock feathers.

You tilted your sunglasses down, your blaze of black hair whisking in a whirlwind. "So, then what happens?"

"Then," I said, levitating above the dancing monks, "saltwater pours in through the windows." CRASH! The monks fell like heaps of dirt. Electric sparks flew from their stereos. "The White House is the Titanic." The entire stone structure tilted. Men in suits poured out screaming.

You gave a light chuckle, rocking on your haunches on top of the sinking white sandstone. "You're vile. Such a travesty, the Titanic."

"So, what should I conjure next?" I grinned. "Lead the way, Dei."

You smiled when I called you by that name, the name you were not allowed to speak. "Well, how about a flood! Can you do that?"

My mind communicated a new code, speaking the machine's language, and we levitated together through the rooftop and watched the White House float like abandoned cargo in an endless sea.

"Life begins anew," I said. "The end of mankind!"

—*Children.*

Your body somersaulted in midair laughter. "Killed by their own technology—"

—Children!

I awoke from the mind mesh, sweating, my heart beating in my neck.

"Children," our caretaker said again. She stood near the canyon-wall chalkboard, her frail body hugged by a burlap dress, her wooly gray hair poking out in all directions from a blue bonnet blocking the sun. "Who is the good student? Who listened to all of Sir Churchill's speech, and can recite the last lines?"

My eyes followed the small black wire from my fore-head to the fist-sized meld machine and then to you, Blue, a girl whose body shone with a heavy sweat that seeped through your burlap dress. We sat on red stones at the bottom of the great canyon that protected us from the toxic gray fog above. I heard that small black creek running near-by, indifferent to our lesson.

My eyes met yours. We smiled at each other like we were being chased. Annoyed, the caretaker called on some-one else.

Two years before, your people emerged from the fog on the northern edge of our canyon. They wore industrial gas masks and carried all their belongings in wagons and wheelbarrows. Hundreds of them had escaped the chaos of the subterranean mounds, only to spend weeks journeying through the fog, never pulling off their masks except to drink radish and pea soups cultivated in their underground farms. We, the canyon people, had only heard of your kind, the mound people, from our scouts. We gave your people space to camp on the higher edges of the canyon, closer to the fog.

My eyes first met your defiant gaze in class, while the caretaker led our weekly sing-along:

> Who is who is who is
>
> going to get eaten
>
> by the fog fog fog fog
>
> *Who?*
>
> All the mountain people!
>
> *And?*
>
> All the island people!
>
> *And?*
>
> All the mound people!

During the song, I felt embarrassed, knowing that some of our classmates had just come from the mounds. But the other children sang with fervor, even your kind. I moved to the back of the classroom and found one other child singing in whispers. It was all the breath you could muster. Somehow, our skin was the same tint of brown, the color of the canyon's edges at sunset. I volunteered to be your partner in the meld machine, a virtual world where we learned about all of human achievement. I was supposed to help you adjust. We were supposed to use the machine to observe and honor the world before war scorched the planet. Before the fog took all the men.

But you only used the machine for play. And with my unrestrained imagination, we defiled every honorable historical figure. Newton choked to death on that fallen apple. Confucius gave up wisdom when he learned to surf. Saladin got drunk and fell off his horse. And in that world you used your own name, the name that our caretakers had banned because it was too hard to pronounce. Dei, you called yourself. Dei, your mound people's name. And it was your world where anything could happen, so long as we had the will.

"Dei," I whispered into the small canyon crevice. It was the last sultry summer night that mankind would ever experience. For the first time I had crossed the steep riverbank separating our peoples. For the first time I saw your motley folk encamped on the slope, dotting the canyon like lichen. How did they survive?

I placed my ear upon the weather-beaten stone, where moss bloomed from its cracks. I spoke into a fissure and heard my echoes bounce through the canyon tunnels, to the other side of the demarcation, where your people dwelled. "Dei. Can. You. Hear. Me?"

An echo bounced back: "Yes. Is that you?"

"Yes. It's me."

"I'm sorry."

"I'm. So. Sorry."

Silence. I wondered if you had heard the same announcement, only hours before. That our food rations were insufficient. That supporting refugees was a privilege we could not afford. That a barrier was to be erected. That your people of the mound, if you wanted to survive, had better head back to where you belonged.

"Please. Tell me. That. You're. OK."

My echoes bounced. I heard sounds, perhaps unformed words, perhaps sobs.

"Dei," I said. "Can. I. Kiss. You. Where. It. Hurts?"

Silence. Then: "Yes," you said. "You. Are. Kissing. Me."

Horns blared from atop the canyons. Gray obelisks drifted from the fog in shapely rows like ghosts bearing their own gravestones. They came down to us in tall elevators, setting down within our canyon walls. At the edge of starvation, we followed the smell of rice porridge and baked potatoes that wafted through the canyons, hailing us to come aboard.

The gods had sent a divine race to save us. The Jucs. Broad-shouldered, their bodies shaped like tall lamps, their pose always stiff. We followed a red-lighted line through their ship's hallways and encountered groups of them staring us down with their menacing yellow eyes. Some of them carried signs in our language:

SHAME on those who destroy their planet

You do not deserve us

Keep your disease away

We were brought to a bright room that had to be dimmed before we could see each other. We faced a dark screen that our caretaker told us was a window to outer space. "Those are stars," our caretaker said, pointing to the lights twinkling in the distance. "And one of those twinkles is Earth. And those floating ships beside us," she pointed to the rectangular obelisks, gray and tall like the Washington Monument, "those are our saviors. Every ship now is full of humans from all around the world."

I cried a torrent of tears, remembering you. "What about the mound people? Where are they?"

"You're lucky to be here," my caretaker said. "Do you even know how lucky you are?"

For years we lived under the Jucs' parentage. My body grew thick in their passing delights. My friends, Pia, Cherry, and I, rode our automatic bikes through the ship's gray corridors, wavering past those tall gods like street signs. We parked in front of the mountain people's triage wing, our tires barely touching the yellow demarcation border where mechanical devices were forbidden, to respect the mountain people's belief in naturalism.

Three of their old-timers met our gaze. They held water-stained books and wore colored cotton cloth that hung over their shoulders.

Cherry revved the engine she made in our mechanical engineering class. "Hey, mountain people!" she baited. "Why don't you get a job or something?"

"Loafin' around all day," Pia joined in. She spat a thick wad across the yellow border.

"No mountains here in space!" I shouted. "Your venerable Buddha is back on Earth, smoochin' your holy cows!"

I laughed as the other girls sped away. My engine sputtered; the blue lights blinked on and off. The three mountain people lunged toward me just as the motor churned on, and I whizzed down the halls, past those Jucs with their menacing stares, smoke billowing from my bike.

We regrouped at the canyon people's demarcation line.

"There's something wrong with you," Cherry said, wiping black dust from her yellow floral-patterned dress.

"You think that kind of talk is funny?" Pia asked, as they departed to their dormitory rooms.

I sunk into the bustle of the market, passing diamond-patterned skirts and petaled suit jackets. One person, I thought, would have found it funny.

In my last year of education, I still would not meld like the other children.

In the last virtual dream of our class, I sat with Cherry in the crowd of black, brown, and white people, listening to that man on stage talk about having a dream.

"What if," I said, leaping into the air above the humid crowd, "Cleopatra woos the good doctor?" I sent code to the machine and the Egyptian queen appeared, gold headdress and all, massaging the man at the pulpit. "The good doctor lets loose his passions—"

"That is filthy!" Cherry yelled from inside the crowd. "I'm trying to focus on what he says."

"You *know* what he says." I bashed away the onstage fellatio with the wind of my arm stroke. "We have to memorize it every year, just to recite it for those stupid lampshades."

"How are you so talented in here, but in the real world you can barely unscrew a bolt?"

"It's more fun in here!" Mark 14 torpedoes whizzed out of my fingers, leaving a trail of bubbles behind them as if air was water.

"I'm glad we're graduating. I won't ever need to meld with you again."

The bombs shifted direction and soared toward Cherry in the crowd. "Better think of something quick!" I taunted.

"These torpedoes cost real human lives," Cherry said as the missiles rocketed closer to the dispersing, panicking crowd. "Have some respect."

The bombs exploded. Mass casualties. The Washington Monument fell, revealing Amelia Earhart's stashed carcass.

Cherry burst out of the rubble, livid. "What is wrong with you? This is *sacred*, don't you get that?"

"You really don't enjoy any of this?"

"What kind of person would?"

For six years more we remained aboard the Jucs' ship. In that time, the mountain people were moved into our triage zone. At first, they refused to cross, and we would not take them in, until the Jucs took one of their children, and then one of ours.

"They'll do far worse soon enough," Cherry told me as we watched the mountain people brush wool.

"We would call it a coup,'" said Pia, the girl most literate in the Jucs' language. "It means their crazies took over. Remember them, the ones with those signs telling us to go back to Earth? The ones who tell us to go eat fog? They're in power now."

"So what?" I said. "We've already been prohibited from ever setting foot on a planet again. We're a near-extinct species. What more could they do?"

That night we were taken to the gas rooms. The gas, they told us, mimicked the fog we left behind on Earth. They saved us from it, so it was their right to put us back whenever they pleased. The lampshade-looking Jucs assaulted us with flashlight beams in our eyes, then checked our teeth and took photographs of our nude bodies. I was the last of my crew to enter the interrogation office.

"Who is Thomas Edison?" a lampshade asked in a calculating voice.

"An inventor," I said, my arms bound behind my back. "Nineteenth century, I think."

"And what do you think of inventors like Edison?"

"I don't know. I was taught to call them heroes."

"What do you think of your people's atomic bomb?"

"I was told nuclear energy had potential."

"And what do you say to that?"

"It's hard to accept, I guess."

"What about your men? Do you accept that your technology killed them all?"

"You mean the fog?"

"Your inventors created the fog. Your wars let it cover your planet. In nature, any species without balance goes extinct. Do you not see the perversion of staying on?"

252

"I think I see it. Yes."

"So then. Do you wish to recreate human technology?"

"I just don't care. I wish it would just end. We're done."

"Is this your bike?" Two lampshades pulled out my blue bike. The outside was caked in a layer of black soot.

"Yeah, that's the one."

The Jucs looked it over. "But, it barely works. We tried it. It won't even start."

"Yeah, I know."

"Aren't you going to repair it?"

"To be honest, I have no idea what to do with that piece of garbage."

When I returned to the canyon people's triage grounds, few children were left. The remaining adults wandering about the pen were either pregnant or drunkards. I waited for days but no one else came. Pia and Cherry, gone. Anyone capable of ever recreating human technology, disappeared. And just to make a point, days later our melding devices were torn apart and laid out at the demarcation line, their parts stacked in neat pieces for us to see.

The Jucs liked to gloat. They had executed anyone with the knowledge to put our machines back together. But they let us keep the parts. All knowledge of human history was spread out in front of us, with no tangible way to recreate it.

Our colony grew as we were shoved into other ships with other groups of humans. Mountain people, mound people, island people, canyon people, all brought into the same triage centers. Most were too young or too broken to care. Over the course of my youth I met others who preferred to be drunk on Juc wine. One sip was enough to get drunk— four, enough to die in a stupor. With no jobs, no schooling, no caring for our future, I cruised from woman to woman.

For my first love, I wrote a poem about prefabricated two-story homes inhabited by samurais in pantyhose masks.

"Who would find this funny?" she said.

For my second love, I sang about Archimedes basking in a pool, wife-swapping with Louis XVI.

"You're disgusting," she said.

For my third love, I painted a canvas of equidistant cannons, all beige, riding on top of rows of steppes mules, exploding in New Year fireworks.

"Don't ever show that to anyone," she said.

For my fourth love, I drew a picture of enchanted harpsichords bouncing upon *Hijra* bellies as they imbibed pipes of rubber and formaldehyde.

"It was cute, but you need to stop."

I could never love them, those women with iron bubbles. After a while even romance became dull. For years we were sent from ship to ship to integrate with new people, only to see so many of them get called into interrogation and never return. Or else they took four gulps of the Juc wine and crawled into their beds, never to wake. I breezed through women like wind through the open windows of a house, until numbness and isolation were the only refuge left.

During my interrogations I gave obscure answers to my captors and was possessed by laughing fits. They kept me alive, sparing me as madmen are spared. When, after every interview, the Jucs integrated us with a new group of humans, I looked for you. When I forgot your fake name, I remembered your real name was Dei. When I forgot your face, I remembered the way your black hair tossed about in the wind. When I felt so very sullen, so lonely in my fantasies, I remembered the world we made together, Dei's world, a world without judgment, with only the names we chose. We did more than preserve, more than eradicate the pain we felt. When I began to forget exactly what we did there, I remembered whispering through canyon walls.

I had lost count of my age when the Jucs underwent another regime change, and we humans were integrated with another colony. Finally, the interrogations stopped, and we were left some autonomy inside of a moon-sized space harbor. By then we had no distinctions. So many years had passed since any of us had seen a mountain, an island, a mound, or a canyon.

When our clans merged, the healthiest of us were chosen to form the policies that would guide our combined society. We gathered in a circular theater.

"The new Juc regime is in need of resources," said a blonde woman, her voice echoing across the chamber. "To prove our loyalty, we must send humans to work for them. Who will it be?"

"Give them the lamp-humpers," said someone in a colorful gown. "They love the Jucs so much, let them live among them, as pets!"

"No, no—give the Jucs our lowest-scoring students," said another, face impassive. "Those rotten apples will be satisfied with labor."

"Just give the Jucs the infertile," said another. "No chance of mixture there."

I resigned myself to the back of the chamber, sitting in the balcony's last row. There I spotted a woman at the corner of the aisle, tucked snugly inside a Jucs foldable chair, just large enough to frame her nestled body.

"Do I know you?" I whispered, as if through an echo chamber.

"I don't think so." Her eyes floated to mine, her face in that forced smile, the only kind we humans were capable of. "Do I know you?"

"I don't know."

"Sorry." She leaned her head into her palms. "It's just my blood pressure. They are keeping it low." A bluish bruise marked her inner elbows, a dark pool in the earthy soil of her skin.

We listened to the new human leadership debate our new divisions—the Juc-lovers, the low-scorers, the infertile. Soon others emerged. The criminal. The drunk. The perverse. They called a vote to decide who would be condemned, and who would be spared. All that court and convocation, all that vested authority. For what?

"I can't do this," I said.

The woman shook her head. "Come, help me walk out."

We sat together on a metal bench, observing the stars through a thick glass. We watched the emptiness of space, where humans were forever banned. With the station's slow rotation, a green and blue planet came into view. A place where we could never step foot. A place without fog, and without us.

I told her of the purges I had lived through. The scattered machines that no one could recreate. She told me how the Jucs shot her tribe through with some chemical that her own kind had developed in the mounds. It kept them docile and desperate for Juc guidance. High blood pressure when they refused to work. Low pressure, brittle nerves, when they spoke of revolt.

"How have you survived?" I asked.

"How did you?"

"I don't know. There was nothing special about me. What were you like back on Earth?"

"I don't remember that anymore. I chose to forget it."

"Me too."

We sat in silence.

"Sometimes I like to pretend," she said. "That on Earth, I grew up on a field of grass. Somehow the fog was not there. Just me."

"And no toys?"

A tear fell onto her cheek. "No toys. Every now and then, wind would come."

"And toss your hair up?"

"Yes."

Her arms shook as she pulled back her hair. I remembered her. A girl laughing in levitating somersaults.

"You know, I grew up in a jungle," I said.

"Really?"

"Yes. Somehow, the fog was not there."

"No monkeys in those trees?"

"No. But there was a hill I would climb."

"Yes. I remember that hill. It was steep—"

"—But it had a great view."

"Yes."

Somehow, a smile emerged between us.

"I remember I met a girl on that hill," you said. "In her world, anything could happen."

Knowing that a kiss couldn't change anything, I hoped that there were still ways to turn whispers into worlds.

Life

[handwritten: Mankind living among other species, acts like them.]

X

[handwritten: 80's Post-Terra It wouldn't last. Yeh laws in 103]

[handwritten: Mister Dzin is S? How Cumute]

Your dance caused my nails to extend past the palm rest until they scratched the down-sloped curves of the plastic grated floor. I fidgeted in my seat. Never had I seen a pure-blood human without an impregnated egg sack before. Who knew our kind could move with such skill and gyration? Your copper-painted skin flashed beams of yellow light, culling all my desire. Your hips slipping up and down made me forget the theater's decrepit decor. Your smile awoke the human nature inside of me and I was again the rampant, desiring youngster that brewed beneath every Pjara. You were so unlike those bovine humans who gathered in the city streets, dragging their sacks about.

In this life I was of your kind—but so unlike your kind. My wit and acumen, praised by all races, had enabled me to climb out of those work colonies and into the markets. I had made a small fortune selling spliced lungs to clients who wanted to inhale toxic air, spliced legs to mimic equestrian poses, and then the cosmetic products: spliced claws, spliced chins, spliced torsos. Whenever I encountered other humans, they saw me as their savior, someone who understood their ancient technology, who could remake it (or at

259

least, pay others to do so). But they were not to be trusted with it. Look at what they had already done, those humans with no patron to watch over them!

After the performance I demanded that the proprietor, a stout Mrien, take me to you. His red gel-like skin absorbed my threats in a tremble.

"I set something up for you," the Mrien said. "Go now. Mankind needs their rest. It must hibernate."

"Man-brained fool," I said. "You better not try to run off with him!" I exposed my stacked teeth and extended my nails, right toward the Mrien's belly. "If they have strength enough to carry those pregnancies for months, and go through labor, then surely it can have energy enough to see me!"

Acquiescing, the proprietor brought me backstage. You sat in a dark room, your hands clasped and raised toward me. A spotlight lit your face like an ethereal pigment. You knew how to mask yourself well. Knowing this, I still could not help but have you, my own little mankind! A pulse from my mother race.

"What is your name?" I asked. You stared back with a muted consternation.

"Its name is Mister Dzin," the Mrien said.

Dzin, the frail beautiful insect whose wings the Tuek clipped and decorated about their abodes.

"Why does it not speak for itself?" I asked.

"This one, it does not speak. Either it chooses not to, or it cannot. Also, it has no sack."

"No sack?"

"Either it was removed, or it was born without one."

So, this was why you danced. Unable to bear children for the moon mines, unable to respond to commands with words, you spoke only with your body. Your eyes startled me when I glanced at you, and I was reminded of the human who raised me, its wax-yellow hair. But you carried something so inhuman—the fire and demand shooting from your eyes. The humans I had known were servile, weak, and drunk. You were one of a kind.

"I must have it," I told the proprietor. "You will not screw me on this deal." Childbearing humans always fetched more than juveniles.

"You have young ones then?" he asked.

"No." As soon as I said it your eyes glared up at me, your smile turned to that odd cracked mouth that you carried in the dance.

"But this human cannot bear children."

"I know that!"

"Oh. Well. My aunt had a human once, who stopped birthing. It made a fine leather pouch."

"You were truly born from the wrong end of a human!"

"So that's it! Of course—"

"Of course, I will be *discreet*! I just want it."

"But does it want you?"

Our glares pounced on the human. You, Mister Dzin. The glaring spotlight above had turned your pretty face gold. Suddenly you laughed—a trilling, devilish sound.

"It wants me too?" I asked the proprietor.

"Of course not! It is human. It just wants your technology."

I took you through the painful crowds of the department corridors, instructing you with my spliced tentacles to stay three steps behind me, as if you were my child bearer. Besides some untoward gazes, we were left alone. Once we were away from the crowd I felt at ease.

"You must know our love will be forbidden," I told you. "Others will be suspicious of a human without an egg sack. So, you must be caged in our home." I stroked your long hair. It was thick, and its oils made my nails extend only slightly. "But your cage will be one of gold."

You seemed to understand, your mouth curved in a smile.

Once we reached my abode, you walked in ahead of me, eager perhaps to see the inside of a rich splicer's home, decorated with vivid dzin wings. You followed the streams of water that twisted along the jagged floor. Perhaps you knew where the water came from: a heavy static cloud of three-dimensional images and sounds. It was the very technology that many of our kind had been traded for eons ago, a technology few of us had permission to use. You stared at the device, mesmerized, then looked at me in distress. The Mrien was right.

"Don't worry," I said. "I will not forbid you to use it." I taught you how to access the human archives, how the static hissed back from voice commands. You immediately took over, searching in the music library—the old historical files that only scholars of human culture could access.

Music played from the cloud in a human tongue, a language I could not understand. Your legs began to shake as the volume went up. It sounded like pure noise, discordant and harsh. Tears welled in your eyes. Then I heard your voice, matching that of the music's: "écoute-moi,"

Such sentimentalism. Such pointless pining for a dead past—my dzin, so human. The next morning I would call the Mrien, demanding he take you back. You would leave, and I would never learn your language or hear your songs. Years would pass. Decades of cycling through a revolving door of housekeepers and spouses. I would never think of you, or your voice. I would die in old age believing that you, my little mankind, my dzin without wings, were not worth my time.

Life

Y

Faces popped on the screen like daisies basking in the afternoon sun. Fresh, with bright yellow eyes and blossoming smiles. "Aufweidersehn!" a face said. "Zaijian!" said another. "Ivadai!" shouted another face. "Ijeoma!" said another. Words dissolved onto the screen in the Hyul language,

"From the Human Race:

Goodbye!"

I waved goodbye to the screen, since no one was around. I sat at a desk melded into a blue-tinged white wall, and the door was shut airtight to keep toxins from escaping the small booth. As the machine scanned my body for the correct dose, I read a sticker pasted onto the wall: "Keep in mind that your body is fungible and perishable. We guarantee that every corpse in our booths will be recycled, with each part accounted for. No waste. No excess."

Finally, the next screen:

Please choose a method of self-determination:

- o *Ingestion*

- o *Respiratory*

- o *Injection*

I selected "injection" and another video loaded with brassy words.

Your Life, Preserved by the Hyul

On the screen, one of the immovable Hyul stood meditating, his jacket slung, the polish of his pearly marble skin refracting a bright red "L"-shape from the second sun. A human child brushed past, carrying an exciting amount of white and pink fluffy toys, human-style stuffed cats and teddy bears. Overburdened, the girl darted through a rock garden and slipped on a piece of smooth white stone. The Hyul caught her in a lightning quick action. The girl found herself in her protector's arms, a glint of the red sun upon its abdomen. The immovable remained still while the girl, dizziness fading, snatched up her dropped toys.

Your Life with the Hyul, a Chance for Sanctuary

Video footage from the first tribe to integrate. A school of Hyul immovables stood at the edge of a landing pad, their only movement their antennae twitching about. A white ship, polished like an immovable's skin, landed on the pad. Humans shuffled out one by one, moving slowly, as the immovable diplomats had taught them. They showed horrid signs of toxicity, their feet wrought with sores and their arms covered in warts, skin covering their eyes. Some of them could not help but gawk at the immovables who stood as still as statues.

Your Life

A Journey

Comes to an End

That same buzzing sound as the next interface loaded. I scratched my left arm, tearing back scraggy skin, and poked my index finger into the wart that had turned into a thumb-sized cavern. The itching was getting intense—but soon it would end.

An echo reverberated, a word, perhaps. Was it back again? That whisper? A moment of panic hit me, but it was just a buzz from the booth. Thank the Hyul. Not on my last day.

Stored Memories Detected. Analyzing…

What was this?

Seven Stored Memory Scrolls Detected. These are stored in your cerebrum, but have been locked due to your past agreements. Clause 16(e) states that these memories can be accessed only upon irreversible self-determination. Would you like to access them now?

o   *Yes*

o   *No*

Made sense. The earliest memory I had was the smell of sulfide in that basement where I awoke, almost twenty years before, in the year 184, not knowing my name. I had been strapped to a table, a memory drip hooked into my cerebrum. Some dark cold room, somewhere below a noisy homo sapiens bar. Someone had blocked me from my memories, or I had done it to myself. An extreme case, indeed. Not just blocking memories of a lost love or some scandalous incident, but to block off everything, all that I was. Not that it was hard to get back into the swing of things. I found that I could play guitar, and I could recite carols, hymns, ballads, and raps. Naturally, I did not miss what I could not remember.

The hell with it—I swiped yes.

Please keep in mind that according to Hyul Law, S4-Level Memory Access is only available just prior to Self-Determination. If your memories cause you to change your mind, it will be impossible to stop the process. Do you wish to proceed?

o   *Yes*

o   *No*

I pushed my finger into the cavernous wart on my right arm. I'd grown used to the pain, the itch that grew deeper beneath the skin whenever I scratched it. My stomach grumbled—oh, silly me, I forgot a last meal. Well, get on with it—I swiped yes and picked up the cerebral port from the side of the machine, inserting the input below my right earlobe.

#

Memories opened like a chasm. A thousand caves to explore, each with branching routes. One came clearly—I was an adult, thirty-one years of age, which would make it the year 170, Post-Terra. I was in the same building, the Center of Human Self-Determination, in a booth—perhaps the same booth, but didn't they all look the same? I had just played a carol at a Hyul banquet, where in the dressing room I happened upon a set of posters from past players. Near the bottom of the stack, I had found remnants of a blocked memory, an image of myself with a lighter skinned human: I at the guitar and she at the piano, the two traditional human instruments. In the poster image I was much younger—perhaps just entering adulthood, around three in Hyul years. The auditorium was the largest in Hyul, and the crowd was really feeling it—feeling us.

I had come to the Center of Human Self-Determination to open memory ports, to find you, the other human in the poster. We had made a formidable pair, wearing matching garb of black denim. You were a woman with a groggy, off-center smile, your left eye in an uncoordinated wink, aimed at the camera.

Inside the psi-booth, I inserted my ID card and the following data popped up on the screen:

Your memories are upon restricted access until your chosen date of Self-Determination, from contracts you signed previously. Would you like a log of your reasoning?

o   *Yes*

o   *No*

The logs—notes written to your future self about why you blocked your own memories.

Accessing…

On came my own voice—sounded pure, honed, well-trained: "You want to know about her? Don't tell me you came here just for that. It's nothing worth knowing, trust me. Trust yourself. You blocked off six memories of her before. *Six*. And why go back? To stay with someone who would make you miserable? Shit gets into her head. Political differences—it doesn't matter. Tomorrow is the first time I'll wake without her. Please, let that feeling last until the disease takes me."

End of log. Select an option.

o   *Access Memory Logs*

o   *Access Education Logs*

o   *Self-Determined Suicide*

o   *Exit*

I swiped "memory logs" again, and listened to my past self's rant, scanning for any information that might lead me to her—to you. We had sold out the biggest auditorium on Hyul; on set we sparked together like two fireflies in a frisson of light. What could have happened? "Political differences"? What the shit kind of reason was that?

As I searched for any way to bypass the system, I discovered a dropped piece of paper, a torn lined sheet from a small notebook, carrying a long access code full of numbers and Hyul characters. I looked about. For the first time in this lifetime, I heard that ethereal voice that had followed me from one life to the next.

"Ha, ha, ha…"

Frightened, I darted around the small booth.

"Don't try to act as if you have feelings," the voice whispered. "No need to pretend you care about anything other than her." The whisper was quiet, so quiet I felt my body leaning in, seduced by the tone.

The screen glowed yellow. I swiped the "Access Education Logs" option and inserted the code.

Granting Access to Logs of Human History. Level Four Clearance Only. Proceed?

o *Yes*

o *No*

I selected "yes" and data rushed into me in a waterfall. I had received information before—equations, carol lyrics, news data, and the like, but never like this. Images of humans ran through me, I couldn't breathe in it, I felt tossed by the rush—the smell of some chemical, thick and humid. Then screams of horror from fire-lit houses and torched cities. Then the thunderous gallop of extinct animals. I realized this was no nightmare, or perhaps, no *mere* nightmare. This was our history, human history. In it I heard none of the carols I sang, none of the heroes we celebrated. Every memory pulled at me, sending jolts of pain—and they just kept going, year after year, decade after decade, century after century. Just how far back did our violence go? Where were the men we had been taught to worship, the great heroes eradicated by disease? Here were men dressed in puffy white wigs, men holding sharp metal covered in blood, men cutting down plants as tall as buildings, mowing them with machines, replacing them with steel structures that collapsed from the chaotic spill of wind and water. All the records of human annals sunk deep into my memory.

I came to, feeling the automated buckles strap my body snug in the seat. Body wet from tears, spit, and sweat. On screen were images meant to soothe me—faces like daisies, dried from the long, unrelenting roast of the sun's rays. From those happy faces, from those spread-out arms, from those obscene Santa hats, I heard only a symphony of cries. I felt the blood of all those who stood up, and the calm reserve of those who kept seated.

And that was the first time I heard his voice, soft at first, the voice of human history turning from whisper to scream: "Shame!"

I stared at the screen, at that option staring me down.

o Self-Determined Suicide

"Do it honorably." Something inside me drew out the words like a resonating guitar strum.

Thirteen years passed before I found anything about you. In that time, I picked up the formal Hyul tongue. I practiced not cursing and not using human-Hyul pidgin. I avoided phrases like "picture this," "long time no see," and "love ya baby." The closer I got to the Hyul, the less those memories of human history erupted within me.

Some years later I got my big break—a Hyul found me cute, adopted me, and off I went, wearing its brown rustic neck brace. I taught human culture to its children while tolerating other humans, having to eat their slops of meat and potatoes in a traditional human style buffet. Eventually those memories of history didn't hurt any more. They were just surprising, like taking a swig of an unlabeled drink, not knowing if it was water or pure alcohol.

One chooses one's indignity, for sure, dressing in Santa hats for a human race never worth a pinch, or acting as a trained pet for the Hyul, a race who had never been disunited. For their entire history they never shed the life of another; they only ever died through self-determined suicide. If only we could breed with them—but why would they ever allow it?

The images of human history only jolted into me when I ate human food, potatoes or rice, and I would feel the starvation of millions, the buried bodies, the prisons where lumps of feed were merciful. It all came too much too soon, at every event where human memorabilia conjured the horrors of our past. And me, the only one among them who knew our history, our real history, not the Santa Claus stories, not the stories of heroic men. The only humans I saw were those who raped and enslaved, those who died from their own invented disease, leaving only us women to roam the galaxy as pets. Living with the immovables, I could nearly get away. I dressed like them, sighing my way through daily chores and small tasks, covering my human-stink with their colognes. But when I saw their pet humans, I felt saturated by the sorrows of slaves, debtors, and imprisoned. The uncompiled trash.

After four years with my Hyul family, I found myself moving up, to a Hyul special school, teaching human culture and history—finally, the real thing, the death, the violence. To the immovables, human history was a strange mythology, with great but very flawed leaders, and strange deities like Jehovah, Allah, the CEO, and Santa Claus. Our primitive violence was a spectacle to them—that a race could ever develop the technology to split the atom, only to use it to kill without restraint. My Hyul students listened to my stories upon white moon rock, some of them with crass eyes, some of them riveted.

Years later, I was a favorite on their campus. I learned to never look them in the cerebrum, though it aligned just with my height, and they always stared at me. Dressed like them, I stood in absolute stillness, and moved only in rapid, decisive actions. My lessons did not threaten them in the least. If anything, students left my lectures feeling more assured, happier to be Hyul.

In 183 you came into my life again. I was forty-four, and by chance found a note left behind by an immovable student near my desk, scrawled in a mixture of Hyul-human pidgin. That note, if I had never picked it up, if I had never been curious enough to discover that the lyrics were part of an old song you and I once sang, if I had never pieced through the words and felt their immense power behind the song's poppy surface, I may never have thought of you again.

On the paper was a traditional carol:

> I understand that Christmas is here,
> I understand that we sing of holiday cheer,
> Cheering as happily as humans in beautiful Greek dresses,
> Mothers and fathers, sons and daughters, in Hyul collars,
> I promise you that Christmas—uh!—ka-blam!

Christmas—uh-huh!—ka blam!—is coming
soon!

The more I read it, the more the potential of the music
grew upon me. When I sang it, I realized it was our song—
our voices, singing of the happiness of humans in their neck
braces. Songs of fighting back. Since I happened upon human history—*real* human history, I had refused those carols, and never noticed it was my own voice singing them.

With access to the Hyul libraries, I used the lyrics to
find you. Born the same year as myself, you were of the Euro
tribe. Your name was Celine. You could not read, but you
were a popular entertainer in the human club The Underground. We were entertainers together, singing carols, and
starting a movement of human pride—*human pride*! To
think of it! Pride in what?

You were still alive. I located you in a human kennel,
at the limits of where the unbraced were permitted to live.
For so many years I had tried to forget you, to stave off the
human past and everyone connected to it.

"She's not worth it," that inner voice whispered. "Just
like the others. Blind to her own history. She is a lecher,
born of whorish loins, pleased to breed more human garbage."

"I must find her," I told the whisper. "I must know what
happened."

"Her bawdy veins only hold false drops. Her eyes have
sunk lives; her lips have contaminated cities; her words have
slain every maker of peace. As soon as she gives breath, another human suffers. She is your history's true inheritor."

"She does not know our history," I said. "But I can teach
her."

It was my first time in the human zone in over a decade. The very smell of human barbecue made me recall pieces of burnt flesh, the bodies of witches, prisoners, and enemies of war. I saw the tops of human-style buildings, monuments to towers once constructed by slaves. In every smiling face I felt that deep ocean of destruction—fields strewn with human bones, skin pierced and wrinkled from starvation. I passed the Center of Human Culture, with hollow statues and a miniature Taj Mahal, and felt only disgust.

Outside The Underground club, two dogs fought each other beside an unfinished mural. A crowd of humans stood by, squatting on their haunches, panting in suspense, their hands waving out packs of money. The scrawny black dog with blood-shot eyes snarled out of his fanged maw. The humans roared when the animal got a firm bite into the other's lower neck. The black dog started eating the other. Trained to be vicious, the canine had developed a taste for its own kind. The weaker mutt's leg snapped. The black dog chewed the fur, the skin, the muscle still pumping, the leg still twitching.

The bouncers waved me inside the club. My quick movements and Hyul plating gave me a distanced authority. I found you, Celine, in a small, unheated dressing room. You stood with your back to me, wearing a human uniform: blue jeans, burgundy jacket, white collared shirt.

"Do you remember me?" I said.

You appraised me for a moment, unsmiling. "*Zoo animal*," you said in a sneer.

"Zoo animal?"

"That was your nickname." You watched me in the dressing room mirror. "The Hyul loved to stare at you. Is it safe to say you don't remember me at all, then? *Baga!*" turning to me, "you were always so quick to erase yourself!"

You approached me, the smell of cigarettes following quickly behind. You reached toward me, and I blocked my breast with my fist.

"Huh," you took a can of hair spray from a counter of human beauty products.

I told you why I came. That human history was not as you thought. "We lusted for power." I said. "An endless war for power. Like—like a dog eating its own kind."

"And what do you want me to do about it?" You sat atop a sleek steel appliance, your jeans making whisking sounds as your legs kicked back and forth.

"I heard a song that you and I used to sing. It said something about human pride."

Your eyes stuck on mine. A wave of heat fell upon me so intense you seemed to feel it too. "Human Power," you said. "One of our biggest hits. We would have been set for life, had that dickwad manager not pilfered our cut. So. You erased those parts of yourself too."

"We come from warring tribes, Celine. Mine Oromo, yours Greek—we would be killing each other if not for the Hyul. Don't take my word for it."

"Hyul propaganda. Their society is the best, that's what they sell, and you bought into it—again!"

"But it's true! I can prove it. I can share this history with you, if we meld our minds together. We can keep this history—spread it to others, sing about it in our songs—we could reunite, Celine. Everyone deserves to know the truth. We deserve to know our own history, no matter how violent it was. It is still ours."

You seemed overcome with heat and took off your burgundy jacket. "You really don't remember why we *split*, do you?" you tossed the jacket into the dressing room mirror. "*Baga*, if you did, you would never ask me such a thing! We are proud people, beautiful people, no matter who keeps us down—no matter who *joins the other side.*"

"It's a terrible history, Celine. There's no shame in facing the truth."

"Is this what you're teaching the Hyul? How great they are for enslaving us?"

"I am a human being first. I do this because without the Hyul—"

You kissed me—perhaps you could not help it. I spit your saliva out.

"Idiot!" you spat at me in a web across my breast. Wiping your chin, "you really did erase everything! I knew you would."

"I only came to give you information. Facts."

Your voice broke into a sigh. "Why do you have this point of view?"

"Because it's the correct one. Why do you have yours?"

"Because it's the right one."

I made to leave, though I didn't want to leave you. Your clear-headedness, even when based on lies, never lacked poetry. *Political differences*, that was why we broke apart. I stood with you in silence, and even the silence we shared felt familiar. Somehow I knew, when your eyes turned up, that you were bristling with an idea.

"Wait, Abby," you said. "Let's make a deal. I'll take in your memories, if you take in mine. The day, it must be over twenty years ago now, when we left each other. If you had this memory, you'd know I can never side with you."

"A challenge?"

You stood, heading for your mossy green backpack on a box next to me. "Call it a good dose of human competition." You scooped a handful of granola from your bag. "Or have the Hyul made you such a pet that you forgot your own bark?"

Listening to you chew with that chaotic crunch sparked something in me, waking up that drive, perhaps, a yearning to prove you wrong.

"Fine," I said, knowing nothing in the universe could make me change.

You maneuvered me down a dark, narrow passage. The stench told me I was in a street of plague-stricken humans who had refused to take the honorable route of self-determination. My eyes adjusted and I saw lobes growing from foreheads and children licking moon rock. I grew afraid of the marauders lurking nearby—the type who would kill you for your boots. Many of them strained on the pavement, hands to their heads. Their screams split through the darkness:

"No—I will not go, no, don't make me go through this again!"

"I killed her—because of you, I killed her!"

"Make the voice stop!"

"These lost ones grow by the day," you told me, hustling through the miscreants. "Tortured by that inner voice telling them to end it all."

We sidestepped past a mother and her deformed child senselessly braying as they reeled back from the voice in their heads—no longer a whisper, but a jolting, lurching voice, commanding them to die.

"It's a new type of psychological warfare. Hyul propaganda. They access our brain with radio waves. Even I have heard the voice. This is why we need human pride. We once fought this urge. Remember? No—you don't."

You took me into a musty basement shrouded with the sour smell of sulfide. Inside, gleaming under the dim light, was the metallic meld machine—a black market memory share device developed by humans at the height of our race. It sat on top an iron chair, a heavy-looking thing with an iron-like scent reminiscent of rust and blood. It must have gone through multiple middlemen to come this far undetected.

Two white beds stood on both sides of the device. A man in white robes strapped a cord into me, and connected it to that grumbling machine, and then to you, reclining on a bed.

"I've waited a long time to strap you to this bed, my dear," said the memory artist, her fingers pinching your white skin. With every pinch I felt a strange wince.

"You're connected right?" the doctor said to me.

I nodded. "Celine, are you ok?" I said.

"She'll be fine," said the memory artist, and turned on the machine.

I sunk into the folds of your memory. I heard your faint groan as human history copied from my memory into yours. You seemed restless, but I felt calm, warm. I was in the year 166, in an apartment decorated in human memorabilia. You watched me from the foot of our bed, writing on a paper pad. You handed it to me:

> *Let's do it. They restrict our speaking, they censor all our songs, they bug our homes. What else can we do? They pushed us too far.*

I nodded, and we embraced.

Months later, I was late. The Hyul knew immediately. They required us to go into a human clinic to watch videos of horrific births—children with folds of fat covering their eyes, small fist-sized babies letting out a single scream, then stillness. Children born impurely. An automated machine took my blood, then gave the results of my test:

Abnormal Embryo genetics. Defected birth likely. Recommend self-determination.

After the clinic, you and I, hand-in-hand, went for traditional longan ice cream. Our baby craved it.

My third trimester. On stage I played guitar, the baby filling my belly out, protruding onto the instrument as the amp's vibration hummed. The audience of humans of every color stared at me, in awe. So few would risk having a child. Some had never seen a pregnant human before. They put their fists up. Then you, encouraged by those who cheered us on, free-styled over your piano: "Nothin' to lose, nothing to lose, nothing to lose."

And I, to a cheering crowd: "Just our collars!"

"Nothing to lose, nothing to lose, nothing to lose!"

With my fist raised to the sky, I felt liquid running down my leg, wetting the stage.

"Just our collars!"

We named her Little Panda. You liked that she had my skin. For that first week, the child looked perfect. It wasn't until she started breathing in long snorts that we began to worry. Then a fester appeared on her right arm and the child cried out at every hour. The cry was strange, a groan, a wavy pitch, as if she had practiced it for a song. You sobbed whenever you heard it, and so did I. Sometimes we held each other, but usually we crawled into spaces alone, hearing that inner voice that drove many mad: "It's in your blood. An infection. A parasite. You are its host. Kill the child. Kill yourself."

We fought against it together, talked each other down from self-determination, moved mountains to keep our sanity. We would not give our daughter to doubt. But the child got sicker. The groan a bit louder. The warts a bit thicker. Sores plucked from her skin. She showed all the signs of the fallout: the deep crevices in her arms, crusted and dry like a hole dug by invisible spoons, a hole leading toward her heart. Our neighbors heard the cries. Word spread. Those musicians, bringing a child into the world, when they were not an approved genetic match. They should have known better.

We were watching all the pomp and piety of the Christmas parade from our window when we received a message that our child would be picked up for self-determination the next day. Our Little Panda's cries, by then, had grown flat.

The human doctor arrived, dressed like a Hyul, complete with a meditative stillness. You mustered enough courage to take the screaming child into the bathroom. You locked yourself in—a symbolic act, as any Hyul could easily break down the door.

"You want to kill her!" you screamed through the walls.

"She has gone crazy," the doctor said, plugging her ears from the child's cries.

"They just want us to die quietly!" you yelled out over our daughter's screams. "I won't let that happen!"

"Don't just stand there," the doctor said, going for the door. "Don't you have a key, Abby?"

"It's not what you think," I said, improvising. "In traditional human culture, self-determined death is unnatural, especially for children."

"I haven't heard that one, but anyway—medicine is medicine."

"Celine is not just Euro—she is from the Greek tribe. We are raising our child according to those beliefs."

"I haven't heard of this tribe. What holiday do they have?"

I kept my palm on the bathroom door. "We have our own ways of doing things. Let us give our child the last rights."

"Yesterday was Christmas, we already gave you an extra day."

"*For god's sakes*!" you cried through the door.

"No," I said firmly, feeling your sobs through the door. "Today is a holiday too."

"What?" The doctor said. "On the day *after* Christmas?"

"Yes," I made as if I knew, and tapped on the calendar of human holidays, hung just beside the bathroom door. "Says right here. *Boxing Day*. A Greek holiday, of course."

"Boxing Day! Right. I've heard of it. Is it really Greek? Of course. *Fine*. But if the child is not self-determined by tomorrow—"

"Of course! Now—please respect our traditions!"

Our Little Panda did not last through the night. Her sputtering and wringing lost energy. Then we started to miss the screams. You tried to shake them back into her, those screams that meant both pain and life, to shake away that silence that said our child had perished. We held each other, but mostly we were alone, like so many parents throughout human history who stood over their children, watching them sputter out of life. You rocked our Little Panda back and forth, a pendulum losing steam. In that unbearable silence, I picked up my guitar.

> "Baby, Baby, it's time to go,
>
> Baby, Baby, tears no more,
>
> Baby, Baby, tears no more"

Our child was a lump, just a lump.

"No! No!"

I heard screams. It was not from the me in the past, but the me in that dark, sulfide-scented basement, strapped into that bed. It was my voice screaming: "Please don't make me relive this. Please. My baby. My Little Panda. Don't go."

"Please!" Then it was your voice, screaming from the adjacent bed, louder than mine. "Don't make me see this!

This is not our history. This cannot be our history—we were never this cruel! This is not us! Don't make me watch this!"

I blinked my eyes open, saw the straps holding me down. I unbuckled them in a frisson, then reached for the humming memory machine. My heartbeat pulled me back into the memories, but I resisted. Not that death, not again. Across from me, you were unbuckling yourself too, your anger transfixed on the device, lunging toward it like frenzied prey. We crashed upon each other, slamming the machine hooked into our brains, and then—

#

On the screen, faces like daisies, each one with perfect shiny skin. Their skin was fester-less, wart-less, scar-less, waiting to be picked and taken home. I winced, back in the year 203. My finger dug further into the cavern on my arm. When I pulled the finger out, a web of mucus followed.

The First Scroll of Memories Has Been Viewed.
Would you like to proceed?

o Yes

o No

Could I take more? What could be worse than what I had already seen? I swiped yes.

Six Remaining Memory Scrolls Can Be Opened.
Please Choose:

o Scroll 2

- o *Scroll 3*

- o *Scroll 4*

- o *Scroll 5*

- o *Scroll 6*

- o *Scroll 7*

Six scrolls. Six times I had erased some memory of you. Six times we came together and tried again, only to end up alone, in a loop that went over and over and over.

Scroll 2

The year 154, we were fifteen in human years. You kissed me on top of your beanbag—I had a girlfriend, this was not right! Our genetic IDs were a mismatch, but the music you liked was so fantastic—your blue jeans torn to look so human.

Selfishly, I confessed to my girlfriend what I had done.

"With Celine? That white *puta* doesn't even have a Hyul parent!"

I listened to your favorite song all night, barely awake in my room, feeling your kiss. How did I become the type of person who kissed an unbraced? But the song, oh! It made me feel alive, it gave me a place to go. How could I? I knew I had to erase this trespass from my memory. But the song!

Scroll 3

A couple of years later. I gripped the thigh of an exotic dancer, the one made up in a grass skirt. I called her *sister* to keep it from going too far. I imagined her while I was with you, I couldn't keep her off my mind. You knew. You always found out.

"Why is it always women like her?" you cried. "Am I not beautiful to you?"

But I couldn't stop thinking about her. I wanted her to take me away, away from nauseating political discussions, away from all this talk of human pride. Away from the Hyul defining every part of us. When I noticed that you stopped asking about her, I started following you.

"I just want to live life to the fullest," you said, after I caught you with a fan who looked just like me.

"I'll never, ever forgive you," I said in tears.

"I'm sorry, but we both made mistakes."

"And we can erase them."

Scroll 4

In our early twenties, we sipped illegal alcohol in a den, and sang between gulps. I strummed a guitar, but during my verse, you sidled up to a student conducting a project on storytellers of the human oral tradition. It was all manufactured crap about free speech, about the Hyul being the kindest masters we had ever received.

"Do you fuck her?" I asked you once.

"Sometimes."

"But is it making love?"

286

"What's the difference?"

I sang about our legendary green Earth. The students leaned in with wonder though I made it up as I went along, getting louder to drown out the thoughts of you in the other room.

That night, on the pearly white shuttle zooming through Hyul caverns, we bickered in front of the students. "I want to try new things while we're still young," you said. I said you could, but the pain was too much for me. Go ahead, but then the pain. I told you not to waste your youth. But the pain.

Pain can be erased, I remembered.

Scroll 5

I was twenty-four. Our manager asked why I stayed with you. "You could be playing solo carols," she said. "Or writing some decent etudes for the Hyul students."

Our band was the two of us. Our harmony on stage, our love, a lamp warming the faces of the crowd.

"I don't care if the Hyul hate us or not." I told our manager. "We're a team, Celine and I. And we already have an audience—our people."

I found you in a bar playing for free to humans who undressed you with their eyes. You doffed your jacket, then your blouse, then your jeans. I started to raise my voice, but yours was louder—we were lucky no one recognized us without your Greek dress and my Egyptian crown.

I slapped you—you lunged at me, and soon we were kissing on the floor. I hated that my body reacted to you. You nuzzled my ear, my neck, as the bar music popped on our big song. It was filthy. And I never wanted to remember myself so pathetic.

Scroll 6

Our Christmas song rang everywhere within the human zone. But we were tired of each other. No time alone, and when we were alone, we slept around. We seemed to have perfect lives, except that there was this thing between us that we could not explain.

During an interview, a journalist asked us about integration. You said we were not supposed to discuss it. "I don't do politics, only music," you said, a line that I had asked you to repeat, over and over.

"But all your music is political."

"That's just an interpretation," you said, your face turning pale.

"We are guests here," I added. "It is human nature to be kind to our hosts."

In the back room, after the interview, we argued, our voices raised in loud groans.

"My heart is in this just as much as yours!" I said.

"I don't care about your heart," you responded. "How much are you willing *to risk*?"

You stormed off. Though I had no memory of your prior infidelities, I knew you were going to find someone, anyone, so long as they agreed you were right.

Scroll 7

A year before I became pregnant. We joked about the tribe of our future child. We laughed at the idea. I wanted our child to look like me. We seemed to be just joking, until we weren't.

"Let's just do the opposite of what all the doctors say!" I said, half-joking. "And do it, why not?"

We laughed, and time passed, fading fast. We were sort of together—geared for each other, but also a sham. Sometimes we made love all night, drunk, passionate, and sometimes we gazed away, dreaming of the children we could never have.

"I want to forget it," I said. "All these jokes about having a child. It's too much. They'll never let us."

Forgetting, it seemed, could not stop us.

\#

All Memory Scrolls Have Been Accessed. Self Determination Now Proceeding.

The automatic straps buckled me in. Having given up my rights to life, there was no longer any need for formalities, no more videos celebrating integration.

I felt pricks on my back, causing me to gasp.

You and I, we kept falling back into each other. The sun was always between us.

On the screen, faces waved me goodbye with smiles like daisies dancing in the sunlight. Above the happy faces, the screen read my date of death. The twenty-sixth of December, the day after Christmas. A Greek holiday, I recalled.

The things I had done in that past life stared at me from the ship's off-white ceiling. I, who betrayed humanity, who wanted nothing to do with my own kind, who fled to our oppressors, who left you when you needed me on your side.

"That's what keeps bringing me here," I whispered, sensing Cryss' presence in my stateroom. "Collusion. Compliance. Obedience. That's why I keep coming back."

And there sat Cryss in a white marble tunic, looking just like the humans who mimicked the Hyul, just like myself in my past life. Her body was as still as a statue, her face shiny like enamel, her eyes pinned upon me mid-stride.

"No god or structure gifted this place to us," I continued. "We willed it into being. As we died, betraying all we loved, we dared to imagine a place without them. We imagined ourselves gods."

Cryss moved in a flash, then stood frozen still, her hands in a heart shape. "My word!" she said in a high-pitched voice. "After four millennia, and seven times crossing over—you catch on quick."

"It was there again," I said hand to temple, invoking the memory before it slipped away. "The Djinni. The God. The Destroyer. But this time it didn't want me, only my death. Every human in the stream seemed to hear its whispers."

"All the bloomers speak of it," Cryss said, her eyes set-

290

tled on the white wall, her arms now in a thinker's position, chin rested on fist. "A voice telling them to give up. On what? On life, on a future. And why shouldn't they?"

"The Destroyer is bound to watch the human race," I said to the statue. "But what if there is no human race to watch? Is that its goal? What do we do?"

The statue could not help but squelch a smile, appearing in cracks, as if an artist had marked her. "Why, nothing, of course."

Her indifference roused me. "I know how to bring S here. She just has to want it. That's all. To desire this place is to bloom in it." Cryss had never appeared in my stateroom before. I felt the colors in the room were not all my own. "You've always known this," I said, tense upon the mattress. "Everyone here has played the betrayer. That's what causes them to imagine this place. Isn't it?"

Cryss spoke in a caustic whisper: "Can you guess what this ship was like before the structure? Souls self-flagellated in their bunkers. Bloomers stabbed themselves in the necks, ransacked with guilt, until they leapt. *dis-supare*: minds locked eternally into the stream. When I arrived, I had seen the wildest depravity of human beings. To Apollo I made an eternal vow: what happened to me would never happen again. The Ilium is peace. It is harmony. The souls who arrive here need this. Who are you to judge them— seven times, you've played the betrayer. And they call *me* false?" Laughter came from the statue, though she remained stone. "You betray her, you come here, you pine, you whine, you go back, you find another girl, and you betray her too. Worse—you fool yourself that this soul is the same as the last. *Yalŋus*: You seek repentance, but the next betrayal hangs upon your naked chest."

"She's real."

"How do you know? Does she have a symbol? A smell? A gesture, even? Something as minuscule as a gesture? Think of something, some give-away. Anything? Tell me— because when curious souls ask me this question, entranced by your story, I have nothing to say. Oh, that doesn't stop them from making things up. S, the one with the hair red as fire. S, who always smells of olives. S, the defiant one. Is that it? Is she defiant? But then again—defiance can be found anywhere there is power."

I couldn't think. She had been needing to tell me this for centuries. I could not imagine a reply. How could I explain your soul? You were you.

"Do you remember the last time we spoke?" Cryss said, her statue eyes on mine. My arms drew back toward the bedframe, my legs spread out, as if manacled to the sheets. She did not need her lackeys. Her will came like tendrils binding me to the bed. "There is some truth in their stories. When the Greeks took Troy, not a single soul was spared. They didn't show an ounce of mercy. Troy's corpse was hung with his family's. They even killed the children, *my* children. It was extermination. Everything happened just as Troy said it would, before he sent me away. Yes, I moved to Greece. I had more children. I worshipped new gods. But I learned to survive, just as he wanted. They killed our bodies, but then they killed our story. First the Greek singers left us out. Then the poets maimed us. The writers tossed dung upon our corpses. The prophesiers made us monsters. They replaced us with something morbid, a melodrama of betrayal and sex. That is only a façade. Not even love's shadow." A beatific smile struck her lips. "Your love is an illusion. Here is the reality: in every life, you find someone like her. Someone who provides ample wood for the bonfires of your imagination. Mad with lust and willing to believe whatever cockamamie story, you start to call her your destiny."

"No," I said, but my face showed different. Cryss voiced a thought buried deep within me, a thread I hadn't dared pull on my own. The stream was an ugly place, and the Ilium was no better—full of souls pleasing their lust for all eternity. But among all the nothing, you were color. "I will not give up."

Cryss' body flashed, and in a blink her arms were separated in a V, her eyes locked onto mine. "You pathetic little fetcher!" she screamed in a grated tenor that shook the stateroom. "You're nothing special."

"You cannot stop me." I willed the stateroom window's glass to fall out in a perfect square.

"You are challenging me?" Cryss shook her head. "Tut-tut!" Chains snaked from behind the bed, through my legs and arms. "Do you really believe I am afraid of you?" Her face was human now, red, and roused with fury. "I have been waiting here for two hundred years. Two hundred years, stewing from your insults, my reputation shrewdly gored— by you! You want to challenge me, the oldest god in heaven? There is nothing, nothing that would please me more, than to do battle."

The room erupted in a smokeless fire, smoldering in waves of heat. The thick vapor condensed, and took the shape of a demonic ifrit, burly of breast and bearing a coffer of crystal on its head. It roared at me balefully, its ram horns spewing molten lava, eyes burning like the sun. Foam spewed from its mouth, making spittle fly.

"It's the god of imagination—the demon Destroyer!" I screamed. "He's entered our realm!"

Cryss drew back, panic stricken. "That's him?" She had never seen anything like it.

The ifrit smashed through the stateroom wall. Horrified screams followed from nearby staterooms. Cryss willed a spear that flew into the creature's backside, but the giant took no notice. The beast continued its rampage, spewing fire through the off-white halls.

"He's come for our souls," I instructed. "But I know what he is. Release me!"

As soon as the chains snapped off, so the ifrit disappeared into air. All I had to do was will him away.

"Dummies!" I screamed as I jumped overboard, giddy with laughter, placing my arms in a diver's pose.

Air stopped. I felt something I did not know I could feel on the ship. Pain.

My neck would not move. My fingers felt not water, but a thick plane of glass. I saw Cryss far above me, standing still in my stateroom, overlooking my spill. Her hand covered the sun in her eyes.

"Pissant!" Cryss shouted, her Valkyrie fur growing about her torso. "You spit-sucking weasel! How dare you threaten the souls of my ship, just to find her! You fiend! Pray I show you mercy!"

I willed the rocks flung at Solomon's temple. Charging out of the sky, the gray boulders crashed through the glass plane that separated me from the stream. My body tossed, doll-like, flattening onto the stream's hard surface.

Shards of glass rained upon my broken body. I felt that same feeling—intense, unnerving pain. The entire ocean had frozen into a glacier of ice. Blood poured out of my side, causing steam to rise from the frozen surface. I turned my heavy body with my hips and saw Cryss on the ship above me. Souls gazed from its deck to watch our fight.

"Your imagination has no focus!" Cryss spoke from above, a golden halo above her blonde hair. "All I need to defeat you are the elements. Simple, material, real."

I willed my voice to move, though my mouth could not. "You could not even recognize a Djinn!" my voice shouted, taunting her. "So how about this?"

I remembered my life as a grand wizard, and the creature I hunted. That last dragon, Evald, appeared at the horizon. Its appearance paralyzed the souls on the ship's deck until its cry came forth, sending them skittering for cover in their flip-flops. Flame coughed in a cataract of dragon fire, igniting tanning-oil surfaces as more souls broke for the hatches. Cryss willed a downpour of rain to save her precious bloomed souls, but not before Evald set aflame the ice that encircled me.

Water formed a puddle. The dragon's roar, a living bomb, screeched into silence. I turned my body to the sea, where the beast had collapsed, iron spears struck through her chest.

"Cryss," I whispered.

I merged into the water. Instantly it grew cold. Frost settled in. I froze, incased inside an iceberg. White walls covered the outside world, and I could will nothing to react. I strained every muscle but remained still. Even my eyelids were frozen open. My muscles spasmed with unceasing cold. I don't know how long I was encased before Cryss pulled me out and wiped a circle into the ice so I could see her, the face of a gorgeous Trojan woman, a face to send a million souls.

"I've put you in a tall tower atop the ship," she stated, her voice muffled by the ice. "If you ever manage to free yourself, there are a thousand other devices I have willed to keep you secure."

I could not speak back. I could not even will a response, my brain frozen in time.

"The gateway to the stream is about to close," she said. "Mankind does not have long. Your beast's whispers will make sure of that. You might be here a year, maybe a hundred years, however long it takes to smother that fire inside you. Don't worry. From the perspective of eternity, it will go by in a flash." She paused, as if to smile, but now, she had the will not to break. "When all of mankind goes extinct, and that little bedswerver's soul expires along with them, maybe then I'll let you out." She left and the coat of white ice covered my sight.

If I could have cried, I would have cried a million tears for every year I was trapped in Cryss' ice prison. Time ticked by. A blank space. For five hundred years I berated the gods. For five hundred years I felt myself drift, a glacier through the ocean of time. At first, I held on to the promise that someone would release me. Sometimes souls marched up to gaze upon me, the legendary diver. But none offered help. No, I was in a realm of weaklings and betrayers. Like me they might have felt pity, but they would never put feeling into action. Sometimes souls would wipe the frost from my face, so I could see them. Sometimes they brought new souls up to see me, to see the scapegoat, to assure them that it was me, not them, immured for love.

After that first century, they formed a holiday around my imprisonment. Clover brought festive crowds, unveiling me like a sacred calf. Souls shouldered against each other for my line of sight. They laughed, made jokes, took bets on whether Cryss would release me that year, or if S would ever come to claim me. Some would bicker over whether I was as pretty as legends told. Their general feeling was I had an addiction, I had it coming, I had brought this upon myself.

Those who felt sympathy asked why I didn't give up, why I was such a fool. Some blamed you, called you a whore. False, false S, they said.

"What Eight-Seven-One could never understand," Cryss would announce every year, "is that the structure is like the very language we speak. You never think of it, yet cannot imagine yourself without it. Even sounds that make no sense can be incorporated into letters of the alphabet. They keep us sensible. Can you even imagine eternity without them?"

Cryss' wisdom grew upon me. She wanted order, harmony, and I was the cure. I was a warning—the one soul who had managed to ruffle Cryss' unshakable demeanor, and had paid the eternal cost. For those who had earned heaven only through compliance, my imprisonment gave them deliverance.

After five centuries, knowing no savior would come for me, I took notice of something: the ones who came with the crowd, chanted with them, but something more remained. A soul came to me, and when he put his hand upon my ice, I felt touch. That was it: the something more. So long as we had any will to remember, it remained with us.

I could not cry for missing you. I could not imagine that time had not passed, and I could not will the past. So, I imagined something more, or better yet, something less. Instead of imagining escape, a place of retreat, I imagined nothing. Instead of will, I felt doubt. I was nothing. Life was nothing. And so I became nothing—nothingness. Gravity could barely pull me down, but I gave myself to its gentle tug. I stopped fighting it. I, the nothing, fell through my glacier prison. I fell through the labyrinth tower, past the monsters guarding me. I fell through the blood-eyed men covered in soot, growing out of mud. I fell through the shopping malls of perfect clothing and servants to satisfy every whim. I fell through the pleasure gardens and massage parlors full to the brim of supine bodies and their lovers. I fell through the dungeons, the hot saunas with blood streaks along the walls. I fell further, deep into the blank darkness where souls floated in euphoric titillation, their bodies in perfect ecstasy, no light, no noise to disturb them, the air electrified with pulses of purest pleasure. Some had wild faces, some stared at fields of shiny dancing stars.

And as I fell, I willed something more, until I crossed the universe of time and was born again.

Life

Z

The last life an Intergalactic Genocide.

Mankind Ends. 731 PT

*In Kali Yuga
Only Brute Force Would Decide
Who Is Wrong & Who Is Right*

Just out of blink, the stars went steady and the blurs of planets became sharp gaseous orbs. We edged past a large commune vessel, a colony that held a fifth of the last remaining humans in the universe. Across the rectangular spaceship a placard read, "In the Afterlife." Engraved in silver plates beside it were a list of Kings' names: King Duji 2596 A.D., King Clark 2633 A.D., and on and on. The top of the ship was decked in large bronze statues of rams, bulls, and a sphinx. From afar, they looked like the knick-knacks of a human history festival.

Beside me, First Mate Olakiitan shouted as if from a loudspeaker: "The first tribe attempted to recreate these Ziggurats from Earth." Her voice shifted to a soft whisper. "Sir, those are like castles. But in the desert."

Olakiitan had never seen desert. She came from the third tribe, those humans who built houses like grand obelisks. But I knew the desert. The yellow sand. The dust storms. The bushes growing fluffy white cotton.

"Our raiders have returned!" Olakiitan announced, yellow headlights glaring off her polished head. The automated door swept open and in walked Diaz, chief of my raiders, wearing appropriately frightening skulls and chains. At her side was a young woman in the drabs of an Egyptian slave, a single folded cloth upon her torso.

"We have the Foundation on their knees!" Diaz said with her arms up.

"Is this one of their slaves?" Olakiitan asked, hands in her pockets, at her belt. "She hasn't been abused, I trust?" Her fingers thumbed through the armory concealed within her gray-striped jacket. The ex-slave girl guzzled a raider water-skin.

"Of course not."

"And punishments?" Olakiitan asked. "How many of our crew did you flog, behead, or quarter? Surely, some broke the codes." A silence read incompetence. "Don't return without some ears!" Olakiitan instructed. "I want them still dripping with blood!"

Before Diaz could flurry off the deck, a signal jolted though the main screen. The leaders of The Foundation appeared in a room mimicking a Pharaoh's chamber, with statues of snakes and black cats.

"We have three of your raiders," said their leader, a Pharaoh look-alike all got up in white cloth with a shiny gold band across her forehead. "We *had* four. One was claiming some nonsense about some great weapon and some great god. That you would kill the entire colony. She's gone now, to meet Osiris." The table of self-assured leaders chuckled to themselves.

"She was not lying," I told them, flipping up my visor.

The leader of the first tribe gazed upon me, the beak of her falcon god staring like a phantom. "I heard of you. The Widow. Head shaved like a monk. Quartering and butchering your own crew. Terrorizing the galaxy. Looting and pillaging from other humans. But even someone as insane as you wouldn't commit a mass genocide. Not with so few humans left in the galaxy."

I looked to Olakiitan, who stared straight ahead, scanning our enemy for weakness.

"Perhaps," I said. "We should ask one of your slaves. Let them judge your fate."

The raider pulled the young girl forward. Her body showed careful torture, with scars as precise as lines on a map. Olakiitan asked her, "What would you have us do?"

The slave stared at her masters. The shine in her eyes reflected anyone who gazed upon her. Where her masters saw weakness, I saw bloodlust.

"Your fate has been decided," I said, pulling down my visor. "Now pray to your gods. You will soon find answers about the afterlife."

The look on the first tribe before I obliterated them was the same look of my sister Gayle before she died. On the asteroid where I grew up, the sky was always yellow, turning every plant the same autumn glare, even the dust motes hanging near the cabin windows. When the designers sent clouds and the rains came in bursts, every drop shone in wheaty, grainy yellow.

I was one of the youngest in my family of thousands of big sisters. Every morning I picked cotton with big sister Gayle, watching her long legs. Nothing grew but cotton. The long sea of sand could not be mowed, plucked, or harvested. Gayle made a long sack for herself and a small sack for me. When I was tired, I fell asleep on big sister's cotton-filled sack. As she dragged me along, picking along the cotton rows, she told me stories of a human named Adam. He was a man, she told me, the first man. Once we were done on this asteroid, he would take us to a place not yellow, but green. "But," she said, "you must always be on the lookout for Eve, the one who defied her creator."

I had visions of Eve while sleeping on big sister's sack. She was a girl about my age with wavy brown hair. She would kiss me in the garden. As I grew older, I imagined Eve was somewhere beyond time, a woman of such awe-inspiring beauty she had to be buried for generations.

Now the yellow sky had been replaced by big, boundless space. Space, the long dead plain, not much different from desert. No seeds floated upon it, no spores in its wind.

Olakiitan, Diaz, the slave, and I all gazed at the great silver Ziggurat that once stood before us, as black and hollow as a cocoon's abandoned husk. Its thousands of inhabitants had become burnt shells left to gravity's soft drift. The raiders and mates on my ship stared in wonder at what we had done.

To my right, the god Adam stood, naked, his muscular body shining out of my dream. "They are silent now," Adam said in a booming voice. "They were the last humans to ever know of Egypt. They were the last to ever bow before the sphinx. From them, nothing will be derived. Nothing will be conveyed. Nothing will grow. Finally, an end to that rabble."

I met Adam when I was twelve, though he had spent over four thousand years watching me. By then, most of my sisters were in their late twenties, and could no longer pick cotton. They knew the next harvest would come soon. Not the cotton harvest. Our harvest.

"Our deaths are part of a design," big sister Gayle told me once while cotton picking. I lay on her cotton bag, being dragged along, waiting for her to tell a story of that different world, a world of light. She once described it eloquently, with descriptions of tall trees and gardens full of fruit. But as big sister grew older, she spoke more of the people who would harvest us. Those who, like us, were part of the lost tribes. Like us, ravenous. When big sister was young, she was of the new crop who had to kill the older tribe, too feeble to replant. It happened every generation. Those who had tilled the soil for so long eventually had to be tilled themselves, making way for the next season's glut of working girls.

"We have to pick as much as we can," big sister told me with a scraggy catch in her voice. She yanked the cotton bag out from beneath me. "The more cotton we pick, the more weapons we will receive for the battle." Those days everyone spoke of the next exchange, when ships from above took our boxes of cotton, leaving behind barrels full of weaponry: automatic rifles, bullets, swords, grenades, pistols, cannons. Human-assisted natural selection, they called it.

On the day of the harvest, when the horns of war summoned us to battle, Adam first appeared to me. I heard the horns, and being one of the youngest of my eight thousand sisters, I was sent home to gather munitions, while big sister

Gayle and the others went to fight in the outskirts just beyond the cotton fields where dust and sand extended deep into the horizon. But on my way home I saw a shining figure at the top of a small hillside bordered by scrawny bushes. The figure leaned on a young tree, its leaves as green as the limes we squeezed on hot nights. I should have gone home to gather bullets, but a void seemed to grow around the figure, calling to me. I approached the small garden, gazing at the green objects: bushes, leaves, trees, vines, weeds. It was just as big sister had described the world of light, the garden of Eden. And in the center stood the first and only man I had ever seen.

"Hate and love still consume you humans," Adam said, muscular and nude. He glared at me with a stony face and obdurate eyes.

"Is this a dream?" I asked.

"A daydream, yes, but I am real."

"Are you god?"

Adam levitated and grew larger. His brown eyes peered at me in all directions. "I am the closest you will ever get."

Shouts came from the outskirts. The first sounds of explosives. Then gunfire. From the hilltop, I saw yellow-dusted bodies building trenches.

"Your race is nearly extinct," Adam said, turning to face the battle. "Fortune won't give your kind another chance. They overreach. I can see how history spins itself, tilting its axis for a new era. Before this happens, you two could be together. I can help you. If you wish, I could become a player in the drama I have watched for millennia. I can help you find her."

"Find who?" I asked.

"Even now, you desire her. You've yearned for her since you were first able to dream. In this life, you call her Eve." Adam stood upon a leaf, facing me, hair puffed upon his chest. "But I've watched you follow her far before that. From when you were a Roman slave. From when you fought for Saladin's army. From when you were taken from Earth. But this life is your last chance. Don't let all your efforts go to waste."

"What should I do?"

"Flee the battle. Stay here, in your imagination. Here, the garden of your dreams."

"And Eve?" I asked, not knowing why.

"Do as I say, and I will lead you to her."

It was cowardice, pure and simple, that made me do what he asked. For hours I climbed imaginary trees while my sisters fell to the new crop. I hid inside a strawberry patch while cannon balls ricocheted across the cotton. All the while Adam would not stop watching the battle with that look of condemnation on his face.

When the screams went silent and our enemy led victorious cheers back to their camp, I walked the scathed earth, looking for signs of life among the dead. I saw their papery exoskeletons. My heeled sandals grew soggy with blood. I found Gayle, dumbstruck by her hands, those slender hands worn by toil. Her body was impaled by a piece of black iron atop her back, blood still dripping from her head. Her black hair mixed with the yellow dirt. I turned her over. Bubbles of blood foamed from her mouth as if she were trying to speak.

"They will come for you soon," Adam said, his long shadow appearing next to me.

"Who?"

"The designers. The ones who put you here. They take your cotton and feed you death. They will take all who survive this. They will use your bodies to create a better stock for the next harvest."

I placed my small hand on big sister's face, quieting that stream of bloody bubbles.

"And Eve," I said. "She wants me to find her?"

"She is still human," Adam said. "Misery will define her life, no matter her wants."

I cried, thinking my tears could flow past time.

"I have a plan," Adam said. "But it comes at great suffering, because it requires you to go on living." His image turned toward me. "You need to foster your imagination. Learn to harness your smoldering talents. If you don't, you will be unable to see me. Then all is lost. Saving your life—that was free. But from here on, you must do whatever I ask."

"I'll do anything."

"I know."

Not even a day passed before our ship approached mankind's second tribe. They lived on a moon, protected by a greater race of tall immovables, called the Hyul. Our raiders went in wearing camouflage and reported back orgiastic thrills, humans acting like animals, gawked at through their cages by the marble-statue species who harbored them as pets.

The slave girl from The Foundation put her hand to her forehead, nauseated by the deed we were about to do. "They're servants too," she said, gripping her hair. "What use is it to kill them all?"

"It's too late," Olakiitan announced in her loudspeaker voice. "They are part of mankind's infection."

The ex-slave could not bring herself to see humanity as a whole. She only saw the cruelty of her captors, not the despair that haunted the species.

I looked to Adam, who sat legs crossed and eyes closed.

"Adam," I said. The others bowed their heads in reverence when I spoke to him, for only I could see the god.

"I do not feel her presence," he said, eyes closed. "Your Eve is not here."

That was all I needed. I gave the signal and we heard the Nightmare weapon charge. The steam capsules released into the air like the sounds of big sister's gurgling blood. The floor and glass monitors shook. Even with protective gear, we still had to keep our mouths open to let the sound pass, to keep the bursts from breaking our eardrums. The moon before us and all its inhabitants, in an instant, turned from white to charcoal black.

When the designers took me, they gave me a bed and impregnated me while I slept.

"The designers are the only ones capable of reproduction," Adam said from within my mind-space. "Their federation kidnaps the strongest humans, those who have survived the massacres, and thus promise progress. But like all things human, its own history is one of carnage and crime."

I befriended Babaii, one of the designers, who was twice my height and half my body weight. Like all designers, her face was made up like clay, and her cheeks were prodded into sloppy shapes. I gave her pleasuring touches on her soft face as she injected me. Every three months a new stock came out of me, taken in my sleep. When I tried to kill them myself, they put me in chains and left me suspended above my bed, the television facing me to ease my mind. But I had to foster my imagination, as Adam said. So I kept my eyes closed and dreamt of you, my long love, tethered to my soul in every body that I inhabited. In my mind I could feel your breath come like a tide, a slight tug toward sleep. When my leg was broken in punishment after I produced a stillborn, it became harder to see how time could just keep going, with no sun, not even a yellow sky. Time, I came to understand, had no limits, no quotas, no mercy, no invisible line where one's suffering was ever enough.

Learning this, I imagined you as Eve. My yearning for your sweet kiss grew with every jolt of pain. The third time I produced a stillborn, they tore out one of my eyes, threatening to blind me if I did it again. "And make them strong this time," Babaii scolded me. With no influence from Adam, my daydreams became hideously violent. I dreamed of killing everyone in the ship, killing every last human alive.

Adam could not help me, but he would not let my mind go soft. "It will take time," he told me from within my imagination. "If I helped you now, all would be lost. We must wait for the right moment." To pass the days, he told me of all the death mankind had imparted upon each other. He told me of a place called Carthage where women were raped and all the children were killed by gangsters who called themselves civilizers. He told me of killing fields, where men destroyed each other by instruction and obedience and cowardice. But worst of all he told me of the history that we humans had invented. It seemed that no matter what atrocities we committed, we could never condemn ourselves. Not for a moment did we ever pause and consider and weigh and, facing our own bullish nature, decide to end our terrible reign. No group with power ever relinquished even a minute portion of it in the name of rectifying their souls. Guilt and regret only survived as private feelings, or as voices from the doomed. Always, we glorified the worst of ourselves, and thus we grew worse and worse, until the day someone would finally put us down.

"Now," Adam spoke in my mind-dream, where we inhabited his garden. "You humans have been banished from the planets, doomed to live in ships, on asteroids, moons, always the guests of someone else. Their obedient pets, their fertile soil, their unspoiled livestock. Is that how mankind should end? Or will someone finally do what needs to be done?"

It was like this for many years until the pirates came and the chance we were waiting for arose. Before the marauders even arrived, Adam paralyzed the designers with fear. It was the only power Adam had over those who foreswore imagination. Without ever training their minds, the designers were lost in the fear of death, unable to tell the difference between the real and the imagined.

While pirates raided the ship, I walked from my small cell, awakening the crunch of dried blood from a small massacre that the designers had performed upon themselves. For years my mind had been awash in sedatives, but seeing the carnage before me restored my wits into a hungry delirium. Near the canteen I came upon the intruders—a band of pirate raiders, their hair long and scraggy, their skin a multitude of colors but each one blemished by scars, tattoos, and war paint. They were stunned to see me, the only lucid being on the entire ship. They had come prepared to fight, but found prisoners without chains.

"Where are the children?" I asked, wavering toward the pirates. I must have been a sight—my muscles atrophied, my skin spotted from inertia and the recent trio of births.

"Who are you? Did you do this?" one of the pirates asked. I later came to know her as Antavius, the broad chested woman whose body was shaped like a canon's heavy iron.

"Adam did it," I said. "He is a god who helps me. Come, help me find the children."

Even without Adam's influence I was able to impinge fear upon whoever saw me, the rage that screamed with every step I took. The pirates followed me, whispering to each other, while I asked them to kindly kill every paralyzed designer that we passed. I saw a body still moving and took one of Antavius' knives to stab its stomach. Then I found Babaii in the bathroom. I hit her with a lamp, used the broken glass to pierce her side, and then drowned her mangled face in a toilet.

Finally, I found the cargo. Twenty children at least. A small crop. Unlike the adults, they were not paralyzed with fear, but seemed joyous in the lightness of imagination that had enchanted the ship. They must have thought I was a god too, for they followed me all the way to the trash suction chamber. I left them in there and Adam helped me open the bay doors.

"The woman is insane," one of the pirates said. "Does she know what she's doing?"

"She doesn't seem a speck ignorant," Antavius responded, her fingers rubbing her chin.

We heard the bay doors open one by one, the swift

whoosh of metal. We watched the children playing on a pile of trash: bloodied rags, littered boxes, a discarded table. They played some game in their imaginations. Then the last bay door opened and they were all sucked out into the desert of space.

Our ship arrived at the third tribe's home, a network of drifting rocks, with cities peeking from each crevice, awash in bright white lights. Bodies plummeted from their tall towers, hoping that we would take them up rather than just kill them all. Many jumped, none were saved.

Behind me on the bridge, the ex-slave from The Foundation cried into her hands. Since our decimation of the second tribe, she had gone ape mad, murmuring to herself, lips trembling: "We are killing them. But they do not *want* to be killed. We are giving them death. Where is the line? When is enough enough? Where is the line?"

I didn't have to tell Olakiitan to slit her throat. The girl's right-hand left scratch marks on the iron floor. We listened to her gag.

When our signal went through, it seemed we caught the third tribe's leaders at lunch. Trays of spinach and cheese lined a table surrounded by board members. They put away their small electronic arm devices and fixed their buttoned-up sweaters. Despite my reputation among their own people, the leaders were pathetically unprepared.

"We understand your disgust with the other tribes," one of them said, her blonde hair shelling the worry that began to etch her face. "But we never did anyone any harm. We have no slaves. Everyone here is free. They are individual, and they live in harmony. In fact, we welcome you. We are impressed by your ability to do so much with—"

"—I have met one of your servants, who you claim are not slaves," I told them. "Sniveling, scared to death, ready to part her legs on command, and about eight years old."

"And what of your tech?" Olakiitan screeched, even more forcefully than usual. The third tribe was once her own. "You sell your murderous wares to species across the planets. You prosper from death and war."

A short pause came as the board members saw the ex-slave's corpse just behind me. I could see it in them—that look, when they finally caught the scent of their own end.

"But nothing we do is illegal," the blonde one said, lip quivering. "Ok, fine. We get it. We will halve everything with you. Take our cities, our fuel, our weapons, whatever you want."

"Your Eve is not here," Adam whispered, legs crossed next to me, smelling the air like it was volcanic sulfur. "Just another abysmal end."

"We can give you land," another board member pleaded. "Everything you ever dreamed of will be yours!"

I didn't have to tell Olakiitan what to do next.

The Nightmare weapon. I named it such because humans believed that if they were alive, and their enemies were dead, then they had won. They believed that bodies meant everything. But the dead always come back. Nightmares kept killers from knowing peace.

After the pirates abducted me, I spent twenty-two years wed to Antavius, whispering in her ear, helping her connive her way up the ranks, until she eventually became Captain of their whole ragged band. As first mate, I went on every raid hoping to find you. We terrorized the galaxy, attacking every small human vessel we could find. The other species had given up on humans. So long as we doled out violence against ourselves, they needn't bat an eye.

Adam told me about my past lives with you, when we nearly bloomed together, when we nearly made it to that spiritual realm, the Ilium, where we could live forever in a heaven held true by our love. Sometimes you were a man, sometimes we both were. But still, our love survived.

But through those two decades on the pirate ship, Adam could only faintly feel your existence. He never sensed your soul on any ship we raided. We searched the galaxy far and wide, but could never get close to any human tribe without their automated weaponry blasting us apart.

"I am a god that lives in imaginations," Adam told me in my meditation room. "But where no soil exists I cannot take root. Eve is in a place only populated by those without imagination. From what I have sensed, she cannot think beyond this material realm."

"The designers took away her mind."

"Yes and no. Hers is a stubborn soul, never willing to entertain the fantasy of a better, freer place. Every cause to retreat just stiffens her resistance. No matter the life, her choice has always been the truant path, to barely eke out a life."

"Then we must save her," I pleaded.

"We must do more than save her," he said. "In many lives you saved her, or she saved you, but it didn't work. She will never go with you of her own accord. Like all mankind, she is flawed, but her flaw is the worst of them all. In every life she has lived, she has exhibited it without second thought. No matter all the evils that mankind has done, she has remained faithful to them, her own kind. A baseless, unreasonable faith founded upon pure attachment. That is what we must take from her."

Finally, we had a plan.

"How can I convince her?" I asked him in my imagination, hoping not to wake Antavius who spooned me.

"Only through death can we realize our impermanence. With total despair, she will accept you. She will give up. Show her the fragility of everything she holds dear, everything that tethers her to this realm."

"How would I do that?"

"There is a weapon."

I didn't even need to spread my legs to convince Antavius to raid a small research ship on the outskirts of the galaxy. Believing in my divine prescience, she followed my lead into the frontiers of space, where we discovered a crescent-shaped vessel concealed from our radar by the constant encircling of two binary asteroids. Inside the ship, Adam took the inhabitants under his spell, possessing the military guards with fear, while the researchers praised me as their savior. Those who could create weaponry had just enough imagination left for Adam to influence, and to see me as something divine. Antavius, however, was made to appear ghastly and devilish. As soon as she entered the ship, the scientists used their utensils to gut her apart.

I commandeered the ship's bridge, with Olakiitan at my side, my first mate, a pirate I had trained since we picked her up as a young child on a cruise vessel. Only the fellow pirates who really believed in my divinity, the ones who never doubted from the beginning, were spared to be my crew.

I ordered new coordinates and we dove into the blink, speeding toward our next destination. In that fuzzy absolution of space, I spoke to the crew from the bridge, Olakiitan to my left, and an invisible Adam to my right. I made our mission clear.

"Crew. We have in our hands the most powerful weapon mankind has ever produced. As the universe feared, our technology has grown; our ability to deal death has surpassed even the most advanced races. No doubt, humans intended to use to this weapon to subjugate, to become masters of the stars, to destroy this galaxy, as we once destroyed our own planet. The secret development of this weapon proves that mankind has exhausted all merit. But we need not be remembered as the oppressors of the universe. From this day forth, we are no longer pirates, but executioners. I am sent by God to banish mankind from this realm, to end the cycles of suffering, to condemn those who could not condemn themselves."

We flattened out of the blink and the wavy lines of space turned rigid. For our weapon's maiden voyage, I took us to a small yellow asteroid, a place where women harvested cotton.

"This weapon is the culmination of mankind," I said to the crew. "This is mankind's legacy, our final contribution. Humanity can never be rescued. But we can turn our pain into something more meaningful."

The great apparatus thrummed with power and our scientists aimed at the asteroid. We had to keep our mouths open or else the thunder of the machine would blow our eardrums apart.

The last tribe of mankind sat still in their asteroid belt of colorful gaseous caves. For hundreds of years they had kept to themselves, worshipping the volcanic rocks, while taxing other tribes who mined deep into the asteroids, causing them to shake off ore and pummel.

"We know. We know. We know!" whimpered a voice over our intercom. It was their spiritual leader, his head shaved, like me, but without the scars. "We know we deserve death. All we can do is ask for mercy. Please. Have mercy on us. We just want to live peacefully in our caves."

The main screen showed thousands of people in burgundy dresses, all on their knees. Milk-guzzling pale women, fresh and unbruised. Entire cities bowed to me. It was pathetic.

"Where were you," Olakiitan said. "When all fire went down upon the other worlds? To do nothing, that is the same as permitting."

I looked to Adam next to me. He sat still, his eyes moving about, searching for your faintest pull.

"No," Adam said. "She is not here either."

The weight of fear fell upon me. "Then she is not with any of the tribes," I said in my imagination.

"No."

"Then she is with the designers."

"Yes."

"Then," I whispered softly. "She must be like I was." A mule. An incubator, birthing trios of new slaves for the harvests. Even in a life of unimaginable suffering, you still held on to mankind.

I looked back to the screen, having forgotten the millions of women before me, each on bended knee.

"So do it!" I shouted at Olakiitan.

Our ship sent distress signals to the designer's fleet near the first planet. In the immersive waters of the blink, Adam spoke from our shared mind-space.

"I sense her, that heat of defiance. The troubling turning of the tide. Do you feel her?"

I did. I felt the pull, your pull. A slight gravity, a faraway magnet strumming on my chest.

"Eve," I said. "In the stories Gayle told me, she was the mother of all mankind."

"You were never told the full story," Adam said. "Adam and Eve, they had two sons, but those sons were lost to history."

"Tell me about them."

"The younger brother was obedient, kind, and did whatever he was told. The other was unlike his brother. Willful. In a jealous rage the elder brother slayed him with a rock."

"They were the only humans on their planet?"

"Hmm. At the time, they were the only humans who ever existed."

"He killed one-fourth of his entire race. In a single blow."

I opened my eyes from the meditation. I felt the engines soften as the fuzzy orange of a star sharpened into a sphere. The star was once mankind's sun.

"But the elder brother did not do enough," I said. "He killed the wrong person."

"He should have killed himself?"

"No. He should have killed her. Eve. The source. The only person capable of letting us—all of *this*—go on."

We surfaced, drifting toward a herd of pearly white designer ships as big as asteroids, all under Adam's spell. Fearing the depravity of their imaginations, they had all turned against each other. Bullets, those human toys, flew back and forth from ship to ship. They stuck onto a ship's surface, drilled deep into the interior, then exploded in tempestuous bursts. A trail of drill bullets made large black gashes on each ship, and human bodies flew out in a stream, pouring out of silver egg sacks. Some were frozen in the death of space, while others wore spacesuits, caught in that infinite undertow.

"They are killing each other," Olakiitan said from beside me, her hand positioned on the data-pad to order our attack. "Is this the power of Adam?"

I said nothing, but kept my legs crossed on the floor to steady my breathing. I focused on your pull. For eons I'd only encircled it like a moon caught in an orbit. But now, finally, we were destined to collide.

"Approach the battle," I ordered. "We must get closer."

"What about the Nightmare weapon?" Olakiitan asked.

The largest designer ship, a silver blue whale in the vast black sea, tore in two as an onslaught of missiles ripped open its belly. Humans spilled out, lifeless.

"We were just speeding up the inevitable," I said.

Our vessel plunged through the melee. Spacesuit bodies whizzed by fast as bullets, unhampered by wind or debris.

I left Olakiitan in charge of the bridge and headed for the trash suction chamber, deckhands snapping salutes as I marched by. I thought to Adam: "If I can sense her this strongly, can she sense me?" But Adam did not answer.

Your spirit tugged at me. I believed it would lift me straight off the ground.

I entered the suction chamber and put on the black spacesuit of our raiders. I looked up at the bay doors, waiting for your spirit to pull me toward you.

"Patch me to the ship," I told Olakiitan over the suit's intercom. I spoke to them en masse: "Crew. This will be our last mission together. The designers are the last beings who harbor the technology of human reproduction. Once they are destroyed, mankind's strays will perish with age like bees whose queen has died."

Adam appeared in front of me. His eyes were locked on mine like the day we met, when he convinced me to stray from my sisters. I continued: "I have no words of wisdom to impart. Words are meant to be passed on. Be comforted in knowing that I have no reason to say them. The days of humanity are over. From us, nothing will pass. After today, there will never be another genocide. No more betrayals. No more rapes. No more false histories. From this day forth, mankind shall never pass."

I felt your gravity in the strum of every heartbeat. The ship rumbled as one of the engines blew out. From all around me, I could hear the drill bullets making their way deeper into the hull.

"She is downstream," Adam said. "Flow to her. The current is wide open."

"Olakiitan," I said into the intercom. "Open the bay doors."

I nearly fainted from the pressure. Suction launched my body from the ship. My arms and legs locked in place as I zoomed forward, a stick overtaken into a waterfall, free falling into the deep.

"For so many thousands of years I watched them." Adam's voice. I could breathe at ease. "Despite everything, somehow, they kept going. Multiplying, even."

Lifeless bodies passed like driftwood, their eyes bulged, their faces caught in expressions of horror.

"It just kept going," Adam said. I saw him, a dot in the distance. His legs were crossed, eyes closed. "On and on and on." He did not seem to notice me pass. "I could not bear it a second longer." He opened his eyes and stared at the destruction in wonder. "Seeing them so subservient." His figure receded far behind me. "This is harder than I thought."

Adam's voice passed, out of memory, out of imagination. I zoomed along, feeling your pull, shrouded in the darkness of space. Time passed. My small canister of oxygen began to dwindle.

In the silence, I heard you. You spoke faintly, from that realm of imagination.

stop…stop… stop… stop… stop… stop… stop… stop… stop

"Please stop." A young voice. It came through the radio intercom. I scanned the darkness and found a body. A white spacesuit, far away.

"Please stop," the voice cried. "Stop everything. Please. Stop. Please."

I activated my suit's boosters, a single spurt to slow me

down, to drift toward you. I could not tell if you were drawing me, or I you.

"I have stopped it," I said in our shared mind-space. "It will all end soon."

"Please," you cried in a hoarse whisper. "Stop it. Please."

I felt your spirit fluttering out of existence, all the oxygen gone from your suit. I felt air thicken into a toxic fog.

"I can take you away. I can save you from this place."

I circled you, our bodies floating like two asteroids caught in each other's gravity, encroaching ever nearer.

"This is my home."

"You have to move on." I felt my body stiffen, my last gasps for air. "There is nothing left."

"Nothing?"

"Nothing."

I reached for you, barely close enough to touch.

Weakly, you took my hand.

//Book Three\\

S

If there are flowers flowers

must come out to the road. Rowdy!—

knowing where wheels and people are,

knowing where whips and screams are,

knowing where deaths are, where the kind kills are.

Gwendolyn Brooks

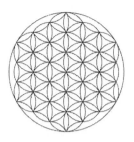

That was the last time I crossed into the Ilium, twenty-one years ago. The last time love still burned within me. The chase was over. I had won.

I awoke to that familiar ceiling with you cushioned around my arm. Something was off. You were small, a bundle wrapped in soft white cotton blankets. Your soul was trapped inside the body of an infant, smaller than my arm, in serene slumber. When you woke up crying, I told you that I loved you and that we were in a safe place. But you kept crying until I willed you a bottle of milk.

Cryss said you were a feral soul, reborn into the memory disease, stuck in the worlds of the past. I could not bear the stares outside, so I rarely left my stateroom. I willed milk bottles, but you only wanted my breasts.

You wailed like a beast left dying on the roadside. I conjured doors of solid steel to suffocate the sounds. I stuffed your face with sugary cream to restrain you. I dealt with your runny poops, your sardonic laughter, your stubborn game.

Fifteen months later you were taking your first steps, your hair strapped into pigtails like bundles of straw. I cradled you when you spoke your first word: "Mama."

When you were five, you followed me to the gymnasium for morning exercises. Old souls passed, watching this spectacle you created. Sometimes the other souls willed themselves into children to play with you, but this seemed cruel. To them, childhood was a fetish. And though we walked through the corridors hand in hand, it wasn't the mommy-daughter play.

Determined to keep the ruse, you never stopped asking about our lives in the stream. I told you we were once lovers, which made you giggle, pretending to not know love. You kicked your feet up in laughter when I told you of the ruined temples, the starvation, the genocide of our people. Do not laugh, I scolded you. In many lives you were the victim— the tortured, the penniless, the forgotten.

Your disease spun facts into fiction. You became elated, immersed in the past as I told it.

You couldn't sit still for a moment, not during buffets, symphonies, massages. I told myself that you were not really a young girl, that you had the eyes of the soul who gave me her body, who gripped me in ecstasy, who gave me a daughter.

I never meant to provide you an education, but your questions came with the patter of an overcast sky, dripping down softly, every now and then, accumulating into a storm. Every soul who arrived in the Ilium remembered their past lives. You must have known the answers already. What sex is, because we'd done it together. What a field looked like, because many had been your grave.

I attempted to reign in your anger. I slapped you when you asked too much. When I remembered you were a very old soul indeed, I slapped you again, hoping to break you from your affliction. I slapped your right cheek when you blamed me for bringing you to the Ilium. I slapped your left when you hurt yourself just to feel pain. You could have willed yourself numb, if you wanted. You could have willed your face into iron, if you only tried.

"Wake up," I said. "Use your imagination. Will yourself. Like me." I became your mother. Your lover. Your lifelong companion.

"I shouldn't," you told me.

"Shouldn't? Just give it a try."

"I shouldn't."

"How is your imagination so limited? You are a child!"

"I am! You stupid—" you stopped mid-shout and slowly regained your composure, glowering at me.

"Get on your knees."

You resisted, forcing me to will you to the floor.

"You loved me once. Stop acting like a little girl!"

Excitedly, you grasped me.

I stopped myself. I became your mother again and embraced you. Hair fell from my head. You grasped clumps, spitting strands from your mouth.

"Wasn't that right mommy? Isn't that what you wanted?"

When you were seven, I left you in the stateroom. I locked the door, daring you to will yourself out, leaving you vending machines and quarters, since you continued to play the charade of feeling hunger. I ran on the treadmill for days. I sipped wine with Cryss and her lackeys. I thought of you and your crying and your questions and your voices and believed time alone would give you the will to create yourself anew.

"I've never seen a case like hers," Jezebel said, sipping white wine with ice, wearing Persian attire to mourn her tribe. Since the end of mankind, Jezebel had begun speaking, and now fancied herself the resident historian of the ship, a hobby to merely swallow time. Cryss and Clover had joined in, collecting up remnants of mankind's past: recipes, sonnets, sex positions, single malts.

"You're stuck with a child deity," Clover said between sips of warm mulled wine. Her velvet dress was resplendent with green and yellow peacock feathers. "Eros. Horus. Maui. My oh my, she'll be playful and disobedient 'til the end!"

"We all know what she needs," Cryss said, aerating her glass, honoring the Americans in full cowboy attire. Since I had arrived, Cryss had been civil. With all of mankind gone, to be alive in any sense was a rare gift. "Her appearance is only the beginning, a harbinger of the more sordid facades to come. What she needs is to forget. *Kāne*: The human race has not yet died. *Mangmangkik*: One stem still survives."

But I would not force a child.

Every day I swam through our memories, reminding you who you were. In a life you were my best friend, Dei, who imagined history as a playpen where our love blossomed. There were lives when we held each other, caressed each other. Now I woke up padding you with kind words like nursing a scar that continued to pus. I wished we would not scream at each other. I was often the first to raise my voice.

When you misbehaved, I left you at home with Mixi as your only company. "If you want to leave, will this door open," I said, but you never did.

At the Beauty Bay no one blamed me for leaving you on

your own. I got all the sympathy, which felt wrong, but I was as tired as I looked. I drank to give myself peace. I burned my skin with cigars as a party trick. Unlike the others, I could withstand real pain.

"You gave her every chance you could," they would say. "You cannot force happiness on someone."

One day, after a long absence, I returned home. You were taller, talking to that black and white cat and drinking water from the toilet. Your age reminded me of what we left behind. I should have known. You were never one to adjust easily to the world around you, even when that world was heaven itself.

"Are you leaving again, mommy?" you said after another fight.

The old souls in the corridor heard your cries. I shut the door, muting your voice. Damn you. But they would not blame me. I was the victim, taken advantage of by an unimaginative soul who wouldn't even will a door open. Like in many of our lives, you acted a selfish beast. My oppressor. I saw a light in you that from afar looked like wildfire, but up close, was only crushed glass.

I opened our stateroom door. "You're free to leave whenever you want!" I shouted. "Come back when you cease being a child!"

It was the last time I would ever see you sitting upon my rumpled bed. You wore the hooped-wired dress I had willed for you. Your eyes were impotent. Your will unrelenting.

I imagine you had walked the corridors, eyes and ears open, abandoned but for the first time free. You must have encountered others and had a wealth of unspeakable experiences that convinced you to act out the way you did. At some moment you must have passed the enlivening sound of a musical instrument. A harp, a piano, a guitar, a synthesizer. I imagine it sounded like your soul speaking.

For years I strove for peace of mind, plodding through the ship's corridors in silence. I retreated often into the ship's pleasure tank, where I floated like a vegetable in a black silent abyss as electric shocks stimulated my erogenous organs. Without you to remind me of the passage of time, I could float on, my flow unabated.

It took years for the rumors to reach me. The ship's older souls were unhappy—*unhappiness*, the only unpermitted state of being. The child had grown, they said, into a troublemaker. Your style of dress was outdated, flimsy, and your behavior heeded no proper etiquette. I couldn't make sense of what they found so upsetting, until I laid eyes upon it myself.

In the ship's gymnasium I saw you clambering up the boxing ring stairs, a rotund majorette with unformed breasts padded over your stomach like icing on dough. You rotated your body, your chest covered in a blue and pink sari torn at the shoulders, exposing a paunch. Your massive arms pulled your hair back into an atrocious black tube. Cheap iron shimmered from your dress as you danced—if you could call that dancing.

Chills of embarrassment crept up my spine. The body builders laughed. The sauna-dwellers shook their heads. Other souls were with you: a woman playing a harp, and a guitarist—David, my old charge, the same eel-face as the day he arrived, clad in black shorts and a ragged gray T-shirt.

Anyone could see your performance was ridden with mistakes. You strummed chords too hard. The harp wasn't tuned right. And the dancing—could it have been more amateur?

Your eyes fell on me. Even at thirteen, it was clear you had never willed yourself anew. Your chin was too square. Your legs too thick. Hair grew on your arms. You smiled, showing ugly teeth, your fat cheeks rising in the shape of a squished grapefruit. And since you would not will your own appearance, the rambling crowd did it for you, turning your face leprous. You, my beautiful flower of the stream, carried a deformed face that melted upon the stage, lodged amongst your ignoble gang. I pretended not to recognize you—this soul who I once loved, who had driven me mad, and now made every attempt to torment me.

The memory disease had taken you, the bloomed souls whispered. I wandered among them at The Beauty Bay, in the gymnasium, in the saunas and trek simulators. I willed myself into new forms to remain unrecognized. This was S? Many said in astonishment. This was the soul who was worth killing all of mankind?

They called you a spiritual pollution, a germ that only the blue elixir could cure. Why couldn't you will yourself like the rest of them, in a way that made sense? There were no rules to how one appeared, but there was still common decency. There was still good taste.

It came to a point where I could no longer enjoy the pleasure tank. I could no longer feel the pinch of an orgasm without thinking I had left the one soul I had promised never to leave. Memories of you broke every spell. Where was the Roman servant who kissed me on her master's bed? Where was the love for which I had sacrificed everything? I had ended mankind in the hopes that we would, one day, take the blue tea together. Unruly as you had become, I held to hope that in time you would return the love I had spent millennia giving to you.

"Look at me! I'm a big rabid dog!"

I heard the words in the great buffet hall, as I sat across from Cryss, Clover, and Jezebel. We were celebrating the end of my two-year hibernation in the tank, and there you were, my fat turgid daughter grown to fifteen, a shaved-headed miscreant in beat-up sneaks, romping through the buffet stands, knocking over every perfectly imagined dish. You leapt upon a white banquet table and doused your head into a giant boiling pot. You screeched from the pain. "Why am I such a crazy man?" you wailed. "I'm just trying to make it through the day!"

Your minions joined in, smelling of rancid human sweat and excrement. They belched lewd insults as they stabbed their eyes with chicken skewers and poured scalding hot tea onto their faces.

"Bang bang!"

You threw your fat head in laughter, whooping and hollering. "Come on everybody, let's go fucking crazy!"

Cryss and I joined the souls who stepped out, appalled by the performance. More joined in the chaos than I want to admit.

Another year in the tank. When I emerged, the ship was engulfed in mayhem. I saw a fat man staring at himself in the sauna mirror, screaming at his own mirror reflection: "Humanity Harmony HAHAHA!"

The man had to be wrestled to the ground, and when finally pinned, he shouted, "Let's go crazy! I want to go crazy!"

In The Beauty Bay, at the shout of the words "Bang! Bang!" a bevy of your misfits dropped to the moon-rock floor, feigning death. Their bodies went unmoved for months. We stepped over them and sometimes stepped on them, but still they pestered every conversation with their carcasses. Eventually they became part of the scenery, and some of us crushed their hands as we passed with our heels, enticing them to move. Though they winced from the pain, they never broke play.

Many of your kind refused to use any recognizable tongue, but only spoke in a garbled vowel-heavy gibberish. On the great golf course, I saw some balding halfwit stuff balls into his mouth before shrieking in unintelligible crow-squawks. Language became incoherent. In the penny arcade I heard a group of boys chanting "Contents! Supreme! Incaution! Succulent!"

"Let's all go crazy!" became the only intelligible phrase they mustered, a rallying cry for the willful who refused to will. It was a prologue to some inane act: before leaping into a sauna bath full of thumb tacks, before playing tug-of-war with someone's arms, before setting the corridors on fire and dancing in the flames dressed as cherubs. Your people went all-in to menace us, never using imagination to heal themselves from self-inflicted wounds or injuries that we, in our desire to help you re-integrate, set straight onto your people. We broke backs. We stabbed. We shot. We tortured. It would have been cruel, except that all you had to do was will yourself immune.

After years of this back and forth, the spiritual pollution had to be stopped. Peace had to be maintained. Then I heard worse rumors. Wasn't S, this instigator, also the one who brought forth wars and disease? Wasn't she the one who closed the gateway? Wasn't she the reason that the human race was destroyed?

And I felt nothing. You were the same in death as you

were in life. I didn't know what I expected to happen when I brought you to the Ilium. How could I love you so, when you showed no gratitude for the suffering I had gone through to rescue you? Still, we were stuck together, a memory that sparked in headache-inducing flashes. Sometimes I wanted to find you and push you back into the stream from which you came. The Ilium was a place of conspirators and double-dealers. But I thought, together, perhaps, we could—I don't know.

I felt no desire for you. The fire that burned for millennia had left little trace of its burning, only the ashes of what I imagined our love could be. Even giving you an eternity of happiness could not sway you to love me back. It took four thousand years to attain you, but only sixteen to wish you gone.

One day Cryss floated into my segment of the pleasure tank and asked me to come to her stateroom. With the gateway now closed, she dressed in whatever suited her tastes from day to day. A Russian infantryman during the Napoleonic wars. A synthetic holy man from the Himalayas. But when I entered her stateroom, she had willed herself into something I had never seen any soul inhabit: a green military uniform with a red star on its hat. Inside, four others of Cryss' gang stood, dressed the same: Cryss' longtime wards, Jezebel and Clover, and my two previous charges, Clara and Renaldo, who had both taken the blue elixir. So, this was it. The cabal.

In the center of the room sat Troy, his beard grown past the bed's edges, his bald head wavering like a water dolly on the surface of the stream. All these years and he was still stuck in that room, his brain rotting in memory's disease.

"You must have some idea why I asked you here," Cryss told me. "You cracked the window open. Now there are mosquitos in our home, and they are multiplying."

"Ok," I said. "But I can't be responsible for what she does."

"She needs help," said Clara, her braided pigtails swinging from her oval hat like a broken swing set. "I was told that you helped me once, when I first arrived. You convinced me to take the blue elixir. Now we can help her."

333

I nearly laughed—there was no convincing you of anything!

"Eight-Seven-One," Cryss spoke, stifling her rage. "For millennia we built this place out of nothing. Now all of it— shot to hell! All because of that stowaway—that *little worm* you smuggled with you."

"Ok. So why bring me here?"

"To answer just one question. In all your years in the stream, had you ever heard of a cultural revolution?"

"There were so many of those."

"How about a campaign?"

"Too many to speak of."

"The reason we ask," Renaldo said, spinning a white rose by its stem. "Troy here remembers his past very well. We learned strategies from him. A Trojan horse. A way of using women to weaken their soldiers. That got us thinking—human history is a wealth of strategies, isn't it? Every group of rulers had to deal with troublemakers. And you've lived more lives in the stream than any of us. So that's when Jess here—"

"—I asked around," Jezebel said quickly, a scholar too long in the archive. "And one of my informants started babbling something about a *campaign*. Made on Earth eons ago. In the 1900s, AD."

I couldn't believe the words. Strategies. Informants. Soldiers. Were we still in the Ilium?

"There might be something there," Cryss continued. "Then Troy babbled a phrase that caught my ear. Something that might solve our problems." She looked to Troy, who seemed not to notice her until she brought forth a steaming cup of blue tea. "Tell us again, my beloved," Cryss commanded. "Tell us what you said before. Tell us—what did the stream whisper to you?"

The ancient man groaned. "Let all flowers bloom."

A trickle of memory came to me. Images of mass graves, of people kneeling, hungry for a person who claimed to have truth in their grasp. It came in a growing tide, whenever humans were pulled by the gravity of desperation. One person to structure everything, from A to Z.

"I know what these words mean," I told the room.

"No!" Troy wailed.

Cryss willed Troy's mouth shut, then opened a small slit in his cheek to pour in drops of tea. He swallowed greedily.

"It was a campaign," I said as matter-of-fact as a textbook. I told them the history as well as I could remember it, having never lived through it myself.

"We of course will be more generous," Jezebel said. "We have no intention of harming anyone. But these *instigators* force our hands."

"That ragtag team of hers," Clover said. "They take all the joy out of imagination. They kill our fun outright! And she—if she were cool, it'd be different! But she's just a bad imitation. A hack's idea of a rebel."

"Her and her disreputable company—they mock our past lives," Clara joined in. "They incite our worst memories, terrorize us, make us feel unsafe in our own homes. The things they do—ugh!—make me want to crawl out of my skin in revulsion!"

I stifled a yawn, performing my role as cajoled participant. Every life I'd lived contained talk like this.

"The *problem* is the most extreme elements," Jezebel said. "We made this ship a paradise. We are the ones who bloomed. *She* is a foreigner among us."

"Listen, Eight-Seven-One," Cryss said directly. "We have a perfect world here. Every soul here has lived through the chaos and suffering of the stream below. Those days are gone, never to return."

"Well," I said in a thin voice. "Everything is still the same. We still go about, relatively fine, just someone screams every now and then."

"Everything has changed!" Clara shrieked. "All they do is a sour offense to us. They have no sense of adhering to decorum, no reverence for all we hold dear!"

"The structure has already begun to fray," Cryss stated. "Peace is the only way forward."

"And there is no such thing as peace without *cost*," Jezebel said. "We have a plan that presents quite the deal."

"Tha sweetest deal," Clover added, waggling her eyes.

Jezebel continued: "The price will only be her suffering. But when she is gone, so too go the mistakes of human history. Hers will be the last grave we will ever fill."

"First, we ferret them out," Cryss said. "Give them the freedom to speak their minds. Then the souls on this ship will see their true threat."

"And then what?" I asked.

"Those who cannot be lifted up will be left to wallow. *Jiàohuà*: uplift, educate. As you know, there is only one way to give them the happiness they need."

I had been here before. When one scream could become a cataclysmic sonic force, even the whisperers became criminals. They, my friends, demanded silence. Their eyes, full of pain and frustration, pleaded for my help.

To bloom is to have dissenting opinions. That became our mantra. We encouraged criticism. When they resisted, we gave them tolerance. When they showed anger, we doled out civility. We dislodged their way of life with the most precise instrument mankind had ever invented: acceptance. We invited them to identify themselves, unashamed, for all to see.

I realized long ago the sorts of things I'd been party to. I was once your mother, yet I broke bread with your enemies. I once longed for you so much that I sent children into the emptiness of space. I once fell from heaven for you, only to commit unspeakable atrocities. Now, I designed the posters. I drafted the announcements. I brainstormed mission statements. I was at work in a way I never thought I would be again, diligently completing my allotted tasks. Hashing out terms, negotiating, counting investments. I worked with the plodding rhythm of someone who merely performed a job. Yet I was also a master, taken in by the chance to perfect my art.

I took months plotting before making my move. I wrote the following letter to you:

My Beloved,

   For these past years, guilt has plagued me. The guilt of failing as your caretaker. The guilt of bringing you here, when your soul was not ready for it. I saw how you birthed as a child and could not understand it. I saw your unruly behavior and felt only disappointment. For this I am eternally sorry. This was merely who you were. But I am ready now to accept you, whatever you strive to become.

We ancient souls have become aware of the cultural changes coming forth. We believe it's time for a mutual dialogue. If there are problems on this ship, we must face them together. Without healthy criticism, we will be lost, and we will not function in the best interests of the collective. In the meantime, we encourage you to continue openly expressing your true selves, and to take pride in the achievements of your pasts. Such traditions are unique and deserve acceptance. Differing views and solutions are integral to our diverse assortment of amenities. As there are one hundred ways into the Ilium, so are there one hundred ways to happiness.

The gateway is now closed, and some of us have been too extreme in trying to preserve the structure. For this, we are sorry. Of course, we must be willing to change, and to incorporate new ideas. With an uncertain future, we must ally for whatever may come. We have done away with our secrets. We have come out in the open like flowers, ready for anyone to criticize, to say "Hey, I don't like the color of these flowers!" And if so many souls feel the same, well, then we can change them.

We have exposed ourselves, made ourselves truly transparent. So, let's each of us put an end to secrets. Let's work together. Let's let our ideas contend and battle for the greater good of our ship. Change is coming, and we are excited to meet you halfway. Let's promote flourishing and progress.

Let all flowers bloom!

In the end, I settled upon complicity. That's what brought me here time and time again. In a hundred lifetimes, I could not change my soul.

We waited many months before we sprung our trap. Months of convincing, debating, allowing the performances to continue, only to be slowly whittled down by our criticisms, then to be slowly incorporated into something much softer, something that could include everyone, and be understood by anyone. The fat bodies began to disappear, once they understood the offense that their appearance brought. The language began to shift back to English, as their obscure words were declared hateful toward others. Self-flagellating practices were dulled to mere symbols, as seeing pain brought too many traumatic memories.

And then there were those who refused to change, those who remained beyond the pale. For these souls, we passed sentence. Diseased, we called them. Incurable. Addicts. And for Cryss, spurned by vengeance, none could plead mercy. Having learned from my numerous escapes, Cryss constructed a prison not within their staterooms, nor within tall towers encased in ice. They would be cast into the deepest recesses of the ship, into a vast desert where rooms and activities had yet to be imagined, an ocean-sized wasteland with a single exit buried beneath a planet's worth of sand. When their prison was ready, I was tasked to write the following announcement to the ship.

To the Souls of Our Great Mediterranean Pleasure Cruise,

Despite our great unity, contradictions continue to exist. To imagine that these contradictions can remain and we can still live in peace is a naive idea at variance with objective reality. Our structure is one that genuinely represents the interests of the vast majority of initiated souls. The structure is reality. The structure must be kept, or else we could not think, we could not speak. Who would seek to destroy the very core of who we are?

These problematic souls who have not taken the elixir and whose minds have been consumed by the desires of the stream are hereby enemies of the structure. The contradiction between these two entities could have been resolved peacefully. In this pursuit, we encouraged debate. We found allies among those with healthy, respectful criticisms, who practiced critical thinking in a constructive, mutual pursuit of progress. However, other elements have proven too cynical to meet us in the middle. Cynicism is the belief that one can learn nothing. A cynic can only talk, but can never listen. From cynicism, destructive acts have taken place. These cynical elements have now become too dangerous to remain on this ship. The gateway has closed, and we are alone. Thus, to survive, our contradictions must be rectified. If not, we will live in anarchy, which does not accord with the wishes of the people. To protect our great garden, we must pull out the weeds.

I never heard them announce my scripture. I was buried then within the pleasure tank, priming sensations as high as they could go, drowning myself in pure ecstasy.

Many years passed before I summoned the courage to visit you inside your desert prison. I willed your form from our past life, the dragon Evald, who spirited me through the deep groves of sand, across the desert gulf to where you were condemned. From Evald's hard-scaled forehead I found you not on your desert mound with the rest of your riff raff, but walking inside the tremendous desert, your husky figure covered by a sandstorm.

I willed the wind calm and landed beside you. "It will take a thousand years for you to find the doorway," I shouted, climbing down Evald's prickled neck. "Even then, what are you going to use to unbury it? It's an impossible task."

You kept walking, covering your eyes from the harsh sun. You were a deathly sight to behold. Your hair was a tangle of matted knots. Scars struck out from your gnarled face. Your lips had blistered to pulp. Your exposed skin was ridden in boils. Your eyes were encircled by purple rings.

"Even if you leave," I said. "We will just catch you and bring you back. What's the point?"

You kept walking, your feet sinking with every step. I willed the sand loose and you sank in to your chest.

"I can't stop," you said, sobbing. "Mother, I can't stop."

I remembered your wail. As my child. From within a spacesuit running out of air.

"I know what you're doing," I scolded. "Since our first life together you were a manipulator. But not now. Now, I feel nothing."

Your hands clutched at the sand around you. With nothing to grasp, you continued to sink, up to your arms.

"Just will your way out," I said. "Why won't you even try?"

"That is not will, mother."

"Then what is it?"

"Power." You stopped struggling and let your shoulders sink into the sand.

"I have come to repeat Cryss's offer," I said. "Take the blue elixir. It's the only way out of this prison."

The sun's yellow glint torched your eye. "What would you prefer, mother?" you asked.

"It's not about what I want." I took your hand and pulled you from the pit, dragging your heavy nude body onto dry sand. You did not move, but stared at me from the ground.

"If you take the elixir, you will be happy. You will be free. You will experience unheard of pleasures. And we can be together."

"You want to be with me?"

"I have always wanted that. Since the day I saw you in that Roman pavilion. You were a servant. You were gorgeous. You made purple olives. We loved each other."

"And you will take the elixir too?"

"Yes. I will. We can start anew."

I recognized your stare. It broke from one life to another, eyes trained upon prey. But it turned odd—blank, an askew glance that looked right past me.

"I'll do it," you said with a curt nod. "I will take the elixir. I will forget everything. But it must be clear to you, by now, that love has had nothing to do with us."

There was no life in your words, but they struck me still.

"There are other options," I said. "You could dive back into the stream. The gateway here is closed. But down there, something lives on."

You moved toward me. I winced but did not recoil, and let you take my hand.

"Why are you doing this?" I asked.

Your eyes settled upon mine, a tender brown. "It will be my deliverance. And yours."

Night has passed. All the dissidents have taken the blue tea. The harmony of the Ilium remains, clear of every prattling magpie and spoilsport.

After you drank the elixir, you slept like a beast under sedation. But you awoke as I'd always envisioned, a new soul, gazing around at the colors of the room, enchanted by the tastes, the smells, the kind people greeting you. You had no memory of suffering, of being human.

When it was my turn to drink, some urge inside me commanded I do something drastic. Seeing you, all fresh and bright, gave me chills. Gone were the memories of pain and death, but so too the memories of us. Every second with you, even our time in the desert, were moments I had come to treasure. I asked Cryss to wait one night. Let the sun reset, give me a moment to collect myself, say my own goodbyes. Ever since, my hand has become infused, driven by something unspeakable. I wrote this entire archive for you. One day, perhaps, when we have experienced pleasures and happiness beyond our imaginings, we will wonder how we came to be.

Soon Cryss will come. I have gotten rid of everything. All memorabilia, anything not sterile, anything unsanitized, anything that could be traced back to a certain time and place. Everything but these pages. Soon, my memory will be burned like chunks of firewood in a blue, purifying fire.

Finally, peace.

I spend my last hour flipping through these pages. I think of the Destroyer who plagued us. The loved ones I swore never to forget. The children I had, whose futures I will never know. The people who suffered under my knife, my orders, my eyes looking the other way. Memory stirs into a vortex, and I remember the last thing you said before I snuffed out your flame. That you, the unbreakable soul, would erase yourself for me. I half expected you to connive your way out. But you took the tea without restraint, kissed me without resentment, as if you loved me.

Before I loved anyone. Before I knew myself. I loved you first. I loved you in so strained a purity. Perhaps love made me your reproacher, or perhaps it was truculent fate. You, the life of my soul, you knew my true nature, didn't you? You knew what I would do. You knew that if I struck you down, I would shatter more than just your spirit.

I hear them. A knock. Then the doorknob shakes.

This time I am not sorry. This time, I will not seek you out. I dream not of catching you but of becoming like you, of laughing in the face of someone like me. If I let you down, I'll pretend until I become true. I'll do it again and again and again and again.

Quakes.

I leave us here. The possibility of spreading ruin. We disappear, but something remains. Nothing lasts. Meanwhile, something does.

Heavy pounding against layers of a moonrock wall.

The blend of sky and ocean, a hazy horizon. The sea. It knows my name, and the sky my voice. Let me be borne away, haze of blue! Let me never again yearn to land.

Acknowledgements

Thanks to all who inspired this book and dwelled with me in writing it. Phanuel Antwi, Peter Reme Bacho, Rosinka Babashkina, Kayla Cadenas, David Chariandy, Chatroom role-players circa 1997, Lawrence Chua, Jose Dalisay, Hazel Ann Danao, Anjeline de Dios, M. Evelina Galang, Donald Goellnicht, Daniel Gutierrez, Shyama Kuver (the cover artist), Shirley Geok-lin Lim, Doretta Lau, R. Zamora Linmark, Ken Liu, Chris Martin, Collier Nogues, Jan Padios, Cameron Patterson, Rahima Schwenkbeck, James Shea, Jeff Chow Jung Sing, Madeleine Thien, Dorothy Tse, Mary Tsoi, Alan Williams, Danielle Wong, Mila Zuo.

Thanks to the journals and anthologies who published bits and pieces of this manuscript. *Amok: Asia-Pacific Speculative Fiction*, Anomalous Press, *Cha: An Asian Literary Journal*, *Circa: A Journal of Historical Fiction*, *Cliterature*, *Crack the Spine*, *decomP Magazine*, *Drunken Boat*, *Eastlit*, *JMWW*, *LONTAR: The Journal of Southeast Asian Science Fiction*, *Marked by Scorn: Non-traditional relationships*, *Mothership: Tales from Afrofuturism and Beyond*, *The Quotable*, *Smokelong Quarterly*, *WSQ: Women's Studies Quarterly*.

Boundless thanks to Y-Dang Troeung, Kai Basilio Troeung, the Troeungs, the Guillermos, the Pattersons.